March &
Feather

March &
Feather

EMMA SASKA

Little Oaks Independent Publishing
Great Britain

First paperback edition February 2023

The text for this book was set in Palatino Linotype. Manufactured in the United States of America.

Library of Congress Control Number: 2022921334

ISBN 978-1-7391706-1-5 (paperback)
ISBN 978-1-7391706-2-2 (eBook)

For Julia,
Who told me about the café where I finished this
dear little story,
and for Ivy Jean, love of my life

WELCOME TO THE HOMESCHOOLERS ACROSS THE COUNTRY FORUM

Please click the link below to read and agree to the forum rules. You may not post on the forum until then. In addition, please always practice Internet safety.

BOARD ► Movies and Television Shows; THREAD ► Movie Recommendations

September 16, 2012, 4:42 pm EST, <u>panda886</u> posted:
I've watched everything my parents own and my friends don't have any good suggestions. So I'd love to see what you guys think I should watch. I'd prefer G or PG-rated movies, but some PG-13 movies should be okay, too.

September 16, 2012, 7:13 pm EST, <u>feathergirl13</u> posted:
I'm assuming you've seen The Princess Bride? *Most homeschoolers I know have. But if you haven't, it's really fun if you like adventure/fantasy films.*

September 16, 2012, 9:02 pm EST, <u>idesofmarch</u> quoted <u>feathergirl13</u>'s post and added:
I 100% agree with feathergirl. It's a classic. Anyone who says differently is selling something.

September 16, 2012, 9:15 pm EST, <u>feathergirl13</u> quoted <u>idesofmarch</u>'s post and added:
You seem a decent fellow. With excellent taste in movies.

September 16, 2012, 9:20 pm EST, <u>idesofmarch</u> sent <u>feathergirl13</u> a private message:
You seem very confident that I have good taste in movies considering you only know I love The Princess Bride.

September 16, 2012, 9:23 pm EST, <u>feathergirl13</u> replied to <u>idesofmarch</u>'s PM:
Anyone who likes The Princess Bride can't possibly like any bad movies.

September 27, 2012, 2:19 pm EST, <u>feathergirl13</u> sent <u>idesofmarch</u> a PM:
I have an idea… You can…is veto the right word? You can veto it though. What if we created Google email accounts just for chatting with each other? That would be so much easier than having to use PMs on this forum. We could use our usernames here as our names there so we could stay as anonymous as we want. What do you think?

September 27, 2012, 3:33 pm EST, <u>idesofmarch</u> replied:
I think that's a great idea. Let's do it.

September 27, 2012, 4:01 pm EST, <u>idesofmarch</u> said:
Got mine all created. I'm idesofmarch117@gmail.com. Let me know when you've got your account up and running.

September 27, 2012, 4:15 pm EST, <u>feathergirl13</u> said:
Yay! Just created mine—it's feathergirl1389@gmail.com. I'm off to email you!

CHAPTER ONE

Four years later...

Ping!

I jump, and my gaze darts around the room, trying to find who has their phone out. Honestly, it's so annoying when people use their phones in class. The least they could do is fake taking notes like I'm doing.

Mrs. Kurtz pauses her U.S. government lecture, and she and my classmates look for the culprit.

Ping!

It sounds really close...

My cheeks grow warm as it dawns on me. I can't believe this is happening! I never leave my ringer on, but I must have had it on earlier to watch a video or something.

I scramble for my phone to silence it, but it's too late. Mrs. Kurtz has already zeroed in on me. She may go easy on me for not paying attention—after all, she's known me since sixth grade—but teachers at Stony Point are super strict about phones in the classroom. I fumble with my phone, but my clammy hands can't manage to hit the little buttons on the side.

"Oh my gosh, I'm so sorry," I babble. "I thought the ringer was off. I swear this will never happen—"

Ping!

My cheeks burn even hotter, and a couple of my classmates giggle. Mrs. Kurtz marches over to the table where I sit. She plants her hands on her hips, but her lips twitch. I'm not used to disappointing teachers, so I shrink down in my seat. Everyone is watching our interaction; they're probably eager for me to get in trouble.

Mrs. Kurtz holds out her hand and says, "Just in case, let's turn off the phone, and then I'll hold onto it. You can collect it from me after class, Audra."

I stare down at the table. I wish I could disappear. "Yes, ma'am."

As I silence my phone, I catch sight of the notifications. Messages from March. Of course it had to be him texting me. When I tell him about this later, he'll get a kick out of being the reason I got in trouble, particularly since I'm a bit of a notoriously dependable, compliant student. To put it simply, I've never been in the running for class clown.

My pen is glued to my notebook for the rest of class, but I really can't be blamed for daydreaming about what I plan to make for dinner tonight instead of focusing on Mrs. Kurtz's Supreme Court lesson. I learned all this stuff ages ago, thanks to my history professor dad, but four years of high school history are mandatory in Virginia, even for homeschoolers. As long as I turn in the homework, Mrs. Kurtz doesn't care what I do in class, but my cell phone going off is kind of inexcusable. Still, her daughter, Lucy, is a senior like me, and we've been in most of the same classes over the years. That's one of the best perks of going to a homeschool co-op: you know almost all the students, and your teachers are usually their parents, so they tend to be pretty chill.

I drum my fingers on my table as I try to remember if we have all the ingredients for a mushroom and chicken risotto. I wonder, too, if Madeline will come for dinner tonight. I liked that she regularly came for dinner on Fridays—that is, until she met her boyfriend in June. Maybe that's just a coincidence; she can't be going out with Trevor *every* Friday. Maybe she just doesn't want to spend as much time with us anymore. I don't know why it bothers me, though; twelve years between us meant we've never been as close as our parents wanted us to be.

With my phone gone, I check the clock on the wall. Thirty-five more minutes, and then I'll be at lunch with my friends. I can stay focused that long, right? Honestly, it would be more efficient if I just took history online. My mom, however, thinks face-to-face classes add validity to my education.

After class, I sheepishly collect my phone from Mrs. Kurtz without reprimand, although the look she gives me is stern. I'll be extra careful in the future. This was too embarrassing to let happen again—everyone's eyes on me, the way I couldn't stop blushing, and the admonishment from one of my favorite teachers.

I shoulder my messenger bag and weave through the church hallways to a quiet corner so I can spend virtual time with March before devoting my full attention to my friends who are physically here. I type in my phone's passcode and open the chat app.

MARCH
Morning! I listened to Back to December on the way to co-op. Your move.

MARCH
Who was this song about again
MARCH
Did you remember to listen to a
Fleetwood Mac song?

I smile. We've had a tradition of listening to a song from the other's favorite artist every day for about a year now. Since I normally listen to Taylor Swift in the morning, too, it's like a little connection despite the miles between us.

FEATHER
Excellent choice. Oh, and it's about
Taylor Lautner. I listened to Sara as soon
as I woke up so I think I win, lol.

MARCH
Wouldn't it be a tie? Neither
of us needed a reminder.

FEATHER
True, lol. How's co-op?

MARCH
As okay as math class at 8 in the
morning can be, haha
MARCH
It would be better if you were here

FEATHER
You really know
how to flatter a girl

FEATHER
Are you still having trouble
making new friends?

MARCH
Nah not really. But the friend groups
formed a long time ago, ya know?
It's hard to fit in when they
don't need more friends.

I don't necessarily agree. If someone's the right fit, a friend group can always grow. I wouldn't have one if the others hadn't widened their circle for me a few years ago.

FEATHER
They're missing out

MARCH
Thanks. 😊 I'll keep trying.
Fellow homeschoolers should
get how hard it is to find
friends right?

FEATHER
You'd think so
FEATHER
I'm here if you want to chat. Just not
in class. Your messages this morning
may have gotten me in trouble...

MARCH
Ahahahahaha really??? 😂😂😂

FEATHER
I forgot to put my phone on silent. 😐

MARCH
Nice
MARCH
Gotta get lunch

FEATHER
Same. Ttyl!

I head to the multipurpose room. My mom will be waiting there with the lunch I packed this morning, but it's a nice enough day that my friends and I'll go outside.

Stony Point Homeschool Academy requires that parents stay on the premises since we're not an official school, so my mother can usually be found in the multipurpose room reading a book or talking with other parents. Today, she sits at a table with some of my friends' moms. They're chatting about college visits, a topic I'm tired of. Most of my applications are in for early admission, but the Stengers are just starting the process, since my best friend Ro is a junior.

My mom slides the lunch bag over to me without interrupting her conversation. I pull out a fork and my Tupperware containers before turning to find Ro right behind me. She pulls her hoodie from her bag and smiles at me.

"Oh gosh, you'll never believe what happened in government class." With a glance at my mother—who will not be happy with me if she overhears this story—I continue,

"I'll tell you outside, if the guys aren't there yet."

I wait while Ro grabs a sandwich from her family's cooler, and then we head out. The two of us settle on stone benches around a patio table. I let the October sun seep through my long-sleeved blouse, while Ro positions herself in the shade. She needs sunscreen constantly, or her skin turns as red as a Campari tomato. I pop open my first Tupperware and examine the chicken sandwich with herb mayo I packed. The country bread isn't soggy, to my delight. I'll have to use this recipe again.

"Okay, so what happened?" Ro asks before cramming turkey sandwich into her mouth.

"So someone's phone went off in history class..."

She gives me a look. "Was it yours?"

My expression must give me away. Ro almost chokes as she laughs at my misfortune. I wait until she's recovered before saying, "March messaged me. Three times in a row."

"Is he okay?"

"Oh, yeah, he was just texting. I should've had my phone on silent, though."

Ro gives me a look. "If it happened to anyone else, they wouldn't care as much as you do."

"I know, but..." I shrug. "I kind of like that the teachers here can count on me to follow the rules."

My best friend rolls her eyes, but she smiles to show she's teasing. "You're such a kiss-up."

I playfully stick my tongue out at her. Some of the other high schoolers trickle into the courtyard. They sit at tables scattered around, and chatter and laughter fill the air. Lucy

Kurtz, with her perfect makeup and bright smile, waves to us from where she's settled with her group of friends, who make up Stony Point's popular crowd—if such a thing is possible at a co-op.

"Have you guys ever thought about meeting?" Ro asks as she shoves strands of her sepia brown bob behind her ears.

"Wait, what? Meet who?" I ask as I take my glasses off to clean a smudge.

"You and March. Have you ever thought about telling him who you are? It's so weird you guys haven't switched to different social media platforms since it's been so long."

I mull over her question as I chew. "I've thought about it," I tell her, "but we've never discussed it. I feel like it would change so much if we knew what each other looked like and where we lived and each other's real names. I couldn't imagine meeting him and calling him 'Joshua' or 'Connor.' It would be too weird."

"But you did think about it?" she presses.

"Yeah. When I had that almost-relationship with Jacob Griffith, I kinda wished he were March. Just because March was already one of my best friends, you know? So then I wanted to find out if I already, by some bizarre twist of fate, knew March."

"Hmm," she muses.

"But the chances of that happening are really slim," I continue. "It was just fifteen-year-old me being a hopeless romantic."

Before she can say more, Joel Mitchell appears in the doorway with another of our friends, Dylan Yanovitch.

Joel, towheaded and tan from years on a farm, is a senior, and Dylan, a junior, is wearing a sweatshirt representing his swim team. They're followed by a couple of this year's new students, Matthew Harwell and Owen Bell. Matthew is loud and opinionated, while Owen's super shy—around us at least. I know he's a senior like Joel and me, from another Southern state—you can hear it in his voice—but that's pretty much it. Somehow, though, he gets along with outgoing Matthew.

Kylie Sung, the final friend in our circle, arrives right behind them. She flings herself down beside me and cheerily greets everyone. She doesn't have any classes until after lunch this year, but she comes early to eat with us.

"What do you have today?" I ask her. Kylie is first-generation Korean American, and her mom makes tons of great traditional dishes when she has time between shifts at the hospital. I've schemed my way into many a dinner invitation, but I can never get the recipes out of Dr. Sung.

"Just leftover spaghetti. Omma worked late, so I made dinner for the littles and me." She opens her thermos and digs a fork out of her bag.

One whiff is all it takes for me to tell the sauce is from a jar. I try not to wrinkle my nose, but Kylie knows me well enough to tell I'm unimpressed with her lackluster lunch. She gently shoves my shoulder and laughs, and I giggle, too.

Matthew, who's on the bench across from me, between Owen and Joel, says, "Hey, Food Queen, care to judge my lunch?" When Matthew got here, he latched onto my passion for cooking and decided I was a perfect target for teasing. I don't understand why; he doesn't bug the others nearly as much, and surely we're too old to pick on people we have crushes on.

I survey his plate. He has pizza, bought from the barebones lunch counter the co-op runs. I tried that pizza once and couldn't finish even one slice. Besides, his comment doesn't deserve my attention when he's only saying it to get a rise out of me. So I roll my eyes before turning to Owen and trying to coax him out of his shell.

"How were your classes this morning?" I ask.

His voice is deep but mellow. "Um, good, I guess." He pauses, and our eyes meet. I smile encouragingly, and he continues, "I really like the speech and debate instructor here. And I've got algebra two with Matt."

"I took speech last year! It was great; Phillipa's dad is such a great teacher." We eat for a couple minutes and then I ask, "So now that we're halfway through the semester, how do you like Stony Point?"

"I like it all right so far. Y'all have more classes than I expected. It's almost like a private school." He straightens his teal plaid shirt, which complements his warm brown skin nicely.

"Yeah, but with fewer extracurriculars," Matthew butts in. "At my last co-op, we had drama and language clubs, a vocal ensemble, and sports teams."

"Sorry we're not up to your standards," I say, but he seems to miss my biting tone.

"I'm not saying I don't like it here. I'd just rather join a drama club than a community theater group."

Needing a subject change, I turn to Ro. "Our moms were talking about your college search when I went to grab my lunch."

"Yeah. My parents want me at community college for a couple years, but I want to go away for all four." She sits up straighter. "You know what would be fun? If we road-tripped to a couple schools during spring break!"

"Who's the 'we'?" I ask.

"You, me, and Kylie! I bet Mom would let me borrow her car for the week. I'm interested in a few schools out west, but most of them are closer, so we could drive to them easily."

Kylie is bouncing. "That *would* be fun. And if Audra has decided on a school by then, we can visit and see where she'll be next year," she says.

Dylan, who was listening in, says, "Are we invited too, or is this a girls-only trip?"

My friends and I exchange looks. "Well it'll be harder to convince our parents if the boys want to come," Kylie says slowly.

"Plus my car only seats four comfortably," says Ro. Her expression is neutral; she doesn't seem as uneasy as Kylie and me about putting up with the guys for a week.

"We could always take two cars. I don't mind driving," Matthew interjects.

I roll my eyes again. Of course he wants to come with, and now that we've talked about the idea openly, there's no way we could invite just Dylan and Joel, the guys we've been friends with the longest. We'd have to invite Matthew and Owen, too. I've known Joel since he ate Play-Doh in church nursery, and Dylan has been part of the friend circle for as long as I've been at Stony Point. I'm much more comfortable around them.

Ever the peacemaker, Joel says, "How about y'all float the college road trip idea with your parents first, then ask if we can go with? We don't want to intrude."

From the look on Matthew's face, I'd say he disagrees, but I'm sure he's also very used to getting what he wants. After all, his dad is a hotel mogul; Matthew is practically a walking advertisement for Spoiled. He wears brands that I've only seen on private school kids, and he's always talking about his trips all over the world. Matthew is the rare wealthy homeschooler; most of us are solidly middle class. If the upper class wants their kids to get a different education than what public schools can provide, they can afford to send them to elite private schools. Matthew would fit right in there with his attitude and charm that he thinks will win over every girl.

I remember his first two weeks here. Kylie told us about this book series she'd found about fairies. She loved it so much and couldn't stop talking about it, but I didn't mind. Matthew apparently did because I saw him roll his eyes when she was describing the first book's plot. That, plus his teasing about my passion, was the catalyst for deciding I didn't want to be his friend.

I chat with Ro and Kylie and eat the perfection that is the rest of my lunch—besides my chicken sandwich, I packed red potato salad, a pear, and a homemade cookie loaded with chocolate chips and M&Ms. Lunch winds down, and I don't get an opportunity to talk to Owen again. He's too wrapped up in a quiet conversation with Matthew. About five minutes before the period is over, I drop my containers with my mom and head off to AP calculus (a.k.a. the hour of suffering).

"Hey, Audra," says Matthew, sliding up beside me in the hall.

I mumble a greeting but immediately feel a pang of guilt. I was the new kid once, way back in the sixth grade. Even homeschooled middle schoolers can be brutal, so I know how hard it is to settle in at a new place.

I should make an effort at least, I tell myself, so I ask, "What class are you headed to?"

"World history." He makes a face, so I don't ask how he feels about it. "What about you?"

"AP calculus."

"They offer that here?" He slides his phone into his back pocket and pushes his glasses further up his nose.

"Yeah. Mrs. Powers has a master's in math and one in science, so she's qualified. There're only seven of us in the class, though."

"So besides food, you like math," Matthew comments as he shoves his hands into his jean pockets.

I can't keep myself from laughing. "Yeah, no. I just don't want to have to take math in college. My sister's the math geek of the family, so she helps me out. My parents make her, anyways."

"Man, there's no way I could do that. I'll struggle through basic college math instead."

I shrug. "I doubled up on a few classes for the last few years, so I might as well do something productive with my time now." I stop walking. "This is my classroom."

"Okay, cool." He starts to walk away but pauses. "See you next week!"

"Yeah, see ya," I reply. I don't bother to watch him go.

After calculus, my brain feels like it was sucked out, ground up, and then put back in. So many of the concepts go right over my head, and all I can do is scribble down notes as fast as I can so Madeline knows how to help me later.

I'm not done with classes for the day, but I'm not a student in the next one. This year and last, I've been a student assistant for the preteen cooking class during the second-to-last period. It's a normal afternoon—someone drops a plastic bowl of ingredients, nothing burns, and one kid hates their food. But it's fun overall; I've learned a lot from the instructor, Mrs. Sanders. She's taught the class since I took it in seventh grade, and I'm so glad she thought I would make a good helper.

Once cleanup is done, I hurry through the hallways, past students I've known for years. We exchange greetings and polite smiles. My mom sits in the multipurpose room as usual, her nose in a book. When I stroll up, I expect her to grab her stuff so we can leave, but she pats the plastic blue chair beside her. I plop down, wincing at the unyielding seat. Most of our classrooms have these chairs, and they are quite possibly the worst in the world.

I wait until she finishes the chapter, and then I say, "Can we go now? I want time to relax before I start making dinner."

"Change of plans," Mom replies as she puts her book away. "Madeline called. She and Trevor want to treat us to dinner downtown."

"You mean I can't make my risotto?"

Mom laughs, so I guess I look absolutely pathetic. "You can make risotto tomorrow night," she assures me. "They're taking us to Fig & Root, which is one of your favorites."

Well, I guess that makes up for it. As my mom gathers up her stuff, I continue, "I wonder why Madeline and Trevor want to go out."

She shrugs. "I'm not going to question it. We don't see your sister enough these days."

I privately agree with her.

Fig & Root doesn't look like much from the outside, but it's cozy and bustling inside, much like I'd imagine a British pub would be. My parents and I beat Madeline and her boyfriend here, and we get a table for the five of us—not an easy feat on a Friday night in downtown Richmond. Dad is still in professorial attire since he came right from work; he's a history professor at the University of Richmond. Ro says he looks like a world-weary man with a penchant for eyeglasses from the '90s. (She's not wrong.)

My parents study the one-page menu, but I people-watch instead since I already know what I'm getting. My order is the same every time we come here, although I've only settled on the fish tacos in the last few months. It took a lot of trial and error but I found what I like best, and now I stick to it. As plates rush past to other tables, I catch glimpses of creamy sauces and sides piled high and whiffs of tomato, garlic, and cilantro.

A group of girls in their twenties are clustered at a table in the back corner. They laugh and talk, and a few words arch over the noise of other diners to reach my ears. It's definitely a girls' night out, and I think about how fun it'll be when I get to do that someday with my friends after a long week at work. Couples having Friday night dates are at most of the other tables. They all look happy, too.

I glance at my parents. I'm not unhappy to be here with them. I love them a lot, and spending time with them isn't a hardship. But it's nice to daydream about life in five or so years, when I'll be going out with friends or, I can hope, a boyfriend—maybe before the next century.

We order our drinks while we wait for Madeline and her boyfriend. Mom and Dad talk about his latest book on war history, which I've heard too much about at the dinner table. So I tune them out and subtly examine the meals on the tables around us. Some people take their time, savoring every bite; others plow through their food because it's just that good. A waiter passes by with a plate-laden tray. A spicy fragrance wafts over from a dish of pasta, and my stomach growls a little. He pauses at the corner table and distributes the plates. The girls immediately pass around dishes and glasses, trying a little of what all of their friends have. One waves a hand in front of her mouth, and her friends laugh kindly. Another takes a bite of a burrito bowl. She groans and immediately gestures for the four others at her table to try it.

They must be having so much fun, I think, smiling a little.

Having exhausted my surroundings, I turn back to my parents. Mom traces the rim of her wineglass, and the three of us sit in silence. As much as I enjoy eating out, I want to be home where I can message March; if I pull out my phone here, my parents will side-eye me until I put it away. They're as bad as the teachers at Stony Point.

"Tell your dad about what you got in the mail today," my mom prompts.

Her words take a moment to settle in; I was wrapped up in my thoughts, and I have to spiral out of them.

"Oh, well, um, I got my acceptance letter for the CIA." I glance up at my dad, then back down at my silverware. I can't hide my smile, but I restrain myself a little. At least I got to have my screaming, jumping-up-and-down celebration at home earlier. My parents are the first to know, but I'll text all my friends later.

"Should you be announcing that so loudly?" Dad's eyes dance. "We don't want to blow your cover."

"Dad," I groan with an eyeroll. He's made a variety of spy jokes over the last several months.

"No, but really, that's great!" he says, smiling widely. "Did you get mail from any other schools today?"

With other parents, I know that question would mean they didn't want me to go to the Culinary Institute of America. But my dad doesn't mean it like that; as a professor, he likes to be involved in my college application process and is convinced every school on the planet wants me. So I reply, "No, but I was really nervous about this one. I didn't think I'd hear back this soon."

"I know. This is a big deal. I'm really proud of you, sweetie." I meet his steady gaze as he reaches across Mom to squeeze my hand.

Madeline and Trevor enter the restaurant, and they stride over to us. My sister has the same hair as our dad, and she got her height from him, too. Trevor is tall and, in heels, Madeline is close to his height. She smiles, lips pressed together and eyes not crinkling. She's as serious as ever. My sister squeezes my shoulder and leans down to hug Mom before sitting across from her. Madeline's straight brown hair swishes against her shoulders, and her glasses reflect the lights' golden glow.

Lamplight reflected off Madeline's glasses as she turned to look at me. I hovered in the doorway to her room, watching her put on makeup and pick a necklace.

"What, Audra?" she said. Her mouth was a thin line. I couldn't ever remember her smiling when she saw me.

"I wanna see a movie at the Byrd, and Mom said I had to ask you to take me," I said, taking a step into the room.

She sighed. "I'm going out with my friends."

Even then I knew not to ask if I could come with; she always said no.

"Oh," I replied, moving back to the doorway. "Well, you wanna play a game when you get back? I got Clue for Christmas, and we didn't get a chance—"

"I'm not sure what time I'll get back, Audra. I haven't seen my friends in months, so we may be out all day." She turned back to the mirror atop her dresser.

I was dismissed.

I look at my sister. I don't know how to talk to her these days unless it's about math homework. We don't share any of the same interests, and she doesn't seem to want to get to know mine.

The waiter comes around eventually, and we place our orders. Mom and Dad order the crab cakes to share, and I make a mental note to ask for a bite since it's a new addition to the menu. If my parents like them, that's a recipe I'll want to attempt to replicate at home. Madeline orders the crab pasta, like one of the people at the table to our left; Mom's gotten that before, so I know it tastes good. Trevor chooses roasted chicken—delicious but not very adventurous. You can get roast chicken anywhere.

Once the menus are cleared, Trevor leans his forearms on the table. Then he moves his hands to his lap and leans back in his seat. Madeline scratches the back of her neck before playing with a strand of hair. The silence stretches on a bit longer until Madeline takes a big sip of water.

Once she's swallowed, she smiles nervously. I tilt my head; if Madeline's smiling, she's trying to get Mom and Dad to do the same and warm them up to whatever she's about to say. "So, um…" she says, "I'm glad you three could meet us for dinner because… We have some news." Her smile grows a little. "Trevor and I are engaged."

Mom coughs and turns to her, and I think my mouth falls open. Madeline pulls a ring out of her purse. She puts it on her hand and holds it out for us to see; the band is gold with a pale blue stone between two small diamonds.

"He proposed last night. He was so nervous, and he accidentally spilled some gelato on his shirt, but it was so cute, and I couldn't help but say yes," my sister continues, all smiles and happiness.

My parents, on the other hand, are frozen. Dad looks like one of us just told him we totaled his car, and

Mom's eyebrows are practically at her hairline. They like Trevor, I know, but this was clearly a surprise for them. Considering he hasn't stopped by the house on his own ever, I'm certain he didn't ask for their blessing. And anyways, he and Madeline have been dating for, like, only four months. Isn't this a bit soon?

After a moment, Mom and Dad voice their congratulations. Another beat passes, and I force a smile.

"Wow, that's awesome!" I manage to say, but I'm not sure I really mean it.

I feel like I'm congratulating an acquaintance, that's how distant my sister is. My mom asks how he picked the ring, but once that topic's covered, they all drop the subject. Dad and Trevor talk about work and sports, and Mom asks about each of Madeline's friends. Normally I'd bring up my Culinary Institute acceptance letter, but not now. I don't feel like celebrating anymore. Our food arrives at some point. My fish tacos smell amazing, but I've lost my appetite. I don't know how I wanted tonight to go, but it wasn't like this—ending in confusion and stiff conversations.

CHAPTER TWO

I yawn and slump further in the backseat of the car. Why my church thinks an 8:30 a.m. service is a good idea is beyond me. I lean back against the headrest and close my eyes to catch a few more minutes of sleep, but my mind floods with memories I stirred up last night while tossing and turning with my sheets twisting around me.

Madeline not caring that I'd made dessert for Thanksgiving. Not sticking up for me, her little sister, when our cousins wouldn't leave me alone. Never playing Uno or Monopoly with me, no matter how many times I asked over the years. An image of her engagement ring pops up, too, and my eyes fly open, sending those thoughts far away. There's no way I want to look at that ring again. Even if it made Madeline happy.

I really don't know why this is bothering me so much. Madeline has already moved out, so it's not like I'd be losing her. I never had her to begin with.

We pull into the sparsely filled parking lot, and I stumble up the front steps behind my parents. A few dozen people are in the hallway outside the sanctuary, but their conversations are only a hum. My mom strolls over to the Wheatons, and I smile sleepily at Holly, one of my best friends. When Holly pulls me in for a hug, I don't want to let go. Her hugs have been one of my favorite things since we were small. My mom has so many pictures of the two of us, hair in pigtails and with skinned knees, our arms wrapped tightly around each other.

Holly's not a morning person either, so she clutches a cup of coffee. She and I mumble our way through a conversation with her older brother and sister before we head into the service. We've been allowed to sit with our youth group friends instead of our parents for a few years, and this morning, we find Joel and half a dozen others waiting for us. The scents of coffee and soap float around me, keeping me awake for the next hour. It's not that I find church or our pastor boring; it's just much too early, and Pastor Newton's voice is very soothing as he preaches on trusting God.

After first service ends, the nine of us head across the driveway to the junior/senior high building for Sunday school. As usual, Miss Elizabeth has brought donuts. Holly and I elbow the boys out of the way; if we didn't, they'd eat every last donut before remembering the rest of us might want one. Food makes them forget their manners.

Holly and I grab our food and more coffee—the latter just for her; I have to suffer since I can't tolerate the taste. Then we settle in two cushioned chairs off to the side to wait for some of the other girls to show up before class. The guys scarfed down their donuts before snagging the air hockey and Ping-Pong tables across the room. Their cheers and shouts echo, and I watch Joel play for a moment before turning to Holly.

"Have you found out yet if you have a solo at Hickory's Thanksgiving concert?" I ask.

We both did children's choir here at church when we were in elementary school, but Holly's stuck with it—for good reason. She's got the voice of a Broadway star mixed with a worship arts leader—clear and melodic but able to hit notes, and she can harmonize well.

She shakes her head. "An email is going out on Tuesday, and I'll know then."

"I'll keep my fingers crossed—and pray about it. Promise." I give her a look, and she laughs. We joke a lot about Christians who say they'll pray for you but don't really mean it.

"Eh, don't hope too hard. I'd rather have a solo at the Christmas concert, and Mr. Hernandez wouldn't give me a solo in both."

"Then I'll keep my fingers crossed for that." I hold up my pointer and middle finger for emphasis before licking donut glaze off them.

Holly laughs. "Sooo, how's March?" She has this look in her eyes I can't interpret.

"Same as always. We haven't talked since Friday afternoon. He's been busy, I think."

She nods, and I eye her, wondering why she's giving me that look.

"Any boys I ought to know about?" I ask since I can't figure out what she's thinking.

"Nah. They're all just friends. Besides, Mom won't let me do anything besides group dates until I'm eighteen," she reminds me.

"Oh, right." Some homeschooling parents are like that. Others are more like typical parents of public schoolers and let their kids date once they're in high school, and then there are some families that do courtship only. Thankfully, my parents don't fall into that category.

"Anything fun happen at Stony Point this week?" She smiles a little, and her pale bronze eyes crinkle at the corners.

"Nah, it was a normal week. Oh, but you won't guess what happened at dinner on Friday night."

"What?"

"Madeline and Trevor told us they're engaged."

Holly chokes on her donut. "To be married?"

"No, in battle." I give her a look. "Yes, to be married."

She shakes her head, her eyes wide. "Wow. Not sure I saw that coming."

"My parents and I didn't."

"I'm surprised Madeline said yes. I met him at your family's Labor Day party, right?" When I nod, Holly continues, "They didn't seem to have any common ground. Different senses of humor and all."

I shrug. "You know him about as well as I do."

"Maybe it'll be a good thing," she says after we're quiet for a couple minutes. "Maybe he'll make more of an effort to get to know you guys now, and if he makes Madeline happy…"

"I *think* he does…"

From the corner of my eye, I see Joel head our way. He pulls a chair over and swings it around so he can sit on it backwards. "What's up?"

"My sister's getting married," I tell him.

"No way," he says, his eyes wide. "To who? I didn't know she was dating someone."

It's not like Joel and Madeline are close, but he tends to know everyone's business just by nature of being an open, friendly person. People like to talk to him—both about themselves and others. I've trusted him with most of my secrets, except for March. I've always been too embarrassed to tell Joel and Dylan about March, since they'd tease me about my "online boyfriend."

"Yeah, she and Trevor have been together since...the end of June, I think. I don't know how they met, though."

"Oh, yeah, Trevor! I think I met him at Labor Day." Joel leans forward in his chair and tips it so it's resting on two feet.

I laugh under my breath. If that's all my friends can remember about Madeline's fiancé, surely this engagement isn't a good idea. I still have to tell Ro, Kylie, and March the news; I wonder how they'll react.

Miss Elizabeth calls out that it's time for Sunday school to start. Joel jumps up immediately to head to the circle of chairs in the middle of the room. His chair lands on all four feet with a thud. Holly takes one last swig of coffee, and then she and I head over, too.

I don't remember anything about today's lesson.

In the afternoon, I lounge in the basement family room with a mountain of calculus homework when my phone buzzes with a message from March. I welcome the distraction because my brain feels like it's crumbling.

MARCH
My dad grilled burgers for

27

lunch. There's a reason
Mom doesn't usually
let him cook.

FEATHER
Aw sorry! I won't tell you what
I made for lunch then.

MARCH
No please tell me. I live…
vicariously (is that the right word)
through you

FEATHER
Yeah, vicariously sounds right
FEATHER
I had taco leftovers and
a salad and a raspberry
cream cheese brownie

MARCH
It's probably a good thing I don't
know you in real life because I'd
eat too much food. I'd beg you to
cook for me all the time.

FEATHER
Who said I would share?

I stretch my arms above my head as I wait for his response. I lean back on the ratty plaid sofa my parents bought before I was born. That message was too flirtatious, now that I think about it. I hope March doesn't take it the wrong way.

MARCH
Aw you wouldn't be that
mean, would you?

FEATHER
......no probably not

MARCH
You're clearly having
a better day than me

FEATHER
Eh maybe not

MARCH
What's up?

FEATHER
Well uh my sister got engaged.

MARCH
That doesn't sound
like a bad thing.

FEATHER
I'm pretty sure her boy-
friend didn't talk to my parents
about it at all. And it's just weird.
To think that she's engaged.

MARCH
Yikes
MARCH
I hope things get less
awkward on that front.

FEATHER
Me, too

FEATHER

As much as I want to keep
chatting, I need to get back
to my homework.

MARCH

Ok! Sorry to keep you from it

FEATHER

Nah it's ok. Wanna talk
later? I want to hear
about your weekend.

MARCH

Sure. After dinner?

FEATHER

Sounds good. Ttyl!

After another half an hour of work, I take a break and go upstairs for some apple cider. My parents fall silent as soon as the basement door swings open. I side-eye them; Dad is prepping dinner, and Mom sits at the table with the newspaper in her hands, but she's clearly not paying attention to it. She never reads the obituaries.

"Hi, sweetheart," Mom says, her tone a bit too cheerful.

"Heyyyyy," I reply, dragging the word out to let Mom and Dad know I'm onto them. "Just getting some apple cider. Don't mind me."

Dad chuckles then asks, "How's the homework going?"

I shrug. "It's *homework*."

I fill my favorite mug—the one March found online and told me about, that says, "May contain iocane powder" on it—and pop it in the microwave. Warm apple cider is the perfect fall beverage. My parents stay silent, like they're waiting for me to leave. In my peripheral vision, I catch them glancing at each other. Yup, they're not going to say anything until I'm out of the room again. It's like they're begging me to eavesdrop. So as soon as the mug is in my hand, I head back to the basement. I shut the door behind me and mimic footsteps going down the carpeted stairs, but I sit on the top step instead.

Just as I expected, their voices start as soon as they think I'm out of earshot.

"We haven't even met his family," my mom says. "What if they're awful, and he's as bad as they are, and we just don't know it yet?"

"That's a worst-case scenario, Kathleen. I'm more concerned about Trevor himself. I know I said this Friday night, but he and Maddie have been dating for, what, three, four months? She can't know him well enough to say she wants to spend the rest of her life with him."

I agree. Yeah, Madeline is twenty-nine, so she's likely wiser and more mature, but there's so much she doesn't know about Trevor—like how he acts when he gets angry, or how he'll react during a medical emergency, or if he'll tolerate her singing country songs in the shower. Maybe she thinks she knows him, but how can she really?

Despite Mom and Dad's disapproval, I have a feeling this wedding will happen. Then we'll never see Madeline after; she stopped coming over as often as soon as she started dating Trevor, so I can imagine how much worse it'll be once she's married. She'll have a new life that will consume all of her thoughts and time. It's probably too late for me to get to know my sister, but now my chance—if I ever wanted one—truly is gone. Soon she'll be wrapped up in newlywed life, and babies won't be far behind; then she really won't care about her kid sister. I've always wanted a sister who cared about me and wanted our relationship to be more than on paper. I want late nights giggling over cute actors, like Holly and Christina have, or nights spent at my sister's dorm room, like Ro got to do when Helen was at Transylvania University.

I've long thought Madeline didn't really want a sister. After all, I was a surprise baby. She was probably content having Mom and Dad all to herself. Of course I didn't understand that when I was little. All I wanted was for her to play dress-up and soccer with me. Yeah, she had papers and exams, but it wouldn't be unreasonable to expect her to take a few minutes out of her day to spend time with her *sister*, would it? By high school, I gave up any hope of having an actual relationship with her, but I guess that desire stuck around, if I'm feeling this way about her engagement.

I lean against the wall and sip some apple cider. My senior year wasn't supposed to have this much drama. All of that was supposed to be left in middle school.

CHAPTER THREE

I get to Stony Point a few minutes before second period. As I walk towards Madame Gibert's French III classroom, I double-check my phone to make sure the ringer's off. I don't need a repeat of last week.

Thankfully, it doesn't accidentally get turned on during French III and U.S. government, which I'm extremely glad for. I don't want any phone interruptions, not even from March.

I meet Ro and Joel in the hall. It's been raining since yesterday, so we'll have to eat inside. The multipurpose room is already noisy when we step through the double doors, which is a bad sign. Little kids' voices echo off the high walls, and the fuzzy carpet on them does nothing to muffle the sound. I can only imagine how rambunctious the elementary schoolers will be once they have lunch.

Joel stuffs his Virginia Tech cap into his backpack, then goes to find the rest of the guys. Ro and I look for Kylie. With three kids under thirteen, the Sungs are perpetually late, so I'm not surprised we don't see her before the guys jog over.

"Will Han told us and some of the other guys about a new game that he's got on his phone, so we're all gonna download it and play and eat together," says Dylan.

He brushes his shaggy brown hair out of his eyes and bounces on his toes.

"Okay," Ro says with a shrug.

This happens occasionally, even with Owen and Matthew at Stony Point now. Joel and Dylan need time with other guys, and we never begrudge them the space. Today, I don't mind at all.

Once Kylie arrives, we grab our lunches and find a semi-quiet corner. Lucy Kurtz's group and a trio of middle schoolers flank us, but at least they're not cheering and groaning every few minutes like the group of guys clustered around Will Han.

Before we eat, I pull a Tupperware out of my bag and present it to Kylie. It was her birthday on Wednesday, and I brought lime curd bars as a treat. There are enough for her to share with us, the guys, and her family, but Kylie squirrels all but three away for later. We scarf them down before focusing on our actual lunches. I have leftovers from dinner; we ordered Chinese takeout since Mom was called in to sub at the middle school and Dad had to work late. At home, I use chopsticks, but they're too much to manage when I'm sitting on the floor at co-op, so I use a fork to scoop up my shrimp lo mein.

"Hey, what are you thinking about majoring in?" I ask Kylie. She has a few different interests, and I can't tell if she prefers any of them to the others.

"Photography, I think, or maybe event planning," she replies. Her expression is tentative, but then she smiles. "I can't decide if I want to plan events or document them."

Ro and I laugh. Only Kylie would say something like that.

"What about you, Ro?" Kylie asks.

She shrugs and brushes hair out of her face. "I don't know. Communications sounds interesting. Psychology, too, but I don't know what I'd do with either." She eyes me. "I wish I knew for certain like you do."

"Well, I've had a whole extra year to look at schools and think over things," I tell her. "Don't worry; you'll figure out what you wanna do. And if you guys still go on that spring break college tour, you might decide then."

I finish my lunch as we talk about *The Great British Baking Show*, which we're watching on Netflix. At one point, I see my phone screen light up with a message from March, but I ignore it for now. Just as the boys benefit from guy time, I benefit from hanging out with just Ro and Kylie.

Our girl time is interrupted, though, by Matthew and Dylan sauntering over. Dylan flicks hair out of his eyes and plops down beside Kylie. He steals some food from her Tupperware. She swats at his hand, but he just grins before popping a grape in his mouth.

"Tired of video games?" Ro asks. She isn't teasing them; her eyebrows are raised, and her head is tilted.

"Nah, we lost," Matthew says with a shrug. "So we figured we'd see what you guys are up to."

"Not much." I crumple up my trash instead of looking at him.

Ro mentions something about UVA football, and that gets the guys going. Since it looks like they're sticking around, I pack up my lunch containers and grab my phone. I don't want to be around Matthew if I can help it, so I'll go message March now.

"I've gotta finish some calculus homework," I lie in case any of them are even listening.

Once I've exchanged my containers for my backpack at my mom's table, I head to the study hall room. If I *look* like I'm doing homework and keep my phone on silent, the supervising mom can't kick me out.

I finished my homework last night, though, so I pull up March's message.

MARCH
I waited til lunch to
message you so I hope you
didn't get in trouble again.

FEATHER
I kept my phone off in class
today, but thanks 😊

I twirl a pen in my hands, then pretend to scribble something in my notebook while I wait for his response.

MARCH
How's your day been?

FEATHER
All right. Yours?

MARCH
Today's been okay. Sometimes
I feel like I'm starting to fit in.
Other times...

FEATHER
I'm sorry 😟

FEATHER
Are you the only one making
an effort? Or are they trying
to include you?

MARCH
It's not like they're excluding me.
But sometimes I think some of them
are pretending to want me around.

FEATHER
That doesn't sound like fun. Is
there anyone else you could
try to be friends with instead?

MARCH
Yeah I've joined a community theater
group and I fit in better there.

FEATHER
I'm glad.

MARCH
One of the guys there works part-
time at a restaurant and he told
me last week they're hiring
more busboys. I applied already.

FEATHER
Hey that's great! Maybe you
could make some friends there too.

MARCH
Yeah maybe
MARCH
How many more classes do you have?

FEATHER

Two. You?

MARCH

Same. Hope yours go well.

MARCH

g2g, lunch is ending

I look up at the clock. The lunch hour here is almost over, too. I've long theorized that March lives in the same time zone—*maybe* one behind—and this cements it for me. I pack up my homework and push in the blue plastic chair before darting out of the room.

"Oof!" I collide with someone right outside the doorway.

"My bad," the person says in a deep Southern accent.

I look up sharply at Owen—has he always been so tall?— and shake my head. "I'm sorry. I wasn't looking where I was going."

He smiles easily and dimples appear in his brown skin. "I wasn't paying attention either," he assures me.

I peer closer. "Everything okay?"

"Yeah, I'm just thinking about the job interview I have later. It's my first since I moved here, so I'm kinda nervous. I hope I'm prepared enough." That's the most I think I've ever heard him say at once.

I try to look encouraging. "You'll do great. You're super chill and polite, so there's no way you won't win them over."

He ducks his head and smiles shyly. "Thanks. I'd better get to class, but see you next week?"

I nod. "See ya," I say with a wave. I blush as I walk away. Why did I *wave*?

After dinner—it's just my parents and me at home, so I finally get to make my risotto—I message March again. I'm cozy in the armchair in my room with the lamps casting a golden glow.

FEATHER

How was the rest of your day at co-op? Any progress on the friend front?

MARCH

Maybe. I could've been reading it wrong I guess. The guys are nice.

MARCH

How was the rest of your day?

FEATHER

Good! Besides my math class haha.

FEATHER

When do you go to the community theater thing

MARCH

Tuesdays and Thursdays except during dress rehearsals.

FEATHER

What have y'all been working on?

MARCH

We're getting close to dress

rehearsals so we did a lot of
blocking and I'm almost off-book.

FEATHER
That's awesome!
FEATHER
Do you have a lead role?

MARCH
Nah but this is my first show
with them so I don't care.
I'm a side character with
enough lines. Maybe next
time I'll be a lead.

FEATHER
I'm sure you will!
FEATHER
Although I don't know how
good of an actor you are, so
what do I know?

MARCH

FEATHER

There's a pause where neither of us has anything to say.
I'm about to ask more about the play when I see the bubbles
that mean March is typing.

MARCH
In more disappointing news
today I found out there are

no Waffle Kings in the
Richmond area. What am
I going to do without cheap
breakfast food???

I start to type out a snarky response, but something catches in my mind. I reread March's message, and it hits me. He said where he lives. Accidentally, I assume. Why would he do that on purpose? I erase my first message and start to type out one letting him know what he did, but I hesitate again. Maybe it would be better if I just pretend he never said where he lives.

I consider his words again. He must mean Richmond, Virginia, right? There are a lot of Richmonds in the United States, but surely none of them are as big as Virginia's state capital and significant enough to be referred to as "the Richmond area." But if I'm right, March has moved to my city.

I stare at my phone screen and almost laugh aloud. What are the odds of that? We've always been in the same time zone—I assumed at least—but now he's quite possibly living in the same city as me. He is one of the other one million people in the Richmond Metropolitan Area, which, in the grand scheme of things, doesn't narrow it down all that much. Considering how large the country is, though, it kind of does, especially when I include the fact that he's a fellow homeschooler. Homeschooling may be more common these days, but still. This changes everything.

What if I do comment on what he said? What if I say I live in the same area? I might actually be able to meet one of my best friends, I think. Of course, there's still the small doubt always lodged in the back of my mind that March isn't who he says he is—that he's just a terrific actor, and he's really a forty-year-old dude in some cabin in Montana who gets a kick out of catfishing and stalking homeschooled girls.

MARCH
You still there?

FEATHER
Oh, yeah, sorry
FEATHER
Um, maybe it's time you tried IHOP?

MARCH
That is a sacrilegious thing
to say, Feather.

FEATHER
Sorry, I know, lol. Trust me, I
understand how you feel about
waffles vs. pancakes. Pancakes
are good but waffles are better.
FEATHER
Maybe you should talk your parents
into moving again. To Pawnee.
Since Leslie Knope claims the best
waffles are found there.

MARCH
I might have to haha. Or maybe
you should send me your recipes
and I can start making my own.

If I can ever stop burning everything I try to cook.

FEATHER
My peanut butter waffles ARE pretty
good, if I do say so myself.
However the recipe is a guarded
family secret. I can totally share
my recipe for churro waffles tho.
They're my sister's favorite.

MARCH
What are you waiting for??

We talk for a while longer about breakfast foods—a
subject we've already covered at length, but it's one we come
back to all the time—and recent movies we've watched. I
don't mention his mistake or suggest we meet. The thought
of that is a little too daunting right now.

He tells me about the camping trip he went on with his
dad and brothers a couple weekends ago, and I ramble on
once again about how much I want a dog. Conversation
with him is familiar and feels like home. It's as easy for
me as it is when I talk with Ro or Holly; the only thing
missing is the comfortable silences I'll fall into with them,
when we've exhausted pretty much every topic and we're
just happy to be in each other's company.

Later, after we've said our good nights, I crawl into bed
with a Sudoku puzzle and my film score playlist. As I fill
in numbers and hum to one of the songs from *Pride and
Prejudice*, my thoughts flit to my earlier discovery. What if
March goes to my co-op? If he started at a new co-op this

fall, he had to have moved recently, so it might not be too hard to figure out if I already know him.

I know most of the guys at Stony Point, and there's no way March could be any of them. But...

I drop my puzzle book and sit upright. What if March is Owen?

CHAPTER FOUR

The next Friday, I'm playing detective. Earlier in the week, I told Ro what March revealed, as well as my theory that he's Owen, but we didn't have time to thoroughly discuss it until today.

"Wouldn't Owen have put two and two together since he knows you like food so much?" says Ro. We're waiting for the others to show up for lunch, but we're stuck inside again this week due to more autumn rain.

I shrug. "I don't know if I've talked about cooking when he's around, though. He may just think I really like food." At that thought, I bury my face in my hands. "Oh my gosh, he probably thinks I'm some kind of glutton."

Ro laughs. "He's a *teenage boy*, Audra. I doubt he cares. But anyway, what do you know about March that could tell us whether or not he's Owen?"

"He likes the outdoors," I say slowly, thinking over everything important I know about March. "He's talked a lot about going on hikes. Um...I think he likes to wear bandanas like they're headbands? He did a few years ago at least. He was always talking about the cool ones he found when they traveled. He might be starting a job soon. He has brothers, and he loves movies. We bonded over *The Princess Bride* when we met."

"Y'all are such homeschoolers," Ro says, but the roll of her eyes is playful, not mean. She opens her mouth to say something else but then shuts it.

"What?"

"You're gonna hate me but...I think there's another guy who could be March. Here at Stony Point, I mean. You do realize he could be at some other co-op, right? The chances of March ending up at the same co-op as you are, like, one in a billion, considering it's already a pretty big coincidence that he moved to the same city as you."

I raise my eyebrows. "Ro, are you going somewhere with this?"

"Oh!" She pauses and fiddles with her water bottle. "What if it's Matthew?"

I groan, then shake my head emphatically. "No, there's no way."

"Um, it's possible. I know he has at least one brother, and he loves Fleetwood Mac—you've told me several times that March does—and both their names start with *M*," Ro tells me, holding up a finger with each statement.

"Okay, that last one is stretching it. My username starts with an *F*, not an *A*." I cross my arms. "Besides, it's just not possible. Matthew is nothing like March. He's too arrogant and inconsiderate."

Ro looks skeptical. "I don't think he's like that."

The rest of our friend group join us in the corner of the multipurpose room, minus Joel since he's got a student council meeting this week. (Yes, even homeschool co-ops have student councils.) I observe both Owen and Matthew, mainly to placate Ro, but also because there is some truth to what she said—Matthew has at least two things in common with March. Of course, there are a lot of people who like Fleetwood Mac and have brothers, but I guess I can't rule Matthew out just yet, no matter how much he gets on my nerves. I have to admit it's a possibility when I see the yellow bandana tied around one of his backpack straps.

Neither he nor Owen does anything that screams March, but my pulse quickens a little when Dylan somehow gets Owen to talk about when he hiked part of the Appalachian Trail. That must be a good sign. When a boy, who looks like he's around eleven, runs over and whispers something to Owen, I add that as another check in the March column. They don't look very much alike, but the kid must be his brother. Why else would he talk to Owen? I feign interest in my salami and provolone sandwich, but I watch Owen instead. His interactions with the boy seem brotherly, although I can't hear anything they're saying.

"Why do people have to play their music aloud in public?" Matthew grouses, drawing my attention.

He scowls at some freshmen a yard or so away from us. One of the kids is holding a tablet, and music drifts over to us. The vocalist sounds familiar.

"Isn't...isn't that Fleetwood Mac?" I ask, my thoughts racing as fast as my heartbeat.

"Yeah. Ugh, I hate that song. It's so grating," he replies. He adjusts his glasses, then turns to Kylie, who asks him a question that I don't hear.

Oh, thank God, I think as my shoulders relax. My heart

rate slows a little, and I give Ro a pointed look. That settles it: there's no way March would hate a song by his favorite band. I can't help but feel relieved; I don't know what I would've done if March had turned out to be Matthew.

Ro leans over. "Okay, you were right."

"Thank God."

"I'm not sure he's—" She nods towards Owen—"either. It just doesn't fit to me. Maybe you could check at the other co-ops? Holly could help."

"Ro, you're a genius!" I exclaim.

I shift on the rough carpet, suddenly worried the rest of our friends overheard us. Of course the guys don't know about March at all, and Kylie only knows the bare minimum—mostly because she's skeptical of anyone online and their intentions. But my fears are quickly allayed; they're busy talking about field trips.

Quietly, I tell her, "I know his co-op meets on Fridays, so it has to be Stony Point or Hickory. I'm, like, 99 percent certain all the other co-ops around here meet other days of the week. I'll ask Holly soon."

Co-ops are supplementary to a homeschooler's education, so most of the ones in our area only meet once a week. I've always taken most of my classes at home, except for electives and what my parents haven't felt equipped to teach me, like AP calculus. Co-ops also provide group opportunities for field trips.

Stony Point does one every fall to Colonial Williamsburg, but I'm not going this year. Between my dad and the annual field trips, I've been there enough that I could lead a tour myself. I'd rather have a long weekend in the Shenandoah Valley—I've been dropping hints to Mom and Dad for the last few months—although I doubt that'll happen either, not with all the wedding planning that'll start soon. I know everyone says New England is prettiest in the fall, but nothing compares to the Blue Ridge Mountains. If you're up high enough, the red, orange, and yellow trees down in the valley stretch until they meet the haze of the next mountain, and you feel like it can't possibly be real.

"Audra?" Kylie says, nudging me.

I startle out of my imagination. "Yeah?"

"You're going to Williamsburg, right? I can't wait to eat at the King's Arms Tavern again. That was so much fun." She grins.

"Oh..." I hesitate; I hate to let her down, but I don't have nearly as much fun there as everyone else does. "I...uh... think I have something else going on that day."

"No way!" Dylan proclaims. "Your mom wouldn't have scheduled something else for Williamsburg Day. It's a tradition."

I scratch at an itch on my knee that isn't really there. What do I tell them? I know if I go and don't want to be there, I'll be a big grump and ruin their day. On the other hand, they'll poke at me until I say yes.

"Yeah, I think it was the only day I could get a dental appointment or something," I lie. "And you know how the dentist is—booked months in advance."

Kylie pouts. "It's your last year."

"I know. I'm sorry!" I don't want her to be disappointed, so I say, "Maybe we could go at Christmas. They decorate it so nicely then, and if it's not too cold..." I wouldn't mind Colonial Williamsburg as much during the holiday season, I suppose. And I *do* want Kylie to be happy.

That seems to appease her, and Dylan distracts her by pulling out her favorite candy. He didn't need to do that, although—just his face is enough to distract Kylie Sung. She's had a crush on him, though she won't publicly admit it, since the seventh grade. I can't imagine dating a guy from Stony Point; I remember their middle school antics all too well, even if guys like Joel and Dylan have outgrown that mischief...mostly.

It's like my thoughts triggered something because now Dylan is holding the candy out of Kylie's reach. She's short— only 5'1"—and his arms are long enough that, even when she jumps, she can't reach. I shake my head and share a private smile with Ro. We've been waiting for one of them to act on their feelings for years.

Lunch wraps up soon, and we all head our separate ways. Just like a couple weeks ago, Matthew joins me, and I sigh inwardly. It would be so much easier to tolerate him if he didn't find a new way to bug me every week.

Just as I'm about to say something semi-polite, his phone buzzes in his hand; a short ringtone plays, too—something regal and commanding with crashing cymbals that sounds familiar, but I'm not sure why. Matthew looks down at his phone, and a sour look instantly overtakes his face.

"Everything okay?" I ask.

He shrugs and clicks the phone off. "Yeah. Just someone I should've blocked a long time ago." He clears his throat and says, "So you didn't make fun of anyone's lunch today."

I glance at him but go with the subject change. "I don't make fun of their lunches!"

He gives me a pointed look.

"I don't! I just have high standards for what my friends should be eating."

"Did my lunch meet your standards?" His hands hang at his sides, and I don't meet his eyes.

"You're not—" I catch myself just in time. What I meant to say would've crossed a line. *You're not my friend* would've been out-and-out mean, instead of just sarcastic banter. "Um, I didn't really notice what you were eating." There. That means I wasn't paying attention to him, which surely can't be as bad as saying I don't care what he does.

"Oh. Well next time, I'll make sure to run my food by you," he says. His smile doesn't quite reach his eyes.

"Sounds good. See you next week," I say before scooting into my classroom.

As I find my spot at the square of tables, I think about the look on Matthew's face. Maybe what I said was still mean enough that it upset him. Or maybe it's not about me; I don't want to be that kind of person that thinks that everything she does is the reason for how someone's feeling. Maybe he hasn't had a great day. Guilt pricks at my conscience for not being nicer to him in light of that possibility. He's still annoying, but I shouldn't be cruel. I resolve to try harder next week. If he doesn't try to bug me, there's no reason I can't be nicer.

My conversation with Ro runs through my mind again.

"Besides, it's just not possible. Matthew is nothing like March; he's too arrogant and inconsiderate."

"I don't think he's like that."

I generally trust Ro's opinions, so if she sees something I don't…

I shake my head a little, which makes my classmate, Aliyah Parker, squint at me. I blush a little and mouth, *Zoned out.* She laughs under her breath and smiles at me, then returns her attention to what Mrs. Powers is saying.

I'm still caught on the idea of Matthew being March. As much as I trust Ro, I don't think she can say whether someone feels like March. She's never talked to him; she doesn't know him like I do. She can help me narrow the field, but ultimately, *I'll* know if someone is March.

I try to fit Matthew's appearance—dark brown hair, brown eyes, glasses he shoves up a lot—with how I picture March. It doesn't fit; March has brown hair in my mind, sure, but he's taller and has gray eyes that sometimes look hazel, green, or blue.

Maybe I have to adjust how I picture March, though, since Owen is currently the strongest candidate. He has short black hair and brown skin, which isn't how I pictured March, but that's okay. Personality-wise, Owen is a much closer match. Maybe Ro sees something I don't in Matthew, but the opposite is true, too. I can't be imagining how obnoxious Matthew is. March would never be like that; yeah, he's a guy, but he's thoughtful, smart, and concerned about others.

Matthew is not March, I tell myself firmly.

I pick up my pen and glance over at Aliyah's notebook to see what I missed. Class is more important than thinking about Matthew, anyways.

CHAPTER FIVE

Madeline and Trevor come to dinner that night, two weeks after their announcement. My dad gets home early from work, and I can hear his and my mom's frenzied whispers as I do my kitchen waltz. Mom put in a pot roast earlier, but I'm in charge of the mashed potatoes and pan-seared vegetables. My parents argue about Trevor as I slice yellow squash and chop broccoli, saying, "We don't know him well," and "He didn't even talk to us before proposing." While I stir the vegetables around the pan, they talk about Madeline, wondering if they should sit her down and have a long talk about hasty decisions. As I remove the potatoes from the stovetop and get ready to mash them, they debate about Trevor again. I'm pretty sure I hear my mom questioning his career choice, but I don't even know what he does beyond working for some company downtown.

Unlike my parents, I don't have strong opinions about the engagement. I don't know Trevor well, but he seems okay. He lives a stable life—he has a job and owns a condo. It's not like he and Madeline are fresh out of college; she's almost thirty and he's thirty-two. They can do whatever they want.

I feel like one of my cousins got engaged; that's how

disconnected Madeline and I are. Yeah, she comes for dinner a few times a month, but she talks with Mom and Dad more, and it always feels like having our neighbors over—coats laid over a chair instead of put in the closet, small talk about the weather and kids and jobs, guests who leave at 8 p.m. because they feel anything later is intruding too long. Besides, in Madeline's eyes, I'm just her kid sister who got scared by the crowd at her big sister's high school graduation and cried.

I stare down at the bowl of potatoes and the masher clenched in my hand. Well. At least the potatoes won't have any lumps. The doorbell rings, and my parents' heated whispers cease. Dinner is going to be a disaster, or, best-case scenario, it'll be an awkwardly silent meal. Oh, this is going to be a blast.

Most of the meal falls under my best-case scenario, which I'm not sure is a relief. We eat, compliments for the food are delivered, and Trevor stares at his plate. Madeline's ring glitters when she reaches for the saltshaker. Mom stares at the ring a little too long but doesn't say anything. Trevor refills his water glass for the fifth time, and it looks like Dad is about to speak, but he takes an extra-large bite of pot roast instead. All the things we aren't saying crackle in the air, though, and I feel like we're on the verge of a storm.

Mom brings out an apple crisp for dessert. It's her signature recipe, the only thing she really loves to bake, and I've been told I can't have the recipe until she's dead. Madeline clears her throat, and we all look at her.

Her fingers fidget as she says, "We set a date. Well

actually, we picked a few, and we want to see which works best for y'all and Trevor's parents."

"We're thinking June ninth, sixteenth, or twenty-third," says Trevor.

My parents turn to each other and do that weird nonverbal parental communication thing. After a moment, Dad says, his voice a bit tense, "I think I have a conference the weekend of the ninth, but the other dates should be fine."

"Audra's graduation is May twentieth, so I'd prefer one of the later dates, just so I'm not juggling two big events too close together," Mom says. Her gaze flits from Trevor to Madeline. "The final decision should be yours, but I appreciate that you want our input."

"Okay, we'll see what my parents think," Trevor replies. He runs a hand over his spiky blond hair.

Just as I take a bite of crisp, Madeline asks, "Audra, would you like to be a bridesmaid?"

I almost choke, spluttering and coughing and probably spewing apple crisp everywhere. Dad gamely smacks me on the back and grins.

"As great as the story would be—choked to death on her mom's legendary apple crisp—I'd prefer that not to happen tonight," he quips as I gulp water.

The others chuckle, but I roll my eyes. *Dads.*

Everyone's looking at me now, and I take time to empty my glass, using the coughing fit as an excuse.

"I'd be honored. Thank you," I finally manage to reply. Because what else do you say to a question like that, asked in front of other people?

Madeline smiles, something like relief flickering in her eyes. "Oh, good!"

And that's that.

Trevor volunteers to do the dishes, and a pointed look from my mom nudges me to offer my assistance. Clearly she and Dad still plan to talk to Madeline alone. So my future brother-in-law washes while I load the dishwasher and dry whatever he hands me. Every conversation he starts ends awkwardly; talking has never been his forte—at least with me. He and Madeline seem to communicate just fine.

"You ready to be done with school?" he asks.

"Uh, I guess. Except I'm going to college, so I've got another four years after this."

"Oh, right." Next he tries, "Heard back from any other colleges?"

"Nope." That's the best I can say? Really? I could've been like, *No, it's too early to hear from most of the schools*, but all I could say was, *Nope*.

"Seen any good movies lately? Madeline's always talking about how many movies you know."

"Haven't had the time to do anything but rewatch favorites. There's one coming out soon, set in Africa about a girl who plays chess, that I'd really like to see," I say.

"That's cool."

Mercifully, Madeline emerges from Dad's study after only ten minutes. She comes up beside Trevor and touches his shoulder.

"They want to talk to you," she tells him. "I can take over for you here."

He gulps, and I don't blame him. Talking with the parents of your fiancée, the parents you didn't ask for a blessing, can't be easy. As he dries his hands, my sister rubs his arm and kisses his cheek. Once he's gone, she turns to me.

"They're concerned, that's all. But I think they'll realize we know what we're doing," she says.

"I know. I'm not a kid anymore," I say shortly. I'm one more comment away from an eyeroll.

She laughs softly. "I keep forgetting that."

She plunges her hands into the soapy water, and her shoulders relax. We're quiet for a couple minutes, but it's more comfortable than with Trevor, like when my parents and I are all doing our own things in the same room after dinner. I strain to eavesdrop on their conversation, but the study door is thick, and I can only pick up a few murmurs. At least they're not yelling. That must be a good sign.

"How are things going at that co-op of yours?" she asks.

I side-eye her. *That co-op of yours* sounds so condescending. "Fine. I'm gonna teach the junior-level cooking class next semester."

"Oh yeah, Mom mentioned that. That's exciting." She doesn't sound like she thinks so.

It occurs to me how weird it is that our mother told her first, that Madeline and I aren't close enough for me to be the one to tell her that the Sanderses are moving, and I get to take over the class. I say, "Yeah, it'll be interesting. I'm just glad I have most of this semester to pick recipes. That's the hard part."

"Really?"

"Yeah, I have so many options, I don't know how I'll narrow it down."

Madeline laughs, and I feel my shoulders ease a little. "I'm sure Dad's willing to taste test and help you. Anyways, how's your math class?"

"Not too bad yet. I'm sure I'll be in over my head soon."

"Nah, it won't be that hard. I know math isn't your strong suit, but you are related to Mom and me. And besides: think how much it'll help when you get to math and business classes in college."

I smile, grateful for her unexpected vote of confidence. "Thanks, but I'm kinda hopeless at this point," I tell her.

I dry my hands as Madeline finishes the last dish, and I edge towards the door to head upstairs. March said he'd be online tonight, and we haven't had a long conversation in a few days. I've been too busy piecing things together and trying to figure out if I know him in real life.

"Hey, Audra?"

I turn back to my sister and blink in surprise.

"I know we're not close, and a lot of that is my fault. I didn't want to make an effort. I was too preoccupied with teenage drama to really get to know you when you were young, and then I was out of the house," she says as she pulls the plug to drain the sink. She doesn't meet my eyes, and her cheeks are a little pink.

I shrug. "It's okay." I'm not sure it really is, but what else am I supposed to say?

"I don't want to keep feeling like a stranger, though. Could we hang out more? Do things together on weekends, like go shopping, or up to D.C., or out to eat..." She nervously tucks her hair behind her ears. "My boss wants to start sending me to conferences along the East Coast, and you could come with me."

I'm not even sure how to respond to that. Spending time with Madeline would be weird. On the other hand, though, isn't that how you get to know someone? Not going on trips with them, I mean, but doing things together. Things like Madeline suggested: shopping and going out to eat. Maybe that's how I can think of this—getting to know a new friend.

"Do you want to do that?" she asks, playing with her engagement ring.

"Okay," I say. We exchange small smiles, and then I head upstairs. I don't feel quite settled, though. Both of her questions tonight have thrown me for a loop, and I have no clue what's brought this on.

There's too much on my mind now, and I hate having so much to process. I was planning to try and ask March some leading questions, see if I can tell if he's Owen or not. Now I'm not sure I have the attention span for that. Maybe I can get some homework done instead; the assignments for my US government class don't require too much focus.

I flip on the lamps in my room. As I plop onto my bed, my phone buzzes on the nightstand, and its screen lights up with a text.

HOLLY
Hey, girl! What are you up to
this Friday?

ME
Well, co-op

HOLLY
LOL, I mean in the evening

ME
Oh. I don't think I have
any plans. Why?

HOLLY
Hickory is having their first party
of the school year, and we can bring
outside guests. Wanna come with me?

ME
Sure! I'll need to check with my
parents, but I'm sure they'll be
cool with it.
ME
I'll have to ask later tho.
They're having a discussion
with Mads's fiancé atm.

HOLLY
Uh oh…

ME
She asked me to be a bridesmaid

HOLLY
Wow really?

ME
Was not expecting that

HOLLY
But it's good she asked
you, right?

ME
Yeah. And she wants to hang out more
If getting engaged to Trevor made her

realize we don't act like sisters, maybe
this wedding won't be so bad after all.

ME

We've never been like you and
Christina, though.

HOLLY

Yeah, but Christy's only three years
older, and we've shared a room
our entire lives.

ME

True. And maybe it'll get better. I've
always wanted to have a big sister
like you see in books or movies.

I wait a minute, then text:

ME

Oh, hey did your director ever send
out that email? Did you get a solo?

HOLLY

Yes! In the Christmas
concert 😄 😄 😄

ME
Yay!!!
ME

I am gonna be front row, cheering
louder than your parents

HOLLY

Please don't embarrass me, lol

ME

Me? Embarrass you? Ha!

HOLLY

😶

HOLLY

I'll let you know when tickets are available 😀

ME

Awesome. Oh, so I didn't tell you but March let something slip about his identity last week.

HOLLY

Omgsh, really??

ME

Yup. He mentioned the Richmond area.

HOLLY

Oh. My. Gosh.

HOLLY

He lives HERE???

ME

I think so

HOLLY

And he's homeschooled. Do you think he goes to your co-op?

ME

Maybe! I also wondered if he went to Hickory with you.

HOLLY
Ooh!
HOLLY
I could try to find him.

ME
That would be great

HOLLY
What should I be looking for? You
guys didn't tell each other what you
look like, right?

ME
Yeah, I have no clue about that. I'm
pretty sure he's a senior, but he could
be a junior. He has two younger
brothers, and he moved within the
last nine months... I think.

HOLLY
Mmkay, I'll see who I can find. And
if you come to that party, you can
do a little sleuthing of your own.

ME
Oh yeah
ME
Gotta go. My mom's calling. I think
Madeline and Trevor are leaving.

HOLLY
Okay, ttyl

ME
Ttyl

I toss my phone aside and trot downstairs. Trevor and Madeline are pulling their jackets on when I reach the entryway. They're both smiling, and the creases are gone from Mom's forehead. I watch as she *hugs* Trevor. Guess the talk with him was in his favor. I hesitate on the bottom step and run my hand over the wooden newel post.

Dad beckons me forward, though, and I move to his side. He puts an arm around me and hugs me. I glance up at him. His smile isn't quite as genuine. Maybe the talk with Trevor didn't go well, and Mom's just better at faking it.

"Well, I guess we'll see y'all at Thanksgiving?" Mom chirps.

Madeline looks at Trevor, and he nods.

"Yeah, 1:00 at Grandma and Grandpa's, as usual?" she replies.

"Yup!" Dad says. He lightly slaps Trevor on the back. "I hope Maddie prepares you for Thanksgiving with the Dunnes. My side of the family takes it very seriously."

Trevor swallows. "That'll be, uh, interesting to experience," he says. "My family is a bit more...low-key about holidays."

"It'll be fun!" Madeline says, looping her arm through her fiancé's. "You'll get to meet all my aunts, uncles, and cousins." Then she glances at her watch. "We'd better head out. I'm going to a yoga class bright and early tomorrow morning."

Mom leans over and hugs her. "All right. Thanks for coming, sweetie."

"Thanks for having us!"

Mom hugs Trevor again. "It was good to chat with you, Trevor," she adds.

Now I really can't decide if the talk went well or not. Mom can be so Southern sometimes—she'll lie to your face in the nicest way possible—but she also values honesty when possible, so maybe she's being sincere.

I hug Madeline when she steps towards me. "I'll text you soon, okay? I'm going to D.C. in a few weeks, so it would be nice if you could come with me."

I've been to D.C. a couple times, but there's always more to discover. My smile is genuine. "That would be fun!"

"We'll talk more about it later," she promises.

I fidget as she and Trevor leave. This could be good. Maybe Madeline is finally going to be the sister I always wanted her to be.

Later that night, when I'm working on an art history assignment, my phone buzzes. This time, it *is* March. I slide my homework out of the way and sprawl on my stomach as I read his message.

MARCH
Hey, what's up? We haven't
talked much lately.

I chew on my lip, feeling a little guilty. It's not like he hasn't been on my mind, but I've been too preoccupied with figuring out if he's at Stony Point, among other things, to message him. We've had lulls before, but I feel bad every time, especially if they're my fault.

FEATHER
Sorry, I've been busy

MARCH
Nah, it's cool. Listened to
22 today. Now it's stuck
in my head.

FEATHER
CRAP
FEATHER
I forgot to listen to a
Fleetwood Mac song

MARCH
I am so disappointed. I expected
more from you.

FEATHER
I am so sorry. Can
you forgive me?

MARCH
I don't know…

FEATHER
Picture me on my knees, begging
for forgiveness
FEATHER
I could bake you something. Obviously
I can't send it to you, but I'll make
whatever you want and send loads
of pictures. That's the same thing, right?

MARCH
Haha not really

MARCH
But I can't stay mad at you
so...you're forgiven

FEATHER
Thank you, I'll go listen to
The Chain twice as penance.

MARCH
Good idea 😊

FEATHER
How is everything? How are you
feeling about the move? We never
really talked about that.

MARCH
Things are fine. My dad's still
super busy, but he's promised
he'll be here for Thanksgiving.

FEATHER
That's good. You didn't answer
my second question, though.

MARCH
Why do girls love talking about
feelings so much? 😶

MARCH
I'm happier than I was before. For
the most part. My ex is bugging me,
but I don't have to deal with her in
person and I can block her on social
media. The move was...

MARCH
I didn't tell you, but I was really mad

for awhile there. Last time we moved,
I was 4 and I don't remember it and
it didn't matter to me. But this time
I had friends, a job, and a life and
I feel uprooted and…what's the word?
Displaced?

FEATHER

That sounds right. I'm sorry. I wish
there was something I could do.
You can always tell me anything, okay?

MARCH

Thanks
I don't want to dump
everything on you tho

FEATHER

Well friends are supposed to listen
and support each other. And we're
friends, right?

MARCH

Of course

FEATHER

Then tell me what you're
feeling. Please?

MARCH

I'm fine. Seriously. The people
here are fine. I just liked the
way things were before the move.

FEATHER

I don't like change either.

MARCH
Let's both never change then.

> **FEATHER**
> I wish it worked that way.

What would it be like if we stayed the same together, the only two people in the world who didn't change? Never had to grow up and go away?

I lean back in my desk chair and think. That wouldn't be so fun, though, now that I think about it. I'd never go to culinary school, never fall in love, never travel the world and eat new, amazing foods.

> **FEATHER**
> I've changed my mind. I don't
> like change, but it's inevitable
> and important for... making us better
> and giving us new adventures.
> **FEATHER**
> And as a wise woman once told me
> "People are always telling you that
> change is a good thing. But all they're
> saying, is that something you didn't
> want to happen at all has happened."

MARCH
I recognize that quote

I smile. March and I watched *You've Got Mail* a while ago together; it's always been one of my mom's favorites, and not just because she and the female lead share a first name. March continues typing for a while, probably erasing and rewriting half his sentences. I picture long fingers, perfect for playing the piano—even though March isn't musical—fiddling with his phone. I imagine him chewing on his lip and shifting so he's leaning against his bedroom wall, which I bet is painted green or gray. He probably has music playing loud enough so any noises from his brothers' rooms are drowned out. I'm about to return to my homework when my phone vibrates.

MARCH
New adventures, huh? I guess
the move counts as one.
MARCH
You have such a positive view of
life and I wish I thought more like
like you do. I'm trying to make the
best of a shitty thing, really. I just
haven't been happy in awhile. That
group at the co-op is welcoming, I
think, but I feel like an outsider.
They've known each other for years
just like my friends at home and
I did. They all fit together, have
inside jokes, and finish each others'
sentences. I'm the guy they roll
their eyes at. I can't wait to graduate
and get the hell out of here.

I wiggle my fingers, all set to reply, but his words give me pause. *Roll their eyes...* I don't think any of my friends roll their eyes at Owen. And now that I think about it, he doesn't have two younger brothers. I've only seen him with a freshman girl and that middle school boy.

Matthew has two younger brothers... The thought pops into my head, and I shudder. At least I know March can't be Matthew, after that incident with the Fleetwood Mac song.

Well, this sucks. I think I wanted March to be Owen, who is contemplative and kind and, if I'm being honest, kinda cute with his dark eyelashes and deep brown skin.

MARCH
Sorry that was a lot to throw at
you all at once

FEATHER
Please, it takes a little more than
that to send me running.
FEATHER
I wish I could be there so you had a
friend at co-op. I've never moved or
switched co-ops so I've never had to
completely start over. Even when I started
at this co-op, we chose it because it was
where my friends were. So, even from
the beginning I've had my group.

MARCH
It's just a year. I only have
to make it for a year.
MARCH
That's probably telling you
how old I am, but it's not
that big a deal.

FEATHER
Isn't it tho? We said we wouldn't
share stuff that would make us
easier to find on social media.

MARCH
Pretty sure saying I'm a senior
won't make that much of a difference.

No, I think, *but since you let your location slip, if I were some creep, I'd have an easier time finding you.*

FEATHER
Ok. I'm gonna go.

MARCH
Sorry I didn't mean to take
anything out on you.

FEATHER
Nah, it's been a long day, and I
still have an art history assignment
to finish. And I don't really want
to fight right now.

MARCH
Ok. Talk to you tomorrow?

FEATHER
Yeah, sounds good.

That was the most frustrated I've seen March in a long time, and it kind of came out of nowhere, I guess. He's good at bottling up his feelings. I don't know what guys do when they hang out, but I bet they don't vent about whatever's bothering them. They should, though; it would be healthier than letting their emotions explode.

Maybe when March had a girlfriend last year, he could talk things out with her, but now… It sounds like he has no one. Except me.

CHAPTER SIX

Holly told me the Hickory party won't be fancy, so I wear a short-sleeved, silky purple top and dark-wash jeans. My parents were fine with my going, and they even let me take Mom's car by myself to pick up Holly. I can't decide if they trust my driving skills, or if they're still too distracted by Madeline and Trevor's surprise engagement.

Regardless, I drive the two of us to the party. Her co-op meets at a church in the West End, but they rented a room in a community center tonight. I've gone to parties with Holly before, so I know some of her classmates. Plus, there's overlap in extracurriculars—homeschoolers tend to flock together no matter where we are. For example, the Hickory student body president was in a junior soccer league with me in elementary school, and Holly's friend, Emily, and I volunteered at the same animal shelter a few years ago.

Holly and I hover by the food table with Emily and a couple other girls as we wait for the party to start.

"Do you think any of the new kids will come?" I whisper when Holly's friends are distracted.

"Hopefully." She shuffles her feet, then says, "There's, like, five new junior and senior guys this year, but I'm pretty sure only two of them moved here."

"March mentioned he's a senior." I can't say anything more because a guy walks over and greets Holly.

As she talks with him, I scan the room, taking in the clumps of teenagers, the music, and the sparse streamers. If this is anything like Hickory's other parties, the chaperones/student council advisors will nudge us into ice-breaker games, after which the "DJ" (a.k.a. a former student who still lives in the area) will turn up the music, and we'll form not-quite-circles and dance. Stony Point doesn't do small parties like this; we have the Fall Fancy in early October and spring formal—they're very careful to not call it prom even though that's essentially what it is. Prom just smacks too much of "secular public schools," I guess. I kind of like these smaller events, though. It's easier to talk to people, and everyone feels more relaxed.

Holly pokes my arm, then inclines her head towards a guy who just walked in. "That's Sam. He's a senior, just joined Hickory this fall." He has ginger hair, a leather jacket, and a confident air. I study him and wonder if I'm projecting, or if I actually somehow see March in him.

"Do you know him at all?"

"Not well. He's in my Spanish class, and I remember my mom and the rest of the board interviewed his family before they were admitted. That's pretty much all I know."

Sam strolls over to a group of mostly guys, and they greet him. I watch for tense politeness or eye rolls, but it's hard to tell in this lighting.

"Do you know anyone in that group?" I ask.

"Hmm…" Holly stands on tiptoe and discreetly peers at the guys, trying to pick out their faces in the dim lighting.

"Oh, there's Caleb. We have a class together. C'mon, I can ask how the algebra test went for him this afternoon."

"We don't have to." I meet her gaze. "If you don't know Caleb very well, we don't have to go over there."

"No, it's fine!" Holly nods to reassure me. "I really do want to talk about the test. It was so stressful, and I want to know if someone else felt the same way."

I follow at her heels but hang back once we reach the group. None of these guys are familiar, and I don't know what to talk to them about. I watch Sam out of the corner of my eye, waiting for a gesture or smile to match him with March. Surely I would know March just by how he acted, even if I've never seen him in person before.

Sam has shed the confident air he wore when he walked in. He's standing on the edge of the circle, staring at his sneakers, although he acknowledges a guy who speaks to him. Our gazes meet, and I smile before directing my attention to Holly and Caleb, who are trying to figure out which one of them got a question wrong on the test.

"Hey."

I jump slightly and turn around.

"Sorry, crap, sorry," Sam says, holding out his hands as if to steady me. "I didn't mean to startle you."

I wave my hand dismissively. "Oh, no, you, uh, you didn't startle me. I just, um, I…" My cheeks warm considerably.

He shoves his hands in his pocket and smiles sheepishly. "I'm Sam. Do you go to Hickory?"

I shake my head. "No, I go to Stony Point, but I came with a friend. I'm Audra."

"Is Stony Point another homeschool workshop?"

"We're actually a co-op, but yeah, I'm homeschooled."

He tilts his head. "What's the difference?"

"You know," I say with a laugh, "I've never been able to figure that out."

"I went to another homeschool workshop before we moved here, so I wouldn't be able to say either." Something about his grin is open and comforting.

"Where'd you move from?"

"A suburb of Chicago." He's holding his jacket awkwardly like he doesn't know what to do with it. He looks around, then tosses it on a nearby chair.

"Oh, cool." I try to think of something else to ask, maybe about Chicago, or maybe I can work the conversation around to his favorite movies or something like that.

The volume of the music increases, and I jerk slightly, trying not to show that I was startled again. Guess the Hickory student council isn't going to force us to play icebreakers this time. Holly tugs at my arm and says something I can't quite hear over the music. With a wave at Sam, I drift with Holly over to her friends, who beckon us from the dance floor.

To my surprise, Sam follows. He and a couple other guys join our circle, and we dance to the cleanest pop songs from the last four decades. I can't contain my excitement when "Shake It Off" plays, and Sam doesn't hide his amused smile as I sing along. He trails behind me again when I go to get some soda after the song ends, and I'd be lying if I said I didn't appreciate the attention. It's nice to talk with a guy who hasn't known me since my awkward preteen years. Unlike Joel and Dylan, Sam didn't know me when I unironically said "LOL" aloud instead of laughing.

"So you like Taylor Swift," he says, raising an eyebrow.

I laugh and scrunch up my nose. "Just a little." I pour some Coke in a cup before handing the bottle to him. "I've been to two of her tours. Best nights of my life."

"That's cool. I like *1989*, but country isn't really my thing," he replies.

"I get that, but I like her early stuff just as much as her recent albums. I love her lyrics and melodies and the way she encapsulates heartbreak and—" I cut myself off. "Sorry, I'm rambling." I look down at my hands and fiddle with my feather ring.

"Nah, I get it," he says, and I look back at him. He rubs the back of his neck.

This is the perfect opening to ask some innocent questions, ones that might tell me if he's March.

"So, um, who's your favorite singer? Or band?" I ask, rubbing at the ridges on my cup.

His eyes light up. "Fleetwood Mac. I got to see them in Milwaukee last year. It was awesome."

Stay calm, I tell myself. *Fleetwood Mac has been popular forever; just because he and March share a favorite band doesn't mean Sam is March.*

But that doesn't keep my heart from racing when a short, stocky kid hurtles over and chatters away to Sam. I barely catch a word he says before he runs off again, although Sam manages to ruffle the kid's hair. Something in me warms to the sincere affection Sam displayed.

Sam watches after the kid for a moment before laughing and telling me, "That's my brother. He's a freshman."

"I have an older sister," I offer, as if he'll reply, "*Hey, my best friend from the Internet is homeschooled, loves Taylor Swift, and has an older sister. What a coincidence!"*

He leans against a wall. "So what do you like to do?"

"I like movies and cooking." I mimic his posture, except I face him instead of putting my back to the wall.

He doesn't bat an eye, doesn't seem to recognize those as two of Feather's favorite things.

Surely March would react to that. Maybe he's better at playing it cool than I thought, though. Then again, March wants to be an actor, I remember.

"What about you?" I ask. As he considers this, I study his outfit. He's wearing a plain navy blue T-shirt and jeans. *Would March wear that?* I wonder and consider the leather jacket he was wearing earlier, too.

"I played baseball with a rec league, and I'm hoping to do that here in the spring," he tells me. "I babysit a bit, too, and ride my bike."

I frown. March never mentioned any of those things. Maybe I don't know him as well as I thought. I suppose he could be different online than he is in person. We show different sides of ourselves to everyone. My heart sinks at my next thought: maybe Sam isn't March. There're a lot of coincidences, though, so I'm not ready to dismiss the possibility. One more thing occurs to me. Maybe he lied, although heaven knows why he'd lie about something like this.

"Cool," I manage to reply.

Something niggles in the back of my brain, a vague memory from when March and I first started emailing. *I lied to him; I said I'd been to France to make myself seem* more exciting. Then he asked about the trip, and I had to make up a whole story complete with Madeline getting seasick on the Seine and how boring I found Versailles. But because of that, I can't rule Sam out yet. I can't explain why March wouldn't have mentioned playing baseball, but maybe he doesn't take it seriously enough to merit sharing.

I see Holly gesturing from the dance floor and breathe a sigh of relief. She's providing me with an escape from this conversation I don't know how to continue. "I'm gonna head back out there." Then I pause. "Um, you wanna come?"

He tosses back the last of his soda and nods.

As I dance and laugh with him, Holly, and her friends, I feel like he and I were supposed to meet, even if he's not March. The DJ plays a slow song like always, and Sam looks at me tentatively. He clears his throat.

"Would you like to dance?" he asks all in a rush.

I take a deep breath. "Okay."

His hand meets mine, and it's warm, and I start to worry that mine is clammy. His other hand lands on my waist, and we sway a little, keeping our steps small. It's not quite like slow dances when I was a freshman and kept enough room for Jesus between the boy and me. There's still a gap between Sam and me, but it's much smaller, and although the small talk is a little awkward, I know it's only because we're getting to know each other.

I glance up at him. I'm close enough now to see he has some freckles dashed across his straight nose. My cheeks warm a little, and my gaze falls over his shoulder until he starts whisper-singing the lyrics of the Ed Sheeran song.

80

He's a little off-key, and he's being purposefully corny about it. I laugh and meet his eyes again. His smile is genuine, his hazel eyes crinkling up a little at the corners. We sway for another minute before his steps slow.

"Wanna try something?" he asks.

I blink rapidly. "Uh…"

"Just a twirl," he promises.

As soon as I nod, he spins me out and then back to him. It's smoother than I expected, especially since I'm not the best dancer. When his hand closes around mine, I feel a little breathless.

The rest of the night blurs together. I'm even in a bit of a fog while I drive, although I make a concerted effort to pay attention, especially since I have a passenger. I somehow make it home safely after dropping off Holly; Mom and Dad waited up, but they go to bed as soon as I've answered their perfunctory questions about the party.

I check my phone after I change into PJs. No texts, no messages, no emails. Well, except for the one letting me know I have a friend request on Facebook from Samuel O'Hara. I realize I haven't heard from or messaged March in several hours. At some point tonight, I stopped thinking of March and thought only of Sam. Something flips in my stomach as I swallow. I don't know what I'm feeling right now—maybe guilt? So I type out a quick message while I'm brushing my teeth.

FEATHER
Sorry for my radio silence today.
Hope you had as good a day as

I did! Maybe we can chat
tomorrow if you're not busy.

I hesitate, then send another message. Maybe his answer
will tell me what I want to hear.

FEATHER
Did you do anything fun tonight?

It's late; he's probably asleep or not up for a conversation.
I shut off my phone and fall into bed, wondering if in the
morning, March's answer will tell me if he's Sam or not.

CHAPTER SEVEN

I finished all my assignments earlier than usual today, so now I'm lounging on the porch. Rajesh, the neighbor dog, barks at me while he passes by. I wave to his owners, Mr. and Mrs. Patel, as they shuffle along the sidewalk. It occurs briefly to me to ask if they'd like me to walk Rajesh this winter, since the cold has started to bother them. For now, though, the last of the summer heat has mixed with autumn briskness, creating perfect weather. I watch a mail truck circle the court at the bottom of the hill, and I listen to the rustling of the leaves intertwined with the creaking chains of the bench swing. It even smells like fall, although I'm pretty sure that's just my cinnamon pumpkin–scented body wash.

March sent me a message five minutes ago. I have just enough time for a short chat before Grandma comes to pick me up. She loves to have me over to bake every now and then, since she knows how much I love her kitchen. She keeps her pantry stocked for her favorite granddaughter—her words, not mine—although I bring any out-of-the-ordinary ingredients. Today I'm thinking of making pear scones or a cobbler of some sort. My grandparents would probably appreciate the latter more. Maybe I'll ask March for his opinion after I answer his question.

MARCH

Do you ever hear a song for the first time and fall in love right away? Love at first note. Because I'm pretty sure that just happened to me.

FEATHER

Ooh what song?

MARCH

Guiding Light by Fox Vance.

MARCH

Foy Vance. Autocorrect. 😑 Anyways, Ed Sheeran's on the track.

FEATHER

Never heard of it, but I'm gonna look it up now. Anyways, to answer your question, absolutely. Except I've probably cheated on all my fave music a thousand times over. I fall in love with a lot of film scores.

MARCH

Any recent favorites?

FEATHER

There's this song from Mr. Magorium's Wonder Emporium—"Night Time"— that I like. And "Rooftop Kiss" from The Amazing Spider-Man.

MARCH
The Amazing Spider-Man is an
all-around great movie.
MARCH
Don't think I've asked this before:
Marvel or DC?

I stare at my phone. How the heck am I supposed to choose? Superheroes in general are great. I hate that people get into big arguments online over which franchise is better.

FEATHER
Why do you always ask the
hard questions???

MARCH
Haha sorry.
MARCH
But I need an answer. This could
make or break our friendship.

FEATHER
Damn it, March.
FEATHER
Um… between Peggy Carter and Cap and
the new Ms. Marvel, I guess I prefer Marvel.
But DC has Wonder Woman and Supergirl,
so I'm not sure I can pick.

MARCH
That's such a girl thing to do.

My eyes narrow. I live in the South, so of course I experience plenty of sexism, but March isn't usually like that.

FEATHER
Excuse you. I think it's a
HUMAN thing to not be able to
choose. Don't be sexist.

MARCH
Sorry. I can make up my
mind easily tho.

FEATHER
Oh yeah? Marvel or DC?

MARCH
Easy. DC.

Even as I type out my next question, a thought runs through my mind—when we talked about movies on Friday, Sam said he liked *The Dark Knight*. Could that mean…? Once I send the message, I think of questions to send rapid-fire.

FEATHER
Pancakes or waffles?

MARCH
At least TRY to make it hard.
MARCH
(Waffles as you already know.)

FEATHER
Pepsi or Coke?

MARCH
Coke

Sam drank Coke at the party, I remember. But maybe that was because I poured myself some and handed him the bottle, and he was being polite.

FEATHER
Winter or summer?

MARCH
Summer

FEATHER
Chronicles of Narnia or LOTR?

MARCH
Narnia

FEATHER
Fantasy or sci-fi?

MARCH
Uh… crap

I laugh aloud. Victory!

FEATHER
Hmm…having trouble deciding?

MARCH
Okay so I can't always make up
my mind. You win this time.
But you have to answer your
own questions.

I wiggle my fingers, then type out my answers. I've had a little more time than him to think about them, though, so it's not as hard as the challenge I issued.

FEATHER

Waffles, Coke, winter,
Narnia, and fantasy.

FEATHER

The Lion, the Witch, and the Wardrobe
is the first movie I remember
seeing in theaters.

MARCH

I think mine is The Incredibles.

MARCH

How are things with your sister?

FEATHER

Fine. I'm actually going out of town with
her next week. She's got a work thing, but
she said we can make a weekend of it.

MARCH

That sounds fun

FEATHER

It'll be something. I'll try and send some
pictures, especially of our meals. She's
letting me choose the restaurants.

MARCH

That was smart.

MARCH

That's nice of your sister. I wish
my dad took us on more of

his business trips. It's not
like we'd have to miss school
or anything.

FEATHER
Oh yeah one of the best parts of being
homeschooled is vacations in the middle
of the year. Except we don't take a lot
of those because my dad is an academic.

Saying that is probably crossing a line I shouldn't have for privacy reasons, but if March is going to let his location slip, I can at least even the playing field a little. Earlier, I almost mentioned where Madeline and I are going next weekend, but I realized that was probably too much. My parents' Internet safety lectures from middle school are still drilled into me.

MARCH
Your dad's a teacher, huh? Wouldn't
he want you to go to a real school
then?

FEATHER
My parents already went through that
with my sister, and they wanted to
try something else. They're big on
tailoring education to suit your strengths.

MARCH
Ah

FEATHER
Do you wish you'd gone
to a real school?

MARCH
Hmm, sometimes

FEATHER
I don't really. I still have friends
and good classes. Even if some
of my classmates are annoying.

MARCH
How so?

I'm tentative about ranting about people March potentially knows (if he goes to my co-op), so I keep my answer a bit vague.

FEATHER
I'm just tired of know-it-alls.
Like, a lot of us are smart and
they don't need to act like
they're the only ones.
FEATHER
There's this one girl who even corrects
our teacher and I'm just like???
FEATHER
And there's another who can be
really nice but it's just so she
can get you to confide in her and
then she gossips. So. Freaking. Much.

MARCH
Yikes

FEATHER
Ugh, ok, I think we need a subject change. I hate thinking about them.

FEATHER
I'm so glad fall is here. You?

MARCH
Eh it's all right. I like spring and summer better.

FEATHER
Fall and winter are best for baking

MARCH
You cook and bake all year tho

FEATHER
Yeah, but winter and fall flavors are the best. They're heartier but gentler at the same time. Cinnamon, pumpkin, apple, pear, chai, stews, pot roast, potatoes...

FEATHER
I just love how warm it all feels. It's like fleecy plaid blankets and coats and scarves and leaves falling. Just in food form. Don't get me wrong: I love berries and pasta salads and cheese-cakes and barbecue foods. But they're more vibrant and not as cozy. If that makes sense. Sorry, I'm rambling.

MARCH
It's not rambling if you're
passionate about it

I lean back on the porch swing, unable to stop a grin from spreading across my face. I feel like I do when I listen to the last song from the *Pride and Prejudice* score: completely, perfectly, and incandescently happy. It's moments like this that make me glad March and I started chatting on a whim four years ago and that I can call him one of my best friends.

FEATHER
Thanks for saying that. On a
related note—cobbler or pear
scones with spiced icing?

After he answers, I plan to move the conversation around to what we did this weekend. Hopefully I can figure out whether he was at the Hickory party or not; his message the morning after said he had an okay night on Friday, but he sent another message that changed the subject before I could ask more. Still, I want to know for sure if Sam is March.

MARCH
What type of cobbler? Is that the
one with oatmeal and brown
sugar crust?

FEATHER
Nooooo that's a crisp. A cobbler has
actual dough. But they both have fruit
Um it would probably be apple or pear.

MARCH
Mmm, apple cobbler sounds
amazing to me.

MARCH
Ugh gotta go. My mom found out
I didn't finish my math homework
and she's nagging me.

FEATHER
It's fine. Good luck with the homework!

Guess I won't get to ask anything about his weekend. I should've led with that instead of talking about food. I guess I can try another day, though. It's really not the end of the world, but I want to know who March is, which is strange. I've never really wanted that before, but now that I know how close he could be, it changes everything. Maybe I need to learn some patience. I tuck my phone away and head inside to gather up the extra ingredients for a pear cobbler.

CHAPTER EIGHT

Stony Point has Maymont days about once a month, March through November. A number of families from the co-op will picnic together and then split off to enjoy the park. Although we eat with our moms and siblings in a big group, my friends and I have been allowed to go off on our own afterwards for years.

Mrs. Stenger and my mom are spreading blankets when the others arrive. We're settling by the mansion this time, although sometimes we'll eat by the farm, mainly for Ro's and Kylie's little siblings, who love the petting zoo. Kylie texted earlier to say she couldn't make it because her parents had to work, but everyone else in the friend group is coming. Matthew arrives with Owen's family, which, despite my efforts to not concern myself with him at all, piques my curiosity. Where're his mom and brothers?

"Hi, Cora," says my mom, and she pauses to hug Owen's mom.

"It's good to see you, Kathleen. I can't believe how nice the weather is today! It's so unusual for November," says Mrs. Bell.

Mrs. Mitchell, Joel's mom, nods. "If this keeps up, we may be able to have a Maymont day next month."

My mom looks skeptical. "I doubt it. December always turns on us."

Mrs. Mitchell isn't fazed. She shrugs and says, "You never know. I'm gonna pray for a warm winter."

Matthew mutters to us, "I hope it snows. It's not winter if it doesn't snow."

I shake my head. "Warm winters are way better. It's usually not that humid, and it's just cool enough to wear jeans. After a Virginia summer, we deserve a temperate winter."

Owen snorts. "Virginia summers are *nothing*. Try living in Alabama."

Alabama! I finally know where Owen lived before. He's remarkably tight-lipped, considering he's known all of us for two and a half months now. I don't even know his brother and sister's names. Right now, his sister is timidly talking with Heathcliff, one of Ro's brothers. Maybe shyness runs in the Bell family.

Ro nudges me when the boys go to grab their lunches. "Hey. Can you please play nice with Matt today? He's a good guy, I promise, and maybe he'll let up with the teasing if you're not so standoffish," Ro says.

I shrug and reply, "I guess I could try." I narrow my eyes a little at her. *Why does she care so much if Matthew and I get along?* "Is something...?" I stop myself.

Ro tilts her head and furrows her brow. "What?"

"Are you guys...?" How in the world do you ask your best friend if she has a crush on your mortal enemy? (Okay, he's not really that, but it's felt like it some days.)

Her expression clears, and she laughs. "Heck, no. I just don't like to see y'all fighting any more than I like to see any of our friends fighting."

I laugh, too, and feel my shoulders relax. Joel calls us over, and we join him and the other guys on one of the blankets. I brought tuna pasta salad and homemade bread for my lunch. At least there's no co-op cafeteria around, although Dylan is crunching celery with peanut butter, and I can't help but wrinkle my nose at that. Peanut butter does not belong on celery; I couldn't eat it even if someone paid me a million dollars.

As lunch winds down, Dylan asks me, "Ready for the French test?"

I widen my eyes. "Ugh, no. All the different verb tenses are killing me. I mean, I've got a handle on the basic stuff, but *imparfait* and *plus que parfait* are gonna be the death of me."

"Yeah, I don't get those. French is more confusing than English sometimes."

"Should've taken Spanish," Joel teases from across the blanket.

"Everyone does that, though. I wanted to be at least a little different," I tell him. My fingernail scrapes against the bread crust in my hand.

"Okay, but *everyone* wants to be different, so are you really different if you want the same thing as everyone else?" Matthew says before biting into a carrot stick.

I shrug. "I don't know. I just knew Spanish seemed so ordinary. So I chose French. And yeah, it's confusing and hard at times, but I like the way it sounds." I glance at Matthew, to see if he has some snarky comment. When he doesn't, I continue, "Plus, it's the language of food. I kind of *had* to learn it."

Something in his face twitches for just a moment, but then he smiles a little at that. I can't help but shoot a look at Ro as if to say, *See? I'm trying.*

Dylan has to leave for swim practice after lunch, but the rest of us are ready to explore. This is Owen and Matthew's first visit to the Maymont gardens. Owen brought his camera, and we're all wearing sturdy shoes, so we wander down the steep trails past the Italian garden to the Japanese garden. Most of the hibiscuses, roses, and other plants are already dormant for winter, but it's still picturesque. I've been here in summer when kids are running around and screeching; it's much more serene today, although the five of us hop across the giant stepping stones in the pond like we're in elementary school again.

Owen's artistic eye catches on everything: the stepping-stones, the brightly colored koi near the surface of the pond, the arched bridge, and the waterfall. He takes pictures of it all including us. At the waterfall, my friends lose their adventurous streak, but I climb the stones beside it, and Matthew follows.

"This is cool," he says, eyebrows raised, and he sounds genuinely impressed.

I shrug. "It's all right," I tease.

He glances at me, probably checking to see if I'm serious or not, then holds my gaze for the briefest of seconds. I quickly turn my attention to the gardens around us. I survey the waterfall a few yards to my left that ripples into a scummy pond and the rocks and plants scattered around. I've been coming to Maymont since I was in preschool, and it's as much a part of me as the rest of Richmond.

Ro calls up to us, "Come on, guys! I want Owen to see the bamboo garden!"

Matthew hops down ahead of me. He pauses, then extends a hand to help me, but I ignore it. Once again, I'm questioning his motives. I can't figure out what's going on in his head ever, it seems. I scramble past the rocks and tree roots with the skill of someone who has visited this spot numerous times.

After Owen takes multiple pictures of the bamboo, Joel says, "We can take the steep but short trail or the longer, more gradual trail back up to the Italian Garden. The steep trail's the one we came down."

"Please not that one," Ro groans. She loves coming to Maymont, but hiking is not her forte.

I'm all set to side with her when Matthew says, "Let's take the longer way. I want to see more of the park."

Promise or no promise, I can't help but be contrary. "We're closer to the shorter path, though," I argue. "Let's just go back that way."

Owen, who's perusing a map, says, "But the other path goes by a mausoleum! I've gotta see that."

I'm outvoted, so I sigh and follow them down the trail. Most of the plants are already in winter mode, like I said, so there's not much to look at. The others chatter away, but I drift behind them, finding no interest in their conversations about sports teams or Colonial Williamsburg. I cross my arms over my chest but drop them after a couple seconds when I realize I probably look like I'm pouting.

Owen slows down so he ends up walking beside

EMMA SASKA

me. He doesn't say anything, but he smiles, his dimples appearing again.

"Hey, did you get that job you interviewed for a few weeks ago?" I ask.

He nods, and his smile grows. "Yeah. I'm a photographer's assistant now."

"Oh, that's so cool! What do you do? As their assistant?"

Owen explains, "I'll go with him and the other photographer for bigger shoots like weddings. I'm mostly in charge of equipment and getting people positioned how the photographer wants them to be. And I'll sometimes shadow him for, like, senior pictures and studio sessions. I'm kind of like an intern except I don't get to take any of the pictures yet."

"That still sounds fun."

"It is. I'm trying to take as many pictures as I can on my own because he'll occasionally look at my work and critique it. I've already learned so much from him," he tells me.

"That sounds amazing. I'd love to do that sometime—I mean, not with a photographer," I say, "but with a chef or caterer."

"That'd be interesting for sure," Owen agrees. He pauses. "If you really want to do that, I think my Uncle Vincent knows a guy who owns a restaurant in the Church Hill area. I bet you could shadow him for a day or get some advice or something."

"Really?" I start to feel a little less ornery. "Thank you, Owen! I'd love to do that, if your uncle would be willing to set it up."

"I'll ask him tonight when I get home," he promises, and his dimples flash again.

His words take a moment to register. Does his uncle live with them? Maybe the Bells moved in with him when they came to Richmond…

"Do you, uh, live with your uncle?" I ask.

He nods. "And my aunt and cousins. I, um… My parents died about a year ago. I moved up here to live with my dad's brother and his family." He adjusts his camera hanging around his neck, and his hands shake a little.

My face warms. I didn't mean to pry. "Oh, sorry, I had no idea," I say. My heart aches for him; I can't imagine losing my parents. If we were closer friends, I'd squeeze his arm or shoulder. That's what I've found is best when comforting Joel, at least. "I feel so bad. I thought your aunt was your mom, and your cousins were your siblings. I'm so sorry."

"Nah, I'm an only child," he says, scuffing his foot at the dirt.

I stop and face him. "I can't imagine going through something like that. I'm sorry."

His eyes meet mine. "It's okay," he promises. "And don't feel bad that you didn't know. I haven't told a lot of people here. They just assume that Aunt Cora's my mom since we have the same last name. And since Jude and Alicia didn't go to a co-op til now, I just let everyone think we'd all moved here together."

"Still, I shouldn't have assumed. We don't have to talk about it anymore, if you don't want to." We're almost to the mausoleum anyways.

"Nah, it's okay. I mean, I don't really like to talk about it, but it's good that you know now." Owen shrugs. "You're my friend, and I don't really want to keep secrets from you."

I smile at him. "You're my friend, too," I say. And I mean it.

Madeline helps me get my suitcase down the brick stairs from the porch over to our gravel driveway. She's dressed in comfier clothes than I've seen her wear in a long time, but I guess she doesn't have to look professional tonight.

Once we're settled in the car and Madeline is fiddling with the GPS, she asks, "You excited?"

I look up from March's reply on my phone. "Yeah," I say. Then I remember my manners. "Thank you again for getting me into the intensive."

"You're welcome. I can't wait to try all the new recipes you come away with," she replies as we pull out of the driveway. She glances over at me. "I wish I were as good of a cook as you are. I don't know what I'm going to do once Trevor's moved in."

"I could…I could give you a few tips. You don't have to do anything fancy. The only reason I do is 'cause I've been cooking for years, but Grandma started me with basic stuff." I reach for the ends of my hair, forgetting that I've pulled it up into a bun. "Um…cookies, mostly, but then soups and spaghetti and breakfast foods."

"Yeah, but all your fancy stuff tastes good!"

I chew on a fingernail; I can't look at Madeline. "Thanks."

I clear my throat after a moment. "But seriously, simple stuff can taste good, too. And I'm sure Trevor would rather you make good food than screw up complicated recipes."

She sighs. "You're probably right. I just want him to be impressed, you know? He usually cooks when we don't go out, so he hasn't had to experience my limited skills yet."

Maybe if y'all had been dating longer than six seconds, you might've cooked for him by now, I think. Thank God I didn't say that aloud; it would've destroyed everything Madeline and I are building.

I realize I've probably been quiet for too long, which can't help the situation any. "Um, well…" I say, scrambling for something less judgmental than what my thoughts are producing. "I could… Maybe some weekend after we get back from D.C., I could teach you some stuff. We could make some of my favorite recipes."

"Really?" Madeline sounds like she doesn't believe I'd actually help her.

"Yeah." I try to infuse that tiny word with sincerity.

"That would be fantastic." She clears her throat. "Maybe you could spend the night? We could make dinner—you could teach me how to cook some stuff—and then we could watch a movie or something. If you don't want to, that's okay," she adds quickly.

"No, I, uh…that would be nice," I tell her. She actually wants to do something normal with me. Bringing me along on this trip is a big deal, yeah, but having me over to her apartment for a sleepover is something I feel like sisters would do. I think that gesture matters more to me.

"You're not just saying that? I don't know what other

women do with their sisters, but I know you like food and you always seem to know what movies are in theaters, so I figured you might like that type of thing."

We're on the highway now, so she keeps her eyes focused on the road. I-95 is the worst, even past rush hour. I watch as my sister chews a little on her bottom lip.

I smile. "Holly and her sister watch movies together, but I don't think there's any one right thing to do with your sister. We don't just have to do what I like, though. We could…" My voice fades as I realize I don't really know what Madeline likes to do.

She's good at math, but that's not something she likes to do in her free time, since her job pretty much revolves around numbers and money. I remember her hanging out with friends a lot in high school, but I was never sure what they did. Homework and talk about boys, I think, but neither of those is relevant anymore.

Madeline takes pity on me and doesn't leave me hanging. "I've always wanted to take a pottery class, so we could do that. My best friend Amber is so artistic. I'd love to be able to create like she does."

"Pottery sounds cool."

I try to think of Christmas presents Mom and Dad have given her in the last few years, since that could be a hint as to her hobbies. All I can recall are gift cards and clothes and…

"You like jigsaw puzzles, don't you?" I blurt.

"Yeah…"

"We should get one of those giant 1,000-piece puzzles and put that together some evening. Or over multiple evenings. I don't know how long jigsaw puzzles take." My hands fidget in my lap, but my energy is less nervous and more excited now.

"Oh, yeah, we could definitely do that!" She smiles at me, but only for a second before her eyes are back on the road.

"I like puzzles, too," I tell her. "Well, I don't do a lot of jigsaw puzzles. But I do Sudoku. Holly got me a giant Sudoku book for my birthday this year, and I'm only, like, a third of the way done with it."

"You're better with numbers than you think, if you're good at Sudoku." Madeline puts on the blinker to switch lanes.

I make a face. "It's more about logic than numbers. Besides, Mrs. Powers never assigns Sudoku puzzles as homework, so I doubt they'll help me with AP calculus."

"They make you think, though. That helps with math and problem-solving in life." Her voice is traced with laughter.

I laugh and shake my head.

The traffic isn't too bad tonight, but only because we're heading towards D.C. instead of away from it. I have never seen traffic worse than on I-95; it's like people merge on and instantly forget how to drive. I'm glad Madeline's driving, and not me. I'd probably have a nervous breakdown.

"Do you remember when we went up to D.C.—what was it, fourteen years ago?" Madeline asks, when we're near Arlington.

"I mean, I was three so…" I reply. "I've seen pictures, though. There's one of me in my stroller in front of the White House."

"Yeah, Mom didn't think it was a good idea for you to go to the Holocaust Museum then, so she took you for a walk and then back to the hotel for a nap," my sister tells me.

"Ah." After a moment, I ask, "Did you bring it up since we're going to D.C. or...?"

"Kind of. But I guess I wanted to confess something." Madeline's eyes are steady on the road. "When Mom and Dad had you, I was fine with it. Or at least, it didn't impact me that much. I had to babysit occasionally, but I was busy enough by high school that I didn't have to spend too much time with you. Which was what I wanted at the time. But that trip...I guess that's when I started to resent your presence. We had to work around your napping schedule and tailor our meal choices to places that had kids' menus. Often, I only got time with Dad or Mom, not both since one of them always had to be with you. And I've been thinking about things these last few weeks, and I realized that trip was the starting point of when I became a bad sister."

I look at her steadily, despite my pounding heart. "I understand," I say eventually. "It hurt, though, as I got older and wanted to spend time with you, and you ignored or shoved me away."

"I know, and I'm so sorry," Madeline says. "I want to try to make it up to you. Fourteen years is a lot, but it doesn't mean we need to spend the rest of our lives distant and treating each other like strangers."

I surprise myself by saying, "Yeah. I think forgiving you is going to take a little time, but I want to get to that point. And I'll let you know when I'm there."

"Okay."

We drive towards the lights of the city, and I realize that the tough conversation we just had made me feel so much more settled with Madeline's desire to spend time with me. Usually, difficult talks leave me unsettled and restless. But not this. I smile to myself. This weekend isn't going to be so bad after all.

CHAPTER NINE

From: feathergirl1389@gmail.com
To: idesofmarch117@gmail.com
Sent on: November 21, 2016, 9:58 am
Subject:

Dear March,
I got back late last night from the trip with my sister. Thursday and Friday, I got to do a cooking class intensive, while my sister was busy. I learned so much, and the teacher was tough, but looking back, I had so much fun. As for the rest of the trip, I had to go with my sister to the conference on Saturday, which was boring. I brought homework and worked on that during different sessions. I had to take a make-up exam that night while my sister watched; I was supposed to take it yesterday at co-op, but I wasn't there so...
Then, Sunday—yesterday—we did fun things. I can't really be specific, but we went to museums and some other places in the area. We hit traffic on the way home, though, which was not fun. I didn't eat dinner until, like, 9:00.
What did you end up doing this weekend? How was co-op? Ready for Thanksgiving?
-Feather

From: idesofmarch117@gmail.com
To: feathergirl1389@gmail.com
Sent on: November 21, 2016, 2:37 pm
Subject: Re: [No subject]

Dear Feather,
I worked this weekend. Played video games. Went to the movies with some of the people from co-op. We saw Doctor Strange. A couple of my friends weren't allowed to go because their parents don't let them watch or read stuff with magic, which I think is stupid. It's like the magic in the Narnia or Lord of the Rings worlds and plenty of homeschoolers think those are ok. Anyways the movie was ok but there's better Marvel stuff out there.
Co-op was the same as usual. Nothing much to talk about there. Not ready for Thanksgiving. It's gonna be the same as always, just the five of us and store-bought everything. My dad is too busy to even consider going to my grandparents', which sucks cause my cousins would make the day bearable. Are you doing the usual stuff for Thanksgiving?
-March

From: feathergirl1389@gmail.com
To: idesofmarch117@gmail.com
Sent on: November 25, 2016, 10:42 am
Subject: Re: Thanksgiving

My mom and sister dragged me out of bed at an ungodly hour to go to a bridal boutique's Black Friday sale. I think weddings are awesome and all, but I did not sign up for four a.m. lines in the cold for a trunk sale. My sister didn't find a dress so it wasn't even worth it.

I enjoyed yesterday, though. Thanksgiving is one of my favorite holidays as you know, and I think this was one of the best yet. I made the pies on Wednesday; this year, we had pumpkin, caramel apple with a lattice crust, and triple-citrus tart with a chocolate crust and berries. Then I helped my grandma with the turkey, which was a big honor. Usually she doesn't trust anyone but herself.

One of my cousins had a baby in the last year, so I got to meet my...second cousin? First cousin-once-removed? What's the right term? Anyway, he's so cute! He's about four months old now and has the chubbiest cheeks. He squirmed a lot but barely cried. My sister and her fiancé were there too, and I enjoyed watching him get whipped into shape by all of my dad's siblings. Grandma seemed to like him, though, which I guess is a good sign. I trust her opinion. She's the only adult in my life who knows about you, and she seems to think you're all right and probably not a catfish. (That's not the term she used, but whatever.)

And now I'm going to crawl back in bed and sleep until Christmas.

-Feather

From: idesofmarch117@gmail.com
To: feathergirl1389@gmail.com
Sent on: December 9, 2016, 5:17 pm
Subject: Stab me with something sharp

I am so done with stuck-up know-it-alls. There's this girl at my co-op who thinks she's better than everyone, even her friends. She says the rudest things and she rolls her eyes at them. I can't believe a HOMESCHOOLER would be that awful. She seemed ok when I first got to the co-op but she's gotten worse and worse the longer I've known her. Her friends probably put up with her because they've known her for so long. Maybe they've gotten used to how she behaves? Or maybe they don't notice. It's kinda low key at times. I only notice the eye rolls because I started looking for them.
But seriously, if I didn't like her friends so much, I'd stop hanging out with them. She's too much to put up with.
On a different note, I'm going to a costume party at the end of the week. Haven't settled on a costume yet, so do you have any suggestions?
-March

From: feathergirl1389@gmail.com
To: idesofmarch117@gmail.com
Sent on: December 9, 2016, 5:52 pm
Subject: Not going to stab you

March,
I'm sorry you have to deal with someone like that. My mom likes to remind me we must put up with annoying people our whole lives, which never really helps with the problem at hand. Speaking from personal experience, though, there's someone who's kinda annoyed me too. My friend encouraged me to give him another chance, and I guess he isn't so bad…So I guess that's the only advice I can give you. Give this girl one more chance; maybe

try to get to know her a little better. Maybe she's shy or has a different sense of humor. Give her a chance to prove you wrong before you write her off completely. And if she's really like you think she is, then just be the bigger person.

One more week of classes, and then Christmas break. :D I'm so excited! As for your costume, I'm not very good at being clever. But maybe something that could be a pun?

-Feather

CHAPTER TEN

Hickory knows how to close a semester, unlike Stony Point. On the first day of Christmas break, Hickory's high school student council throws a costume party, open to students from all the homeschool groups in Richmond. Usually I go with my Stony Point friends, but they all had plans, so this year I go with Holly. It's kind of sad that they're missing my last Hickory masquerade; I want to take all the opportunities we can get to spend time together before Joel and I go off to college. Especially since we won't all have spring break together; Kylie, Ro, Owen, and Dylan got the go-ahead from their parents to plan their college road trip. In the end, my parents said it wasn't a good time for me to go—too hectic, with Madeline's wedding planning and it being my final semester of high school. At least Joel, who applied early admission to Tech, and I—and I guess Matthew, too—will be together.

Holly and I get ready together at her house. She's going as Jane Porter from Tarzan, complete with a tiny hat perched on her brown hair, and I'm wearing my go-to costume: Princess Buttercup. In the past, Joel has played along and dressed as the Dread Pirate Roberts/Westley, but I'm flying solo tonight. My hair has been in braids all day, so it's perfectly wavy when I brush it out. I saved up and bought my red-orange dress from a cosplay designer this year; before, I wore a cheap medieval-style dress reminiscent of Buttercup's wedding gown, but this is much better.

Mrs. Wheaton drives us to the community center Hickory rented out for the night. Their usual venue is too small, and I think they started using this place three or four years ago for bigger events. The entry hall is decorated with greenery and twinkly lights above tables where we present our pre-purchased tickets and receive stamps on the back of our hands. Then we enter the gymnasium.

My mouth gapes. Hickory really went all out this year. Even though we're on a basketball court, it feels much more elegant with sparkling trees lining the dance floor and swaths of fabric covering the high ceiling. There's an actual DJ—not just a Hickory alum—on the stage at the edge of the room, and although music isn't playing yet, lights by his station pulse different colors.

Holly, eyebrows raised, says, "I think Calvin blew our entire budget. Spring formal is gonna stink compared to this."

I laugh. "I'll bet ticket sales helped," I reply. "Didn't you say, like, two hundred people are coming?"

"That's what I heard at the last meeting." Holly waves to one of her classmates straightening up the food table. "I'm gonna go say hi. You can come—"

"Nah, I'll stay here," I interrupt.

I'm already scanning the fifty or so teenagers for Sam; we've chatted a bit online since the last party, and he told me he'll be here tonight. I don't see him—or anyone who could be March—but I smile and say hi to some classmates from Stony Point as they walk past. There are already a bunch of kids I don't recognize; they must be from other co-ops. I'm pretty sure I know all the groups that meet on Fridays, but maybe I don't, and March goes to that one. If he's not Sam, that is.

"Audra!" I look up to find Ron Weasley walking towards me, a big grin on his face. Actually, it's Sam, but his costume is pretty convincing, which makes me pause. He looks like he didn't throw something together last-minute like March's email implied.

"Hey," I reply.

To my surprise, he hugs me. Then he steps back and scans my outfit. "Hmm…this is a hard one." I roll my eyes good-naturedly. "You're Buttercup, right?"

"Yup."

"Nice. Man, everyone here is so creative. I saw a girl in a full-on Disney princess dress and then there's a bunch of Star Wars characters."

"Oh, and there's the rest of your trio," I say, as I point to a boy with glasses and a scar drawn on his forehead and a girl wearing a bushy wig.

Sam's eyes light up. "Be right back," he says before bounding over to them.

I smile. He's friendly and outgoing, more so than I imagined March to be. Then again, you have to be pretty outgoing to message a girl after only a brief interaction on a forum.

Sam takes a selfie with Harry and Hermione, and a bunch of other partygoers swarm them. He's going to be busy for a while. I look around for Holly, but she's still with her Hickory classmates. They're gesturing wildly and laughing, and I know I could go join them, but now that more people are here, there are more possibilities for March. But all I see are girls with cat ears, pirates, and cowboys.

"'No more rhymes now, I mean it,'" someone says behind me.

"'Anybody want a peanut?'" I reply automatically.

I turn back to find Matthew grinning at me, and I sigh inwardly. Of course he knows my favorite movie. His expression shifts a little, becoming a bit more subdued, but he doesn't walk away. I give his costume a quick onceover: white shirt, black vest, pants tucked into tall boots, and a holster belt slung around his hips.

"Sorry, who are you supposed to be?" I say.

"'We're gonna have company!'" he responds, which I think is supposed to be a quote from some movie.

I shake my head and tell him, "Not ringing any bells."

"What?! You've never seen *Star Wars*?" he practically shouts. I shake my head, and his eyes grow even wider. "And you call yourself a homeschooler."

I roll my eyes. "I haven't heard *that* before. Seriously, though, who are you dressed as?"

Matthew straightens his back and puffs out his chest. "Han Solo."

"Cool, I guess?"

My eyes start seeking out someone else from Stony Point that I can foist Matthew upon, but there's no one nearby. I glance back at him. He looks so earnest, like a Lab puppy, so I take pity on him and throw him a bone. If I'm the only person he knows here, it wouldn't be nice to leave him alone, no matter how much he annoys me.

"Do you have any big Christmas break plans?" I ask.

"I'm going back to Ohio for a week before Christmas. See my friends, visit my old favorite places, that sort of stuff," he tells me.

"Oh, that sounds nice."

"What are your plans for break?" he asks.

I shrug. As I answer, my gaze dances over to Holly, and I pretend she can hear my telepathic pleas for rescue. "I'll bake a lot. Probably do stuff with my sister. Christmas with my family. Nothing that exciting."

He shrugs in response. We make small talk about our classes at Stony Point and the homework we've been assigned for break. We both wave to Lucy Kurtz, but she doesn't come over to us and Matthew doesn't go to her, which means I'm stuck with him.

I don't know what Holly could be talking about that's keeping her for so long. I wish the DJ would start some music so I'd have an excuse to leave Matthew and go to her myself. I don't see Sam anywhere now; he probably found some Hickory friends and got caught up talking with them.

I turn back to Matthew as we hit another conversation lull and say, "So what, more specifically, are you going to do in Ohio?"

"Eh, I don't really have specific plans except for what friends I'll see. Other than that, I guess we'll do whatever we feel like."

"Oh."

This conversation has hit its natural end, but I can't help but feel that I need a reason to leave. Matthew glances away. I follow his gaze to the food tables in the far corner of the room.

When he looks back, he asks, "You hungry?"

"Not really," I say. Mostly because I don't want him to feel obligated to get me anything. I also can't help but hope that maybe he'll go by himself, and I'll be free to talk to other people.

"I hope they have Airheads Xtremes. That's my favorite," he tells me.

I sigh inwardly. Of course he likes sour candy. But I'm trying to be nice, so I say, "I like gummies best. Especially Sour Patch Kids. I don't eat a lot of candy, though."

"Oh, right, you probably like *actual* food more," he says. There's a hint of a smile on his face, but his words still bite. Why can't he let it go, that I think some food is better than other types? Why does he constantly have to harp on my interests?

Sam appears through the throngs of people, and my shoulders relax. Even if I could've used a rescue ten minutes ago, he chose a good moment to return. He's holding a plate with a variety of treats, and he extends it to me once he's within reach.

"Want one?" he says, gesturing to a lemon bar and a brownie with swirls of peanut butter running through it.

There are few desserts I don't like, and Sam has managed to offer me two from that very short list. While I scramble for a polite way to respond—maybe the same excuse I gave Matthew a few minutes ago—Matthew steps in.

"Don't you know Audra's a food snob? She turns up her nose at, like, everything," he says. His smile looks genuine, but that's all for Sam's benefit, I'm sure. When it comes to his interactions with me, I don't think Matthew has a nice bone in his body.

Heat rises in my cheeks. I retort, "That's not true! Maybe I'm picky, but I don't hate everything."

I'm glaring so hard, I'm surprised Matthew isn't lying dead on the floor.

Sam's eyes dart from Matthew to me. "So, uh… Do you want one of these, Audra?"

And I'm back where I was before Matthew Harwell butted in.

"Oh, um…I'm not big on lemon bars and I don't like peanut butter with chocolate? But thanks for offering?"

Sam's posture eases. "Can I get you something else then?"

"You don't have to—"

"I don't mind," he interrupts.

I smile and can't help but contrast his reaction with Matthew's. "If there's anything else chocolate without peanut butter or nuts, I will happily eat that."

"Sounds good. I'll be right back."

He disappears into the crowd that's grown considerably. As soon as Sam's out of sight, I wheel on Matthew.

"Did you really have to do that? Why do you constantly make fun of me?"

He holds up his hands. "Whoa, I wasn't making fun of you. You just looked a little panicked when that random guy offered you food, and I thought I'd help."

"I don't need your help!" I seethe. "I'm perfectly capable of taking care of myself. Just leave me alone and go fight Darth Vader or do whatever Han Solo does!"

His face hardens, his mouth thinning to a tight line. "Fine, whatever. You don't have to be a jerk about it."

He whirls on his heel and stomps off. Good riddance.

Sam returns at the same time as Holly; he brings two chocolate cupcakes and offers both to me. I force myself to relax as I accept the first one. None of this is his fault, and I want to enjoy myself with two people who are actually nice to me.

Holly and Sam chat about Hickory stuff as I eat both cupcakes. The room continues to fill, and I start to recognize more people. I brush my fingers off and try to be discreet about staring at Sam. I want—no, *need*—to know if he's March or not. Guess I'll have to do some covert sleuthing tonight. I mentally run over the concrete details I have for March to figure out which will lead to the most natural questions I can ask Sam.

Before I can start my subtle interrogation, the lights dim, and the chatter dips and then soars in a wave of excitement. We turn to look at the DJ, who is clearly riding on our cheers. He lets the murmurs build to a crescendo before he waves his hands and starts the first song.

Sam turns to me. "Ready to dance?" he shouts over the music.

I nod, and we wade through the throngs of students onto the dance floor. I lose myself in the freedom that laughing with friends can grant.

My eyes find Matthew during a later song, and my

smile fades. Maybe he was just trying to help, even if he kind of went about it the wrong way. I look away again. He didn't need to help me; he brought my reaction on himself. I am absolutely done putting up with his crap. I told Ro I'd try, but he's made it impossible to be his friend.

Some early 2000s slow song starts. Holly gives me a significant look and then drifts off. I roll my eyes; my friends aren't subtle at all when it comes to their matchmaking. But Sam extends his hand, pulling me into his arms. We sway back and forth, and I remember the questions I wanted to ask him earlier. I thought of four areas to cover that might lead to the answers I want: hiking, his family, his pets, and his social media usage. If I can get Sam to mention he was or still is a member of forum websites, I think it would be clear he's March.

"So, um, what have you been up to this fall?" I ask as my hands twine around his neck.

"School mostly," he says with a shrug. "New co-op, new teachers to get used to. Um, and I've started helping with one of the elementary Sunday school classes at church."

"Really?"

His cheeks turn pink. "Yeah. Kids that age are fun. Most of them don't care if their questions sound kinda dumb, and they want answers to everything, which makes me think harder."

Most teenaged guys don't see elementary school–age kids as people, and, admittedly, I find them annoying most of the time. The fact that Sam thinks they're cool and likes to work with them makes him a much better person than me.

"Anyway," he continues, "My dad and I went to the mountains a couple times, too. Virginia is way better for hiking and camping than Illinois is."

I didn't even have to ask him about hiking. That was easy.

"The Shenandoah Valley is so pretty. I love the Blue Ridge Mountains," I tell him.

"Yeah, they look cool in fall. I can't wait to go again. Do you hike a lot?"

"Maybe a couple times a year? There are some cool trails that lead to waterfalls. Those are my favorites."

"We should go sometime this spring!" he replies.

I nod enthusiastically. "Oh, and the Shenandoah National Park is also super dog-friendly," I say, steering the conversation to another thing I need to check off the March list. "I don't have a dog, but I always thought it would be so fun to hike with one."

"I have a dog," Sam replies.

Check, I think.

He continues, "She's not very athletic, though. Maybe we can borrow someone else's."

I laugh. Then I ask, "What's your dog like?"

"Oh, she's totally spoiled. Lap dog, will only eat people food, sleeps in my parents' bed every night. I'm her favorite, though," he tells me.

The song winds down. I'm not any closer to knowing if he's March or not. Yeah, hiking and a dog are checks in the "yes" column, but they're not concrete answers. I can't think of any subtle way to ask about his social media and forums, which would give me a big clue.

"Do you have any pets?" he asks before twirling me one last time.

I shake my head. "Our cat died a few years ago, and I don't think my parents are ready for another one."

"That sucks."

I shrug as we walk to the edge of the dance floor. "I don't mind too much. I'd rather have a dog."

"What about your siblings? Do they want another pet?"

The next song is one of those group dances I can't do, so I'm glad to stay on the sidelines and talk to Sam. I say, "Eh, my sister probably doesn't care. She's already out of the house and can get her own dog or cat if she wants." I pause. "You have a brother, right?"

That's probably the safest question; otherwise, he might wonder how I know he has two brothers—even though I'm not certain Sam does. I've only met the one.

"Two, actually. Ben's the oldest; he's a sophomore at University of Illinois. And Gabe is fourteen and a total nerd."

My brow furrows. March's brothers are younger than him. At least, I thought so. Maybe I'm remembering wrong, or this is another thing March lied about, or…maybe Sam isn't March after all.

Maybe March isn't who I thought he was, if he's willing to lie about big things like his movie choices and his siblings. What if he's not who he says he is, and this is all one big prank? Maybe Sam is just an ordinary guy, and March is a pedophilic, middle-aged man in Montana.

Maybe I really have no idea who March is.

My heart thuds louder and faster than the beat of the music. I have to get out of here, go and think somewhere.

"Oh. That's cool. I'll, um, be right back."

I make a beeline for the bathroom before he can reply. There are a couple girls fixing their makeup at the mirrors, but I ignore them. I lean against the cool tile wall and pull my phone from my skirt pocket. Seriously, this costume was worth every penny. I leave a couple texts from Kylie for later and open Google Chat.

FEATHER
Have you ever wondered if we've met? Not even in our hometowns but on vacation or at a homeschool convention or something. Or maybe we follow each other on Twitter and don't realize it.

I backspace until the text box is blank again. That's not a topic I want to confront tonight. Instead I type out a message that promises to be just as—if not more—nerve-wracking than that last one.

FEATHER
Have you ever lied to me?

This'll be a real fun topic. Besides who's to say he won't lie and say no?

He doesn't answer right away, so I slip into the end stall where at least my emotions won't be on display for everyone. I scroll through social media instead of waiting for three little dots to pop up. I even stalk Sam's pages a little. We friended each other on Facebook after we met, but I didn't really check his page out or look to see if he was on Twitter or Instagram. Spoiler alert: he is. He tweets a *lot* about baseball, but his Instagram posts are few and far between. I don't learn anything I didn't already know, unfortunately.

With a sigh, I lean back against the wall, then remember where I am and quickly shove away. As far as bathrooms go, this one isn't nasty, but it's still a *bathroom*. My phone buzzes, and I pull up March's reply.

MARCH
Once I told you I had
to go do homework but
I really just wanted to
play video games

FEATHER
I'm serious, March.

MARCH
A couple times. Nothing big tho.

FEATHER
You don't think lying is a
big deal? How have any
of your friendships worked out?

MARCH
I'm not lying all the time.
I've just told, like, one or
two white lies. And I don't
even remember what they
were about.

Is that another lie? Or has he really not lied about his favorite movie, his brothers, and more? Maybe Sam isn't March.

MARCH
Have YOU ever lied to me?

Guess I deserve him throwing my question back at me. I remember what I've told him. My lies are tiny, told early in our friendship when I was trying to impress him. Maybe his are the same. I'd like to give him the benefit of the doubt. Besides, four years is an awfully long time to keep up an elaborate charade with no results. If March really were old and creepy, he probably would've given up a long time ago for an easier target. And besides, Grandma seems to think he's trustworthy from what I've told her about him, and she's a tough cookie.

FEATHER
I don't know

MARCH
Then you can't judge.

FEATHER
Yeah, yeah

MARCH
What made you ask

FEATHER
I've just been thinking about stuff

MARCH
Hmm
MARCH
Well I hope you're having
a better night than me.

I frown. Why isn't he having fun? I can't stand the thought of March not being happy.

FEATHER
Why? What happened?

MARCH
I'm just kinda over the
people here. Ready to go home.

FEATHER
HOME home or your house?

MARCH
Both I guess

FEATHER
😟
FEATHER
I'm sorry people suck.

MARCH
Thanks
MARCH
Bake anything good lately?

FEATHER
I've started making Christmas cookies!

MARCH
What kinds?

FEATHER
Spritz cookies and chai sugar
cookies with cinnamon icing.

I attach a picture of the latter type cooling on baking racks, then say:

FEATHER
They're Taylor Swift's recipe.

MARCH
Of course they are
MARCH
What else do you bake
this time of year? Can't
remember, but I know
you've told me before.

FEATHER
Usually a couple other types of
cookies and I'll make pumpkin pie
and red velvet cheesecake for
Christmas. Haven't decided what
I'll bake for New Year's yet.

MARCH
Man, you make me wish my mom
liked baking. Our Christmas
desserts are blah compared to yours.

I start to type out a response but catch myself. Saying, "Maybe someday I can bake for you" would be crossing a line. It's way too flirtatious, and I don't like March like that.

I don't think so at least. Not to mention, we never talk about meeting; in fact, his location slip is the closest we've come to bringing it up.

What else can I say in response?

The bathroom door opens, and voices spill in. I hear the other stalls fill up and realize I should probably vacate this one.

FEATHER
g2g, will message you later

I put my phone away and flush the toilet. There's a bunch of girls I recognize from other Hickory parties clustered around the sinks when I exit. They make room so I can wash my hands. The water streams over my fingers as I consider March.

He's not here. He's not physically in my life. There's no logical reason for me to have a crush on him, especially when there's someone like Sam—a guy who I'm pretty sure is expressing interest in me. Friendship with guys can be weird, so I'm probably just confusing platonic feelings with romantic feelings when it comes to March.

I shake the water off my hands, then dry them with a paper towel. As I head back down the community center hallway towards the gym, someone catches my peripheral vision. I glance over and see Matthew leaning against a wall. His posture is relaxed although his brow is furrowed as he stares at his phone. We make eye contact as I pass. I glance away and bury that needling guilt.

I go find Sam, who has joined a circle of Hickory

students; they're dancing to a Chainsmokers song. He takes my hand and pulls me into the group, but he doesn't let go once I start moving to the beat. Our eyes meet, and I smile tentatively. Maybe Sam isn't March, but I don't think that really matters.

CHAPTER ELEVEN

Merry Christmas!

I tuck my phone back in my pocket and pull a fuzzy blanket tighter around me. Dad built up a fire on the hearth, but it's still an unusually cold Christmas in Virginia. Mom is next to me on the couch. Trevor, as the newest almost-member of the family, sits by the tree to pass out gifts. He glances back at Madeline, who's teasing Dad, and his expression softens.

Huh, I think.

Despite the time I spent with Madeline over the last few weeks, I still wasn't sold on her engagement. But if Trevor looks at her like how I've seen Dad look at Mom, then maybe they'll work out. Maybe there's more to the relationship than Madeline and Trevor show us.

I consider my sister, who's snuggled up in a UNC-Chapel Hill sweatshirt. At least with me, she's always been a very private person. I suppose she tells our parents more, but maybe she's grown more independent since she moved out. And heaven knows I don't tell Mom or Dad everything.

Mom unwraps a gift from Dad and exclaims over it. I wonder how Christmases after this one will be different.

Madeline has always spent the holidays with us, but next year, she'll have a husband and in-laws. Trevor's family is up in Maryland; I'm sure they'd like to see their son for at least some holidays.

Will it just be Mom, Dad, and me next year? Or will my sister and brother-in-law skip Thanksgiving in favor of his family and spend Christmas with us? I have no clue how it works when you get married, but it doesn't seem easy to juggle.

I straighten my shoulders. I should appreciate this while I have it.

"This one's for Audra!" Trevor announces.

We lean towards each other, and I take the package from him. The tag says it's from Madeline, which surprises me. Every year that I can remember, she's given me a gift card to a place that Mom has clearly suggested—that is, not one of my favorite stores but usually one where I can get a cookbook or maybe some clothes.

I look over at my sister. She smiles encouragingly, so I start to tear the Christmas ornament paper. The box is flat, like something you'd find a starched button-down in. Instead, I unfold the tissue paper to discover a T-shirt that says, "As you wish," surrounded by other *Princess Bride* quotes. Next to the shirt is a movie theater gift card, something I'll thoroughly enjoy using. The entire gift speaks volumes: Madeline is finally paying attention to me and my interests.

"Thank you," I breathe.

"Do you like it?" she asks. Her hands fidget in her lap.

"Yeah. It's awesome." I lift the T-shirt out to examine it further.

"What does it say?" Mom says, leaning closer. I show the shirt to her, and her mouth moves as she silently reads the quotes. She chuckles midway through. "That's very clever."

I smile again at Madeline and thank her. I'm glad I got her a more personal gift than usual—a cookbook that has a lot of the basics.

The rest of the morning passes in a flurry of wrapping paper, cinnamon rolls, and texts to friends. Holly and I chat for a little bit, but I don't expect to hear from Ro until tonight at the earliest. With so many siblings and cousins, her Christmases are always chaotic. Kylie and I video chat briefly, but her little sisters keep interrupting to show off their new dolls. Joel sends a video of his sister's new kitten to our group chat, and we get to witness the pandemonium that is Yanovitch Board Game Extravaganza before Dylan gets banned from using his phone during family time. Matthew likes several of the messages but doesn't contribute much himself.

As the sun fades into the tree line, I head upstairs, my arms loaded down with presents to put away. My stomach is full of Christmas dinner—roast beef, creamy mashed potatoes, carrots drizzled with a warm apple dressing, roasted broccoli, and rolls with cinnamon butter—and genuine laughter drifts from the kitchen where Dad and Madeline are on dish duty.

"Audra," Trevor says, and my foot hovers over a step.

I grab the banister for balance and turn back to look at him. He crosses his arms over his chest and looks down at the ground.

"Would you, uh, like to play a board game or something?" he asks.

132

I narrow my eyes. He's never wanted to do anything with me before. Madeline must've put him up to this.

I tell him, "I was gonna watch a movie…"

"What movie?"

I hesitate. Do I really want to admit I've never seen Star Wars before? Christmas break seemed like a good time to finally try them, but I was hoping to keep it a secret, so no one razzes the "film junkie" for never seeing a so-called classic. I'm definitely not telling March.

"Um, *A New Hope*," I finally say.

Trevor looks up, and his face brightens. "I love Star Wars," he says. "Could I join you?"

Dad pokes his head out of the kitchen. "Did someone say Star Wars?"

"Yeah, Audra's gonna watch the first one," Trevor tells him.

Dad's mouth falls open. "What?" he exclaims, his eyes widening as he looks at me. "You've never wanted to watch them before! Let me finish the dishes. We gotta watch them together." He disappears again, and I faintly hear him tell Mom and Madeline that they have to hurry.

I groan. This is exactly what I wanted to avoid, this pressure from someone who grew up seeing the original trilogy in theaters and will expect his film-loving daughter to appreciate them as much as he does.

Trevor has the sense to look a bit sheepish.

"I'll go get the TV ready," I say morosely.

We end up watching the first three movies in one marathon session broken up only by French silk pie and homemade gingerbread, both piled with teetering mountains of whipped cream. And it's not just Trevor, Dad, and me. Mom and Madeline join us, although they're more confused by everything than I am. They don't tend to watch sci-fi movies; I at least have seen superhero films and some of the big-hitters that garnered awards attention. So I know how the genre works. Plus, I don't live under a rock, so I basically know the Star Wars characters and plots already.

After the movies are over, I'm glad I didn't tell March I was finally watching some of his favorites. They're well made, but I just don't see the appeal. For the most part, I prefer women-focused media, and Star Wars is about so many guys. Maybe I'll like the new trilogy better, though, since there are more female characters.

How do you tell your best friend you don't like his favorite movies? There's no way that'll be an easy conversation. I don't want to disappoint him or have an argument. Not that March would disrespect my opinion, but most people get a little heated when it comes to defending their absolute favorite things. I'm sure I'm like that when it comes to Taylor Swift or *The Princess Bride*.

It's late enough that Madeline and Trevor leave after *Return of the Jedi*, and Mom and Dad trundle off to bed. I stay downstairs on the couch, wrapped in my blanket, taking in the peacefulness of Christmas aftermath. The only sound I hear is intermittent car tires crunching on the snow outside. It's been hours since I checked my phone, and I find it on an end table. I skip over the emails and Facebook notifications and go right to Google Chat. There's a message from a few hours ago.

MARCH
Merry Christmas!

He's probably gone to bed, or he's still busy with his family, but I reply anyways.

FEATHER
Did you get anything good?

Then I check my other notifications just to clear them. None are important. I'm about to head up to bed after that—I've turned off most of the downstairs lights and gathered my things—when my phone buzzes. I plop back on the couch.

MARCH
Uh, did I ever
MARCH
My parents got me tickets
to see Ed Sheeran this fall.

FEATHER
Oh my gosh!!!
FEATHER
So jealous.

MARCH
It's gonna be lit.
MARCH
What about you?

FEATHER
Hmm nothing too exciting. I've

been begging my parents for a dog
for years but instead they gave
me a stuffed one.

MARCH
That's a poor substitute.

FEATHER
It's the thought that counts, I suppose.

I consider everything I'm not telling him as the mantelpiece clock ticks away, thrumming in the late-night quietness. The conversation we had about lying is still on my mind two weeks later. I wonder if keeping secrets or withholding information counts as lying. There's a lot of things I don't tell March besides what we've both agreed to keep private.

His next message isn't about anything important, and I'm about to type out a reply when my thumbs freeze.

If Owen, Matthew, and Sam aren't March, then who is? Is it that other guy Holly mentioned, the one whose name I can't even remember? Or… Every other possibility is worse.

March lied about when his co-op meets, for no logical reason.

March is younger—or older—than I think he is. Not significantly so. But maybe he's started college and is still pretending to be in high school. That would be to protect his privacy, I suppose. He straight up said he was a senior this fall, but maybe that was a cover. Which wouldn't be the end of the world, I guess. I can't blame him for lying if that's the case. My parents would tell me to do the same thing.

Then I consider what is quite possibly the worst option: March doesn't live in Richmond. Perhaps he chose a random place in hopes it would get me to reveal where I live. Or he's somehow found out where I live and was trying to get me to admit it. Either of those sounds terrible because they would mean March is an absolute creep, who I don't truly know at all. I don't want to believe he'd be like that, since he's my best friend, but who else or where else could he be?

I set my phone down. I don't want to end Christmas like this, worrying that my best friend is tricking me. Especially because I've already gone down that path before and resolved why March can't be anything but what he says he is with maybe a tiny bit of fudging.

MARCH
You still there?

FEATHER
Yeah, sorry!
FEATHER
Got lost in my thoughts. It's been a busy day.

MARCH
Everything good with your sister?

FEATHER
No, yeah, she and I are fine!
Christmas just tends to make me think about serious stuff.

MARCH
Anything I can help with?

FEATHER
Thanks, but I gotta deal
with this on my own.

I couldn't really tell him I'm worried he's catfishing me, could I?

I try to think about this more rationally. He's probably the kid from Hickory that I didn't meet. Or he meant a different Richmond area. Or there's a co-op I somehow don't know about that meets on Fridays. I shouldn't assume the worst.

FEATHER
It's late. I should go.

MARCH
Ok. You don't have to tell
me what's going on, but
I'm here for you.

Well. *Way to make me feel crappy for suspecting you're not who you say you are, March.*

FEATHER
Thanks, friend. 😊
FEATHER
I do have a new job starting
in January, so I guess prayers
that it'll go well would be nice.

MARCH
You got it.

FEATHER
😊
FEATHER
Night, March.

MARCH
Night, Feather.

The click of my phone echoes through the living room as I turn it off. I'm going to pray extra hard about my job, too. Taking over teaching the cooking class is exciting but so nerve-wracking. I hope the first one goes well.

CHAPTER TWELVE

That was a disaster.

I can't believe the class went so poorly. I never thought my first day as the head teacher would be perfect, but I didn't think it would be *that* bad. The kids didn't listen to me, they just wanted to goof off, and it was like they'd only eaten sugar for lunch.

Clean up goes quickly, thanks to Mom and Mrs. Cho's help. But all I want is to get out of here. I wish I could be home right this second, to close myself in my room and cry. My mom, though, lingers to talk to some of her friends. I studiously avoid eye contact with everyone and pretend there's something interesting on my phone.

When the tears stinging my eyes get to be too much, I mutter something about needing to use the bathroom. I hurry off, not to the bathroom where girls I know will walk in and start rumors about me crying, but to a classroom that's always empty in the afternoon. I close the door behind me and leave the lights off. I find a corner where no one will see me from the glass panel in the door and slump against the wall. The cool drywall presses through my long-sleeved tee, and I shiver. Tears start to bead and drop, catching on the rim of my glasses. I tug the frames off my face and swipe my shirt hem against the lenses.

I don't want to see Ro right now, even if she's still in the building. But I have to talk to someone. I have to get all these feelings off my chest. With shaking hands, I pull out my phone and open the messaging app.

FEATHER
Are you busy?

I chew on my nails as I wait. Chances are slim that he's not in class, at work, or with friends. Tears continue to well around my eyes. I'm glad I don't normally wear make-up to co-op; I would never be able to explain away my appearance if I emerged with mascara and eyeliner running down my face.

MARCH
What's up?

FEATHER
I've had a really bad day

MARCH
What happened??

My fingers slip over the letters, and I keep jabbing the wrong ones. Out of frustration, a hiccupping sob escapes my lips. Finally, I send the message, typos and all.

FEATHER
My jon stsrted today and
it didn't go well

FEATHER

Sorry about any typos

MARCH

I'm so sorry

FEATHER

I don't know why I expected it to
be a good first day, but I did
Anyways, everything went wrong
and it was terrible

MARCH

What can I do to help?

FEATHER

I just need someone to talk to. My mom
doesn't know how upset I am; I was too
embarrassed to let her know so I ran off to cry

March is typing...

That message keeps appearing and disappearing. I
can only imagine what he thinks about me being an
overemotional teenage girl. I've kept my emotions pretty
close and never really told him when I've cried before. It's
not because I want to hide things from him, but I tend
to be private about that sort of thing. So does he, for that
matter.

MARCH

You can say no, but...I don't think
I can make you feel better over
Google Chat

MARCH
Here's my number. Call me if
you want to talk to someone.
MARCH
513-555-1610

I stare at my phone. All I can do is blink and attempt to process what he's suggesting. He doesn't care if I hear his voice. He gave me his *phone number* without giving my real identity a second thought. What if *I* were a catfish? He's basically saying we can stop being so anonymous with each other, that he wants to know the real me.

Is that what I want? For him to know me as Audra? For me to know the real him? I'm scared he won't like me once he learns all my imperfections and realizes all the things I've kept from him because the Internet makes that easy.

I sniffle, producing the most awkward snort. I take a few long breaths, wipe my eyes, and slide my glasses back on my face. Then I dial his number because I really do need someone to talk to, and March gets me like no one else. The phone rings twice and then—

"Hello?"

"March?" I say, my voice thick from holding back tears.

"Feather," he replies, and he sounds almost…relieved, although I'm not sure why. Maybe he was hoping I wasn't catfishing him as much as I hoped he wasn't catfishing me. "Are you okay?"

"Not really," I say. A sob bubbles up in my throat, and I swallow it. "The rest of my day was fine, so I can't believe this has upset me so much."

"This job means a lot to you. I get it."

We're quiet for a minute.

"Do you want to tell me what happened?" he asks. His voice is a bit wobbly but clear. It sounds familiar, like baking a favorite recipe.

"I've, um, taken over teaching a cooking class at my co-op, which I should be, well, great at since I've had so much cooking experience. But the kids didn't listen to me, and the recipe was a disaster. We did mini quiches, which I thought would be easy, and they were bacon and cheese. Kids are supposed to love bacon and cheese! But half the kids didn't want to try them once they were done, and the other half didn't understand my instructions—and that was my fault—so theirs didn't turn out." I actually sob this time. "I don't think I can do this. I don't think I can teach the class anymore."

"Feather, hey, it's okay," he says. My name is made soft by his voice, and I want to hear him say it all the time. "Bad first days happen. You can't give up. I can't let you start to hate something you love as much as cooking."

"I don't think the kids will ever listen to me," I tell him. "Maybe—I don't know. Maybe it's better they get a parent who's willing to teach."

He's quiet for a moment. Then he says, "How would you feel if you gave up? How would you feel if there were no parents who wanted to teach the class and they had to cancel it instead? Does this change how you feel about cooking and becoming a chef? You've talked about that for years."

Tears start trickling down my cheeks again. He's not wrong; I just wasn't ready for such direct honesty right now, I guess. "Well, now I feel even worse."

"Crap, I'm sorry."

Long silence again. I want him to keep talking, to listen as the cadence of his voice swells. I imagine how it might sound when he's smiling, and all of a sudden, I'm picturing what his smile might be like and I have the urge to kiss the corners of his mouth. The thought freezes me in my tracks. I stare at the windows covered in thick blinds across the room and study the way the light streams through the cracks and gives the room a golden glow, tinted gray by the color of the walls.

Maybe I've denied it for a while or maybe this is something recent, but I have feelings for my best guy-friend.

I like March. Romantically.

My toes curl inside my boots, and my free hand grips the hem of my shirt. My heart is beating faster, and I press my hand to my chest, as if that'll calm it to a normal rate.

"You still there?" he asks.

"Yeah," I reply. I try to calm my breathing, so my mini freak-out isn't audible. "I, uh, can't believe you were so willing to let me call you."

"It's been four years; I decided if you were a catfish, you were a dedicated one. Anyways, it felt…it felt like it was time."

My phone buzzes against my cheek, and I glance at the screen. "Hold on," I tell March. "My mom just texted me. She's wondering where I am." I type out a response. "I told her to give me a few more minutes."

"If you need to go…"

"I'd rather stay here. And I'm glad you let me call you. The timing does feel right." I pause. I should be honest with him. "Oh, and, um, one more thing?"

"Yeah?"

I take a deep breath. "I don't know if you remember, but last fall, well, you slipped up and said where you live, or approximately where you live. And, um, here's the thing. I think we live in the same area. I think you moved to my city."

"Wait, really? You live in Richmond?"

"If you mean Richmond, Virginia, then yeah, I do."

"Wow, this is crazy." He laughs, a bit awkwardly, but something feels off. Like…almost like déjà vu. I'm not sure what, though. "I actually… Well, I kinda mentioned where I live on purpose. It's been four years, like I said, and I just, I don't know, it felt like it was time. I said that already, didn't I?"

"Yeah, but that's okay. I think I agree."

He clears his throat. "Why didn't you say something then?"

"I thought you'd done it by accident, and I was kind of pretending it didn't happen." Then I admit, "I also started freaking out, wondering if I knew you in real life or something."

My phone buzzes again, and I groan. It's my mom again. She wants to leave now, which is ironic since she was the one dawdling earlier.

"I hate to cut this short, but my mom is getting impatient," I say just as March asks, "Do you want to meet?"

Then, sounding resigned, he says, "Oh, okay," at the same time as I reply, "Can I get back to you on that?"

Our laughter intertwines like our voices did just moments before.

"Text me anytime," he says, his words laced with a smile. "Or don't. Do whatever makes you comfortable. That's all that matters to me. I mean, I want to meet you—I've known that for a while now—but only if you want to. You can say no. But you can say yes, too." He's stumbling over his words a bit as they fly out in a rush, and I smile, too.

"I'll let you know, promise." We say our goodbyes and hang up. I wipe my eyes one more time and sniff to make sure my nose won't run until I can get Kleenex in the car.

The hallways are filled with students and parents, all getting ready to leave for the day. Homeschoolers—and their parents—can talk for hours, so I won't be surprised if my mom is talking to someone else when I find her. I clutch my phone and fiddle with my feather ring. I'm almost to the multipurpose room when I turn a corner, and my shoulder clips someone else.

"Oh, sorry!" I say at the same time as the other person.

I look up and meet brown eyes the color of my favorite fall jacket. Matthew. His smile is fleeting, and his glasses scrunch up. He usually leaves long before this class period, so I'm surprised to see him. He's wearing his coat and smells cold, so maybe he or his mom forgot something. Matthew's eyes search my face, and I realize I'm holding eye contact. He tilts his head ever so slightly.

"Are you okay?" he asks, and I have a feeling he's not asking about our collision, since that was minor. I wonder how much of my breakdown is still evident.

I nod and am about to reply when something connects in the back of my mind. Something about the question he just asked sounds familiar. I can't place what...

"Have you seen Joel?" he asks. He laughs. "I know you guys don't have an afternoon class together, but I forgot he borrowed my algebraic calculator, and I kind of need it before next week."

My reply catches in my throat. His voice. His laugh. If I didn't know better, I'd say he sounded like March. But that can't be right. *Moved within the last year...new co-op...likes the outdoors...has a dog...loves waffles...two younger brothers... Fleetwood Mac...*All things I considered before when Ro suggested Matthew was March, but I brushed them aside because I didn't want him to be my best friend.

"No, I just got out of class, and I'm looking for my mom," I finally say when I realize I've been staring like a half-witted person.

I glance down at my phone; the recent calls page is still open, and an idea hits me. As subtly as I can, I tap March's number. Then I hold my breath.

"Oh, okay," he replies. "I'll, uh, see you next—"

His phone vibrates. It's probably just a coincidence. There's no way he's March; I'm just imagining things.

"Hang on just a second," Matthew says to me, and he turns a little bit away as he quietly answers the call. "Feather? Is everything okay?"

CHAPTER THIRTEEN

I don't reply. I hang up and slip my phone into my pocket. Matthew repeats my screen name before realizing there's no one on the other end. Looking dazed, he shakes his head and turns back to me.

"Sorry about that," he says.

"No, it's fine," I manage to say.

"So, um, see you next week?"

I nod and hurry off to the multipurpose room. My ears are ringing, and I don't make eye contact with anyone I pass. Matthew is March. March is *Matthew*. My best friend, apart from Ro and Holly, has been at my co-op since September, and I didn't know it. This all seems too unreal.

"There you are!" says my mom.

I blink a couple times and uncurl from my thoughts. Mom holds out my coat and bag, and I move as if I'm on autopilot.

"I know today didn't go how you want it to, but you can't run off like that. What happened isn't that bad. You haven't spent a lot of time with younger kids before, and teaching is a big responsibility. It's not something everyone is good at, but you're good at leading. The class will get easier as the semester goes on."

"Yeah, okay, Mom," I mutter. I shove my hair out of my face. "Can we just go?"

"Of course. I wanted to leave fifteen minutes ago, but you'd wandered off," she replies. As we head for the door she continues, "Madeline's coming over tonight to talk wedding stuff—decorations and guest lists mostly, I think. Do you have a menu to pass onto Amber for the bridal shower?"

"Not really," I say.

"Well, finalize that when we get home, okay?"

"Okay."

"The shower's coming up awfully fast. Amber's counting on you," she continues.

"Okay, I got it, Mom! I'm not really in the mood to think about cooking today, so it'll have to wait until tomorrow. I'm sure it's fine if I email it anyways. Just please stop nagging!"

My mom stops walking, right in the middle of the parking lot.

"Can the attitude, Audra Lynn," she says, her tone reaching scarily low levels. "I know you're upset—" *Yeah, and shocked and confused and a million other feelings*—"but you do not get to take it out on me."

"Yes, ma'am," I mutter. I resume walking to the car in hopes I'll avoid further embarrassment. There's nothing like your mother laying down the law in the middle of the co-op parking lot where everyone you know can witness it. Why can't she let me have a bad day? Why do I have to act like things don't affect me?

I toss my bag in the back before slumping into the passenger seat. My mom turns the radio to her favorite country station, and I suppress a shudder. I pull out my phone and open the Google Chat app. My fingers are poised to message March, but then I remember.

Do I really want to keep messaging March now that I know he's Matthew, the guy I've only just started to warm to, the guy that seemed like such a pretentious asshole for so long? We're talking about the guy who introduced himself as Peter Harwell IV's son (as if that would mean something to me), discovered my food obsession and latched onto that as something to tease me about, and rolled his eyes when Kylie was chattering away once about fairies. I start to put my phone away, but it buzzes in my hand. March/Matthew messaged me.

MARCH
Did you butt-dial me earlier?

How do I respond to that? I've got to lie, obviously—if I reply at all. I glance at my mom, who's absorbed in driving. There's no way I can ask for her advice. She got mad when I offhandedly mentioned last year that a female friend from Twitter and I exchanged email addresses. I'd probably be grounded for a month if I told her I'd been chatting with a boy for years and that he now had my phone number. It wouldn't matter that the boy turned out to be Matthew; she'd only focus on how dangerous the Internet can be.

Just to be inwardly rebellious, I reply to March's message.

ME
Not exactly. I meant to call you

real quick but then my mom found me
and I had to leave. Sorry about that.

MARCH
Nah it's fine
MARCH
So my parents gave me the ok
to have a party at my house
for the Oscars

I stare at my phone for a moment, deciding how to reply. I feel so numb, still processing all of this, but I think I need to at least try to reply. What if he can tell something is up? If I'm lucky, he might dismiss it as residual gloominess, but luck has not been on my side today. Finally, I settle for something that sounds like what I'd normally say, just with muted punctuation.

ME
That's exciting.

MARCH
It's gonna be small, just my
friends from co-op and the
theater group. Except I'm not
sure I should invite that one girl
I've mentioned before. You
know, the stuck-up one.

ME
So don't invite her.

I can't imagine whom Matthew is talking about. No one in our friend group is stuck-up. Maybe he's talking about another girl at the co-op.

MARCH
She'd know I was leaving
her out. All her friends
would be invited.

ME
Invite her then. Maybe she'll
be nice since others will be there.
Or maybe she won't come.

MARCH
Yeah maybe. I was wondering
if you'd like to come though.
I know you wanted to think about
meeting me but I'd like it if you came.
MARCH
We could meet at a different place
beforehand so you aren't just randomly
coming to my house, haha.

ME
Oh. Um…

I keep typing out various replies, not sure how to answer.

MARCH
You can say no. I won't be mad.

ME
Today has been a lot all at once.
Can I think about it?

MARCH
Sure

ME
Ok, I'll message you later.

I turn off my phone and shove it in my pocket as we turn into the driveway. Dad isn't home yet—he's at the university until five on Fridays this semester—so the house is cool and dark. I flip on a few lights and feel myself relax with the silence. Mom and I don't speak as we unpack our bags. I'm still a bit grumpy with her, and maybe she's realized her advice wasn't helping because she's not offering any more. I grab a Babybel before retreating to my room.

Ro's at work, so I can't text her, but maybe Holly isn't busy right now. I start to text her but hesitate. It might be best if I keep this to myself for right now. I don't want my friends chiming in on what I should do, not yet at least. They mean well, but I just want to process everything on my own for now. Like I said to March/Matthew, today has been a lot all at once.

Instead of texting one of my friends, I pull up Matthew's Facebook profile and stare at his picture, trying to reconcile the slightly less sure boy with the more thoughtful, confident, flirtatious person I know online. Then I note his birthday and practically face-palm.

I know he didn't like that one Fleetwood Mac song, but I should've figured things out sooner when I friended Matthew on Facebook and saw his birthday—November 7, which is, of course, the same as March's. It's even in his username: idesofmarch117.

But they still don't feel like the same guy. Matthew seemed confident about moving and starting at a new co-op; it was like he wanted us all to believe he had everything under control. Matthew teases me about everything and doesn't understand that I don't like it; March only teases me when I'm being too serious and uptight. Sure, I don't hate Matthew like I once did, but he isn't March to me. But I do have feelings for March—he makes me laugh, he wants to talk about my interests, he supports my dreams, and he cares if I'm having a bad day.

I close the Facebook tab and chew on a fingernail. Matthew cares about Feather. He interrupted a conversation with me because he thought she was calling him again. He wanted to make her—my—bad day better. Still, he would never feel the same way about me, Audra. I'm Feather…but I'm not. She's funny and wiser than I'll ever be. I suck at advice, but she's whom March always seems to turn to.

I'm frozen with indecision. I don't like Matthew like I do March, but they're the same person so technically I like Matthew…right? My head hurts.

I have no idea how he'd react if I told him I'm Feather. He'd probably laugh and wouldn't take me seriously. Maybe he'd even pretend he had no idea what I was talking about.

Flipping aimlessly through a random book, I mope until dinner. At the table I stare at my plate and shift my food around, only occasionally taking a bite. Dad asks about my day, and I share the surface details about the cooking class disaster. He doesn't respond with advice about how I should've reacted, which relieves me.

"You know, my first day teaching was a nightmare," he says as he serves himself more casserole. "Madeline was a little under a year old, and we lived in Pennsylvania, since I started out at Arcadia. Anyway, I had one of the introductory level history courses at nine a.m. To start with, I got there late, partly because Madeline was teething and had kept us up the night before and then partly because I'd misplaced my roster. Then I went to the wrong classroom at first—"

"Oh, no," I say, starting to laugh.

"Thankfully, that class's professor pointed me in the right direction. Once I got there, though, half the class didn't show up. Well then I couldn't get the overhead projector to work, so I had to use the chalkboard, which meant subjecting those poor kids to my handwriting. All in all, it wasn't a good day, but it was just one day. I've taught for twenty-eight years now, and there have been very few classes as bad as that one. And my first day at the University of Richmond was much better." He meets my gaze. "I know you feel like your class can't possibly get any better, but it will, I promise."

I smile. "Thanks, Dad." I shift in my seat and wriggle my sock-covered toes.

He reaches over and squeezes my hand. "I believe in you, kiddo."

Sometimes something as simple as that can make all the difference.

To make up for snapping at my mom earlier, I clear the table and load the dishwasher. I know she wants me to finalize the bridal shower menu, but I can't fathom thinking about cooking right now. When I'm done with the dinner cleanup, I retreat upstairs and curl up on my bed. My phone doesn't buzz, which I'm glad about for once. I'm not sure how long I'll be able to hide I know who March is, especially since he wants to meet me. I lie there for a while longer, numbly running over it all again and again in my head.

"Audra?" says Madeline as she knocks on my open door. She's only been at the house a few minutes, and it's quite a change for her to come up to my room so soon.

I roll over so I'm not facing the wall. "Uh, come in, I guess."

She closes the door behind her, which I appreciate, and then comes and sits by my legs.

"Mom said you had a bad day."

I shrug. "It wasn't great."

"Wanna talk about it?"

"Not really… I've already had to discuss it all with both Mom and Dad." She's still watching me. I hesitate, sigh, and sit up. She's not going to give up. "But, um, something else happened."

"Yeah?"

I tell her all about March, starting at the very beginning.

She holds up a hand, cutting me off before I've even gotten to today's events. "Wait—you've been texting someone you met *online*? Didn't Mom and Dad ever have the stranger danger talk with you?"

I roll my eyes. "Yeah, and this is exactly how I expected Mom to react, not you. Besides, we haven't been texting. We emailed and IMed, and then we both got the Google Chat app last year."

"What if he's some fifty-year-old dude in Florida? He could be a really good actor." Madeline's brow is creased.

"Well he didn't sound fifty years old."

Madeline jumps up, and I realize how my words sounded to her. She starts pacing. "I thought you said you guys didn't text! How have you talked to him? How did he get your phone number?"

I sigh, exhaling loudly through my nose. "Can I finish the rest of my story? I think you'll understand why it's okay."

Madeline sits back down, but she doesn't look convinced. I tell her about my meltdown, the phone call, my realization during the call, and running into Matthew. I don't censor my thoughts, and everything comes out in a big jumble. When I'm done, she takes a moment to think. I fiddle with the ruffled edge of a throw pillow and consider how unfamiliar this is. I was eleven when Madeline moved out, too young, really, for serious sisterly chats. The last few months we've been closer, but it's been the two of us in the car or cafés or restaurants, never my room.

"I can't tell you what to do," Madeline says finally. "How would you feel, though, if Matthew had found out you were Feather and didn't say anything?"

"I'd be mad," I admit. "But that's…different. March has always seemed more open about saying how he feels, even if he doesn't want to discuss it—or at least I thought he was. I keep my feelings close around the guys, so, I don't know,

I would feel weird telling him. Besides, I'm sure he doesn't like me like I like him, and having to interact with March in person would make that so much harder. I don't think I'm great at hiding my feelings."

"Well, what if you as Feather agreed to meet him but never told him you'd realized who he was before?"

"I'm not a good enough actress to pretend I didn't already know. Besides, I wouldn't want to keep such a huge secret from him. But I still don't know what I want to do."

"Why?"

I bite my fingernail, considering her question. "I can't predict how he'll react and that scares me," I respond.

Madeline rubs my arm. "Sometimes there are situations where we can't be ready for any outcome. That's life. That's what makes it an adventure. You've always liked adventure more than me."

"Yeah, travel adventures. Food adventures." I gesture vaguely as if that'll help me make my point. "Unknowns when it comes to people terrify me."

"Give it time then. You don't have to decide what to do right now. You've had a full day with lots of upheaval. Why don't you come and have some tea with Mom and me? We're talking about bridesmaid dresses tonight."

Madeline looks so enthusiastic that I muster up a smile and trudge downstairs behind her. Maybe she's right; maybe I just need more time.

I let myself sleep until 9:30 the next morning. When I drowsily make my way downstairs, I find a note on the fridge. Mom and Dad are at the grocery store apparently. I shuffle around the kitchen and pull out baking ingredients. March—Matthew—was right. I can't give up cooking, not for long at least.

As the oven preheats, I set my phone in a small bowl to create a speaker. I tap through my music until I find one of my baking playlists. This one is meant for dreary days when I want to feel soft and content. It's mostly acoustic stuff with a few older jazzier numbers thrown in. I hum, barely above a whisper, as I find the various measuring cups and spoons in the drawers. The sky is gray with snow clouds, and the outside light washes out the yellow kitchen walls.

I measure and level flour into the clear bowl. What are the chances that March would end up at the same co-op as me?

Baking powder, baking soda, and salt go into the bowl. Why did he have to be Matthew?

I move automatically, the rhythm of baking a dance I could do in my sleep. I stir the dry ingredients and pull out another bowl for the wet ingredients. Why did I have to put the pieces together and realize March's identity so easily?

I spoon peanut butter into the measuring cup. Why did I have to fall for March?

I squeeze honey into a measuring cup, and I feel my shoulders relax. Maybe this'll be okay. Maybe Matthew's reaction will be good.

But I don't want to meet March, I realize. Not yet at least. I just can't deal with the way I'm sure Matthew will react. Maybe he isn't even truly March; maybe the boy I know from the Internet is just a façade, a really good act. Deep down, I know this can't be true, but I want to believe it so I don't have to end this golden relationship where everything between us seems perfect.

Norah Jones is singing about "fields where the yellow grass grows knee-high," and all I can think of is how wonderful it would be to go to Tuscany and provincial France. I'd love to cook in Europe.

But do I actually want to cook for a living? That's what I thought I wanted, but maybe my mom is right—maybe I'm not meant to lead a kitchen.

I pause. What am I going to do with my life if I don't go to the Culinary Institute of America and study to run a restaurant? Of course I applied to other schools just in case, but they were just back-ups. I never seriously considered anything but the CIA.

"Shoot," I say aloud.

My eyes run down the recipe and then flick back to the bowl. How much honey did I add? The recipe calls for three-fourths of a cup, but I feel like I did an extra one-fourth cup. I poke my spoon at the honey in the bowl. Does it look like too much? I decide it does, but there's an easy remedy: I'll just double the recipe. My parents can take the extras to their Sunday school class tomorrow. Or we'll eat peanut butter muffins for the next week.

As I go through the motions of adding extra ingredients, my mind wanders back to my school dilemma. I got accepted to five other schools, and I haven't told any of them yes or no yet. But what would I even study at them? I applied to them mainly because my dad suggested them;

the University of Richmond was top of his list, of course. I'd get free tuition if I went there. But the Culinary Institute was my dream.

I push my sleeves up before filling the muffin tins. Maybe I could be a food critic. I love trying new foods as much as I love making them; the past few months trying new restaurants with Madeline have proved that. If I made that my career goal, journalism would probably be the right major.

The muffins are in the oven now, and I set the timer for fifteen minutes. After I pile the dishes in the sink, I lean back against the counter and sigh. My favorite cover of "La Vie en Rose" is playing, and, despite the cold dreariness hanging over Richmond, I feel warm inside. Baking really does make me feel better. I can't give it up after one bad day. Besides, I hate change too much to do something that radical.

Half an hour later, when I've settled in my room with a muffin, a banana, and tea, I look at my messages for the first time since last night. There's a text from Holly about nothing important, and one from Dylan, asking what he missed in French yesterday. More importantly, there's a message from March. I take a deep breath as I open his.

MARCH
You feeling better today?

Part of me wants to not reply, to shut him out until this whole mess vanishes. The other part of me knows that's unrealistic and, well, mean and unfair to Matthew. Also,

I'm a creature of habit. I can't just stop talking to someone I've talked to practically every day for the past four and a half years.

ME
A bit yeah

While I wait for his response, I pop a DVD into my laptop. Saturday mornings are meant for Disney movies, and there's something about *Beauty and the Beast* that always makes me feel more like myself again. That movie, muffins, and the 2005 *Pride and Prejudice* score—which I'll probably listen to later—are my tried-and-true cures for bad days.

MARCH
It's ok if you don't feel like talking
about it anymore. I'm sorry
yesterday sucked.

ME
I have to learn to deal with
disappointment. Life isn't
perfect, and the sooner I come
to terms with that, the better.

I need to take those words to heart and apply them to the March situation, too. He doesn't reply. Sometimes there are things you don't have responses to, so I'm not bothered. Then I realize there's something else I need to address.

ME

Hey, so, I've been thinking,
and I'm not sure we should meet.

MARCH

Why

ME

I don't think I could lie to my parents
about where I was going, and they'd
never let me go if they knew I was
meeting a stranger from the Internet.

MARCH

I get it. Haven't told my
parents about you either.

ME

Maybe this summer.

MARCH

Sure, just let me know. Whatever
you're comfortable with.

MARCH

How are you feeling about
your job and everything?

ME

I can't quit. That would be a crappy
thing to do to the kids and the co-op
board. I guess I have to stick with it.
But I don't think I'm ever going to
love this job.

MARCH

So what does that mean for your
cooking and baking?

I pause, working out how to say what I'm thinking. My dream since I was twelve is no longer the same, and I don't want to admit it aloud or in writing. It's not any easier to share than the fact that I've figured out March's identity, and of course both those things had to happen on the same day. A dull throb pulses through my head as the stress starts to bubble up all over again. I raise my head and take a shaky breath as I stare at the ceiling. I will myself not to cry.

You can do this, I tell myself. *Maybe March can help you work things out. He has before. If he doesn't know you're Audra, things can't have changed that much for him.*

Slowly, I type and retype the message, trying to express my thoughts in one fell swoop.

ME

I don't think I want to go to the Culinary Institute anymore. I'm not made for life as a chef.

MARCH

You aren't going to quit cooking at home though, right?

ME

No.

MARCH

Good. It's always made you happy as far as I can tell. One day shouldn't change that. What will you do instead?

ME

I kinda like the idea of being a food

critic. Maybe I'll study journalism.
Maybe I'll start a food blog.

MARCH
Yo, send me the link if you do.

ME
Okay.

I hear the door from the garage open. Mom and Dad are home—the perfect excuse to tell March I have to go. It's harder than I thought to pretend everything's all right, even when he can't see or hear me. I will have to make up my mind soon; I can't go through life constantly lying to my best friend.

CHAPTER FOURTEEN

Mom drops me off at Starbucks early on Tuesday afternoon. I'm loaded down with homework even though Friday was only the first day of the semester. I have AP calculus and US government assignments, plus notes from French to share with Dylan since he was at a swim meet.

Kylie and Dylan are here already, and they've claimed the long table against the wall. Papers, flashcards, and textbooks are spread across one end as they study for their algebra II test. I plop down by Dylan and arrange my stuff before going up to get my drink.

"No school today?" asks the barista as he takes my order.

I'm used to this question. People's reactions to my response are always fun to gauge.

"Oh, well, not really. I'm meeting up with friends to work on homework," I say.

His brow wrinkles, and he tilts his head as he looks over at our table.

I sigh and take pity on the barista. "I'm homeschooled," I explain.

"Oh." His expression shifts to something skeptical. He hurriedly rings up my purchase, and I sigh again. Typical.

When I return to the table with my drink in hand, Ro and Owen are settling in. Ro smiles at me, and I have a feeling that, if we were alone, she'd press me for details about what's going on. I was a bit evasive in the text messages I sent her this weekend. Owen peels off his coat, revealing a green-black-and-cream shirt. I've never seen him wear the same flannel twice. As I'm musing over this, he pulls a jar out of his bag and hands it to me.

"Aunt Cora sends her regards," Owen says, a smile tugging at his entire face.

I examine the peach preserves and return the smile. "Your aunt is the best. I can use these to make an amazing quick bread."

"Cool. They're good on pancakes and waffles, too," he tells me.

His hand brushes my arm as he moves back to his seat. I watch him for a moment and wish he were March. Everything would be so much easier if the boy who had been kind to me from day one was the same one I'd been emailing for four years.

I suddenly remember I have something for Owen, too, and I pull a small, round container out of my bag.

"Owen! Happy early birthday!" I say, before handing over the cupcake.

His eyes light up. "Thanks!" He pops off the lid and immediately swipes his finger through the frosting. "Cream cheese?"

"Yeah. And red velvet cake." I fiddle with my feather ring. "That's your favorite, right?"

"Definitely." He wraps an arm around my shoulders, and I return the hug.

Joel and Matthew arrive eventually. We all work quietly

for a long time, each of us plowing through assignments and papers. Coming off the month-long winter break is never easy. I try to not pay Matthew too much attention, but it's hard. I keep looking over, studying his face, trying to see March in him.

Eventually, I manage to focus on my own work, although I catch snippets of my friends' conversations. Owen and Matthew start talking about something unrelated to their homework—some movie I've never heard of, I think. Ro jumps in with a witty jab, and Matthew laughs. I catch a glimpse of his smile; it seems genuine. Besides, he's never seemed to have a problem with my best friend. She's not the girl he hates.

Dylan and Kylie finish studying, and Dylan turns to me so we can work on the French assignments. I catch him up on what he missed, and we work over the assignments in the textbook. Our teacher told us we have a speaking and listening quiz coming up next week, so Dylan and I decide to practice having a conversation. This requires most of my concentration, but out of the corner of my eye, I watch Kylie start to interact with Joel and Matthew. Matthew doesn't seem too annoyed with her, but I can't really tell.

What am I doing? I'm not going to be able to watch Matthew with every single girl from co-op to find out whom he dislikes.

I finish before everyone else, which wouldn't matter except Ro is my ride home. I wish I'd brought something fun to read, like that new French cookbook I got with a Christmas gift card, but at least I have my phone with me, which gives me an idea. I scroll through social media sites for a little bit before checking to make sure the ringer is off. I go to March's contact page and type out a text. Then I erase it and write something else, which I promptly delete and rewrite again. Finally, I figure out a good casual message to send.

ME

So bored

I keep my gaze centered on my phone, but in my peripheral vision, I watch for Matthew to move. A few minutes after the text should've gone through, he reaches for his phone. I tap over to the text I sent and watch as the bubble that indicates he's replying pops up.

MARCH

Why?

ME

Finished my schoolwork for the
day. There's nothing else to do.

MARCH

Bake? Watch a movie? Talk your
mom into going to Starbucks
where I might be right now?

If only he knew, I can't help but think.

ME

There's gotta be dozens of

Starbucks in Richmond. How
do you know we go to the same one?

MARCH
oh right, darn

ME
And idk, nothing's holding my
interest right now. If it weren't so
cold, I'd go for a walk or something.

MARCH
Sorry. Wish I could help
MARCH
Actually...hold that thought

Matthew stands up, and I quickly click over to Twitter. He walks behind me and disappears at the back of the coffee shop. I breathe a sigh of relief—until my phone buzzes incessantly and March's name appears on my screen.

"Crap," I mutter aloud.

"What's wrong?" Owen asks, and my head snaps up.

"Uh, it's my sister. She's calling. I've gotta, uh, take this," I say, grabbing my coat and hurrying to the door. As soon as I'm outside, hoping I don't sound too out-of-breath, I answer the call. "Hey."

"Okay, I'm studying with friends so I can only talk for a few minutes, but I didn't want to leave you to die of boredom."

I smile. "Thanks."

"You doing better after this weekend?"

"Yeah. I'm still deciding things, but I feel better. I haven't talked to my parents about it all yet, but I don't *think* they'll be mad—as long as I have a plan. So I'll talk to them once I have one."

"Sounds good."

After a few seconds of silence, I ask, "What are you studying for?"

"Oh, I have a math test on Friday. I'm not worried about it, though."

"What about your friends?"

"Um, some of them were writing papers, and two of them have a chemistry exam next week, and a couple were doing French homework, but I think they finished because one of the guys is working on something else and the girl was glued to her phone when I left the group. I don't get her at all. She's with her friends, but she seems to think whatever is on her phone is so much more interesting than us."

He keeps going, but my tongue is frozen, and my legs are rooted to the ground. I can barely process this. When Matthew went to the bathroom or wherever he's hiding, the only girl on her phone was…me.

"You know?" he says, but his voice is faint in my ears.

I'm the girl he hates, the girl he thinks is stuck up, the girl who annoys him out of his mind—and not in a good way.

"Feather?"

"Uh-huh," I say, hoping that's the answer he was looking for. "Sorry, my mom's calling me. I've gotta go," The lie slips off my tongue, and then I hang up.

I slump into one of the patio chairs. My mind can't form a complete thought, but I have enough sense left to put the

phone back up to my ear and fake a conversation with
Madeline, in case one of my friends comes out here.

I will not cry, I will not cry, I will not cry, I tell myself
over and over. I don't want to go back inside until I've
got a grip on my emotions. To be honest, I don't want to
return to our table at all. I don't know if I can face *him*.
But the wind tugs at my hair and my gloveless hands are
numb, so finally, I stand up and pocket my phone.

"Everything okay?" Owen asks when I drift back inside
and settle into my seat.

I look up at him and try to look normal. "What? Oh
yeah, there was just some, uh, bridesmaid dress drama," I
manage to say. I can't look at Matthew at all. It's a good
thing March and I decided not to meet. He'd probably take
one look at me and then walk out.

"Do you need any help with your homework?" I ask.

Owen's smile is warmer than a summer day, and it
helps steady me. "Nah, I'm good. Thanks, though."

Flipping her ponytail, Kylie says, "Audra's kind of a
math whiz. If you're studying for that algebra test, you
should take her up on the offer."

I roll my eyes. "I barely passed algebra II, Kyls. My
parents are making me take AP calculus. Otherwise I
wouldn't make myself suffer."

"*Barely* passed?" Ro pipes up. "You got an A."

"It was a painfully earned A. Madeline's the only reason
I got it," I retort.

I catch the look on Matthew's face, the way he's almost
glaring at me. I close my mouth and don't say anything
more. I shift in my chair and play with one of the buttons

on my coat. Now I feel stifled, like I can't talk to my friends or be myself without Matthew judging me. I wish I'd never found out he was March.

No, more than that, I wish he'd never joined Stony Point or even moved to Virginia. Then I wouldn't feel so numb.

CHAPTER FIFTEEN

After another Friday when I struggled yet again to keep my emotions in check around Matthew, I settle in my room with a notebook. It's time for me to sort out who March and Matthew are once and for all. So I make two columns on a page and label each with his names. I need to see how they're similar and how they're not, so I can understand all of this. I list things like music taste, families, and hobbies. I keep going with the list for a while, but I don't feel any differently when it's done. Sure, the similarities are there, but I wouldn't have pieced it together on my own if I hadn't started looking for March last fall and heard Matthew talk right after that first phone call. Never in a million years would I have looked at Matthew Harwell and said, "Yeah, that's March."

The problem now is he hates me, and I don't know how to change that. I've always been myself, so he hates Feather, too, who is just as opinionated as I am in reality. I don't know how to lie about my opinions, and I'm terrible at faking anything. There's a reason I've never done any church musicals or taken drama classes.

Maybe I need to bake again. Except it's too close to dinner. After dinner then. Until then, though, I'm stuck in my room with my all-consuming thoughts. I wish I could get Matthew out of my head; he doesn't deserve to be there.

Later that night, my parents take glasses of wine to the family room and settle in for a movie night. I'm welcome to join them, but I'd rather have some cathartic baking time. I flip through the recipe cards in my lavender recipe book, but nothing catches my interest. Maybe I've bookmarked the perfect recipe online... As I look through the web pages, I find a crop of pies from when I went through my pie phase last spring.

Well, now I have too many options. There are several different kinds of slab pie: apple, peach, strawberries and cream... On another food blog, there's a recipe for an apple pie baked in a cast iron skillet. And there are pies like blueberry-peach, sour cream and blueberry, cinnamon peach, French silk chocolate... Maybe I should forgo all my college plans and work at a pie shop instead.

I laugh aloud at that thought.

But for now, I check my pantry and fridge for ingredients. I generally keep a piecrust in the freezer for spontaneous baking sessions like this, so I pull it out for a quick thaw. I also find frozen blueberries, and we always have sour cream in the fridge, so that settles that. I've never been able to replicate the sour cream and blueberry pie at that shop downtown, but this one looks pretty close.

Since my parents are in the other room, I plug my earbuds into my phone and then hit shuffle on one of my film score playlists. As I measure, pour, and stir, I start to think of my movements like a dance. With the background music, it's a waltz. The only difference is that I don't have a partner—except the utensils cycling in and out of my hands. Once the dough and blueberries are thawed, I layer everything in the patterned pie plate my grandparents gave me for my birthday. I handle the dough carefully before spreading out the blueberries and pouring in the custard. The streusel on top is the last step; once that's sprinkled on, I slide the pie into the oven and move into the cleanup ballet.

The kitchen starts to fill with sugary aromas. I pause in wiping down the counter, lean back against it, and inhale deeply. I haven't thought about March—Matthew—at all in the last forty-five minutes.

Well, now I have, which ruins that nice streak. I don't understand boys at all. They're just...weird. I shake my head. I've got to stop obsessing about this; I need to think about something different again.

Madeline's wedding...college—no, I really don't want to think about that. Baking...I want to learn how to make macarons soon. There's probably a class I can take downtown. Cooking...I should probably learn how to grill; maybe Dad can teach me this summer. I hope he and Mom are enjoying their movie. I check the clock; I don't think I'll have time to watch a movie tonight, but maybe I can squeeze in an episode of some show. I wonder what March did tonight, if he watched a movie or did something else.

"Crap," I say aloud. I'm back to thinking about him. With a groan, I fall into a chair at the table. Why can't I get him off my mind?

I can answer my own question. It's because I like March as more than a friend, but I don't know how to feel about Matthew—besides being dismayed that he more than dislikes me. Everything is just too confusing.

My phone buzzes in my hand. When I look down, the screen has lit up with a message from March. I can't remember if I have read receipts turned on or not, so I just read the message preview.

MARCH
You've been quiet these
last few days. What's up?

I imagine replying, *"Oh, not much. I found out you hate me, and I'm still trying to process that on top of figuring out what to do for college. Wbu?"*

I text Sam instead about going to a movie next week, and then go check on the pie.

Holly takes one look at me at church and knows something is amiss. It's impossible to hide any feelings from your friend of fifteen years. It's how I accidentally spoiled the surprise party for her thirteenth birthday, and how I knew she was upset about her dad's cancer diagnosis before she could even tell me the news.

I shake my head, not willing to discuss this where anyone, including Joel, could overhear. That's how we end up secreted away in the church library during second service, instead of over in the junior/senior high building.

Ostensibly, the library is closed during the sermons, but it's never locked.

"Okay, I want to know what the heck is going on," Holly says as she tosses her gray coat over a chair, "but first I need to see if that book is still here, the one Mrs. Burleigh tried to have removed when we were in middle school."

I help her search; she's talking about a Christian guide to puberty for girls. It was published in the early 2000s, but some parents—particularly Mrs. Burleigh—couldn't stand the idea of letting their precious children access any kind of information or resources about periods and hygiene. Because heaven forbid, we understand our bodies.

We find the book eventually, shelved among the other 'R' authors. The little due date card and pocket inside are practically a history record—I even find my name, printed in bubbly, sixth-grade handwriting.

"I know who March is," I say before we sit down at a table.

Holly trips over a chair leg but catches herself. *"What?!"* she exclaims. Then, "Is it Sam? Please tell me it's Sam. He's so kind, and you guys would be cute together."

"That would be the easier option, wouldn't it?" I sigh with my whole body and gesture for her to sit down. "It's not Sam. It's this guy from Stony Point named Matthew."

"Oh yeah, Ro's mentioned him, I think. But what's wrong with him being March?" Before I can answer, she continues, "Did he find out you're Feather and reject you? I don't care if Rowena thinks he's nice. I'll fight him."

That brings a brief smile to my face. "No, but thanks. He doesn't know yet."

Then I explain why I haven't told Matthew about my realization. When she has heard the whole sorry account, Holly sighs. She's quiet for a few minutes as she rubs a section of hair between her fingers. I play with my lip balm tube while she thinks.

"I don't think I have any advice," she says eventually.

"That's all right," I am quick to reassure her. "I think, sometimes… Sometimes it's nice to just talk about what happened, and to have a friend who wants to listen."

Holly's expression is gentle. She reaches over to hug me, and my lower lip quivers involuntarily. It's been a strange couple of weeks. I wish I could tell Ro and Kylie what's going on, but I don't want them to feel like they have to choose sides. Sure, I've been their friend longer, but they genuinely like Matthew. I don't want my senior year to be marred by friend group drama.

When Holly releases me, she says, "You'll figure out what to do. Even if it takes time."

I hope she's right.

CHAPTER SIXTEEN

It's always a bit startling to find a song that reflects my exact mood. As I mope about the house, gentle piano notes haunt my thoughts. They're from a song in a mini-series I watched recently, and the music backs the main character going through a similar sort of hurt and rejection.

The notes plod down in slow succession, growing heavier as the song progresses, and I feel myself descend further into melancholy. I've never considered myself an angsty teenager, but we're all allowed our moments.

With a blanket wrapped around me, I curl up in my checkered armchair and clutch a mug of tea. I stare across the room at nothing in particular. As the strings settle lightly in the background, giving the song a more fragile tone, I realize not even baking will fix this. That pie a few days ago distracted me, but it was only temporary. The heavier notes of the piano echo through the silence, and I try not to think about my broken plans for college and a career.

Days pass in a blur of concerned messages from March that I ignore, a cold kitchen—where, at the most, I make toast and boxed mac and cheese—and scattered plans for my future. All the while, the violins from the song darkly fill the corners of my mind. When I pass Matthew in the hall at co-op, my heart plays the piano notes from the start of the song. Every time I think of March now, all I can see is *his* face, and I hate that such happy memories are made painful. Perhaps Matthew looks at me, but I pretend my French folder is much more interesting. It's more than a tactic to avoid the way he'd shun me, though; it's also to prevent the tears trembling around my eyes from spilling over. I've cried twice at co-op before, and that was two times too many.

The rat-a-tat-tat of the song's drums rattles words loose in classes and at lunch, so I'm not quiet enough that anyone notices something is wrong. But my food tastes like dust, and I'm pretty sure my lack of appetite attracts a little attention from my friends. Ro presses me over text in the evenings, but I lie and say everything is all right. I don't want to cause drama in the group, and if I tell her, she'll probably say something to Joel, the peacemaker, or she'll go after Matthew herself in my defense. I don't want everyone to start fighting and taking sides any more than I want Matthew to find out I'm Feather.

I sigh—something I've done a lot lately—and curl up in my armchair again. Between my meltdown a few weeks ago and the March revelation, I don't know who I am anymore. I don't have a dream to pursue and, according to my so-called best friend, I'm actually an awful person.

It's as if my hands are moving of their own accord as I pick up my laptop and type in a web address for a site I haven't visited in a long time. Forum sites have been fading for a while, and there was nothing keeping me tied to Homeschoolers Across the Country once March and I started emailing and IMing. People there were nice, but I had never made any other good friends, and it was hard to keep up with them anyway since our only place to chat was the forum.

My breath catches as I click on a link in the control panel. All of my old private messages are still there. Those first week and a half of conversations with March are here for me to peruse.

September 17, 2012, 11:29 am EST, <u>idesofmarch</u> sent <u>feathergirl13</u> a PM:
So what's your favorite subject?
September 17, 2012, 4:42 pm EST, <u>feathergirl13</u> replied:
Sorry it took me so long to reply. I had extra assignments today since we have a field trip tomorrow. Um I think I like art appreciation best. My mom isn't artsy so she doesn't expect anything I do to be great. You?
September 17, 2012, 5:00 pm EST, <u>idesofmarch</u> said:
I like English because my mom lets me study movies and plays too not just boring old books. And I like learning Spanish. Are you taking a language?
September 17, 2012, 5:05 pm EST, <u>feathergirl13</u> said:
Yeah, Latin. It's ok. I get to switch to French next year.
September 17, 2012, 5:09 pm EST, <u>idesofmarch</u> said:
Boooooo. You should take Spanish.
September 17, 2012, 5:12 pm EST, <u>feathergirl13</u> said:
EVERYONE takes Spanish though. I wanna be different.
September 17, 2012, 5:17 pm EST, <u>idesofmarch</u> said:
French isn't that different. Take Chinese or something.

September 17, 2012, 5:22 pm EST, <u>feathergirl13</u> said:
But I like the idea of learning French! It's the language of food—
bouillabaisse, flambé, croutons, hors d'oeuvres, roux...
September 17, 2012, 5:29 pm EST, <u>idesofmarch</u> said:
Do you cook or something?
September 17, 2012, 5:31 pm EST, <u>feathergirl13</u> said:
I love to cook. And bake.
*September 21, 2012, 7:18 pm EST, feathergirl13 sent
idesofmarch a PM:*
So why do you love Star Wars so much?
September 21, 2012, 8:34 pm EST, idesofmarch replied:
I love the action and how inventive the original trilogy was. And
the plot twists. George Lucas made us care for the characters,
which can be hard to do in only a few hours.
You really should watch it.
September 21, 2012, 8:38 pm EST, feathergirl13 replied:
I don't really like sci-fi though...
September 21, 2012, 8:40 pm EST, idesofmarch replied:
Aw okay... 😠

*September 24, 2012, 1:57 pm EST, <u>idesofmarch</u> sent
<u>feathergirl13</u> a PM:*
What types of things do you bake?
September 24, 2012, 2:05 pm EST, <u>feathergirl13</u> replied:
Mostly cakes these days. I'm trying to master them.
September 24, 2012, 2:11 pm EST, <u>idesofmarch</u> said:
What's your favorite kind of cake?
September 24, 2012, 2:14 pm EST, <u>feathergirl13</u> said:
Depends on my mood. Right now I like carrot cake and pumpkin
cake. What's your favorite type?

September 24, 2012, 2:17 pm EST, <u>idesofmarch</u> said:
Have you ever had those chocolate cakes where it's like liquid inside? Those are the best.
September 24, 2012, 2:22 pm EST, <u>feathergirl13</u> said:
Oh molten chocolate cakes are AMAZING. So hard to make though.

The conversations continue in that pattern for a few more days. We even talk about how old we were the first time we saw *The Princess Bride,* and I learn that his parents would also mute the moment in the Inigo Montoya-Count Rugen duel where Inigo says "son of a bitch."

I open my secondary email account next and find the starred messages. Most of the inane stuff was deleted long ago, since I saw no reason to keep it. The earliest emails are still there, though. I swallow as I open the first one.

From: feathergirl1389@gmail.com
To: idesofmarch117@gmail.com
Sent: September 27, 2012, 4:26 pm
Subject: Hi!

Dear March,
So we should probably set some ground rules. My parents are big on Internet safety, and I don't think they'd even like me emailing you, but if we're careful, it'll be ok. Here's what I was thinking: we keep our real names, our locations, general ages, stuff like that private. We can maybe talk about where we, like, go on vacation and our families, but if we can use it to Google each other, then we shouldn't say it. Does that sound good?

Anyways, do you have any siblings? I have an older sister, but we don't hang out much. Or do you have pets? We've got a cat. I don't like him very much most of the time. He likes my dad best.
-Feather

From: idesofmarch117@gmail.com
To: feathergirl1389@gmail.com
Sent: September 27, 2012, 4:39 pm
Subject: Re: Hi!

Feather,
I think this is the beginning of a beautiful friendship.
What older movies have you watched? I know you like a lot of fantasy but please tell me you've seen the classics. I think I can forgive you for never seeing Star Wars if that's the case.
Let's see... what little things can I tell you about myself without saying too much? I think you've got a good idea—no names, no locations, nothing about what we look like, no ages. (Though I think we know generally how old we both are.) Anyway. I've got two little brothers. They're ok. We got a dog 2 years ago. Her name is Kelly.
We already talked about favorite foods. Do you read at all? Do you have a favorite book? What about sports?
-March

I swallow something that feels like a sob and a laugh all at the same time. My words sound so young, so eager-to-please. I miss that feeling. I didn't realize at the time that those conversations built the best friendship I've ever had. It's so strange to think that I never thought of that when March and I met. Did either of us expect we'd still be chatting four and a half years later? I'm not sure I did.

The soft piano notes creep back into my thoughts as I consider how much time and emotion I invested in March. Now I'm not sure it was all worth it.

The song is short, so I memorize it eventually. It has become part of my being, absorbed into my bones and released with every breath. I wouldn't be surprised if I'm humming the tune as I do my school assignments each day.

One Wednesday, as I'm working through an essay prompt, my mom approaches.

"You haven't cooked anything lately," she comments.

I shrug.

"The cookie jar is looking a little empty... Or you could make dinner tonight, if you like," she continues.

I shake my head. "I've got a lot of homework."

"You can take a break."

I look up, my focus broken. "No, I shouldn't. I have an essay to write, a pre-calc assignment, and reading and questions for Mrs. Kurtz's class."

My mom chews her lip. "As your primary educator," she says, "I think you can take a break. Your essay doesn't have a hard and fast deadline, so that can wait 'til later. Or maybe I'll change the assignment so you have to bake something..."

"No, you don't need to do that!" I drop my pen and scramble to catch it before it rolls off the table. Mom grabs it, but she doesn't hand it back. Instead, she sinks into the chair kitty-corner from me.

"Audra, what's wrong?"

"Nothing; I'd just like to finish my homework." I splay my hand over my notebook paper as if she'll take the essay away from me, too.

Of course that doesn't convince her; she's been a mom for thirty years. I'm sure Madeline wore out the White Lies and Excuses book years ago.

"Are you fighting with Ro? Or Holly?"

I shake my head.

"Is it boy trouble?"

I shake my head again, even though that's part of it. But I'm not telling my mom about March when my friendship and feelings for him don't matter anymore. She'd just focus on the fact that I made friends with someone on the Internet. It won't even matter that I was cautious; she'll just lecture me about stranger danger.

"Is it school? You know you can always come to Dad or me if you're struggling."

"No, it's not that. I'm staying on top of my homework." *Or I would be, if you'd stop interrupting.*

She checks her watch. Hopefully she's realized her questioning will get her nowhere. "It's probably time for Rajesh's walk. Why don't you bundle up and head over to the Patels'? A walk might do you some good, too."

I make a face. Sometimes walks do help me process things, but I doubt one will today, when I've already been swimming around in my thoughts with no land in sight for days.

But Mom is right—it's about the usual time I take Rajesh out. When winter hit this year, I offered to take the Patels' dog for daily walks. I don't earn much, but I don't mind. Any time spent with a dog is fun, and the Patels are my favorite neighbors. I can't let them down.

So I throw on a coat, boots, and gloves, shove my phone in my pocket, and head outside. I squint against the glare of the sun reflecting off the snow. A car rumbles by slowly because the snow is packed down on the street. Plows never come through our neighborhood; if there's a major storm, we'll be snowed in for days. It drives my dad batty. He spent half his childhood in upstate New York, and they apparently handle snow much better than Virginia does.

I shiver. This'll have to be a short walk, but as long as Rajesh can burn off some energy, the Patels will be happy. They somehow adopted the most rambunctious King Charles Spaniel in the state.

I stomp the snow off my boots as I climb the steps to their front porch. Their car is in the driveway, so I knock instead of using my key. Mr. Patel answers after a minute, and his smile is bright enough that I feel my moodiness melting just a little.

"Come in, Audra." He steps aside, before turning to look down the hall. "Rajesh! Look who's here!"

Nails scrabble against hardwood floor as Rajesh rounds the corner. I crouch down to his level, and he throws himself at me. I stroke his silky ears as he pants happily. Then I reach up and grab a leash from where the Patels hang them by the door. Once it's secure and I have a poop bag shoved in my pocket, I stand and open the door.

"Brr! Glad I'm not the one going out in this weather!"

Mr. Patel says. "If you have time after the walk, stay for awhile. Nitya can make some chai, and you can tell us what you've been up to since Christmas."

I hesitate, but then I nod. "That would be nice," I reply. I smile briefly and head out with Rajesh.

The same song and my thoughts chase us down the block. Rajesh trots along beside me, and I try to focus on him and the way his paws make little indents beside my boot prints. Although the wind is biting, the bright sun provides a little warmth. The further I get from home, the fainter the song grows as I think of other things—books, the colleges Ro and Kylie are considering for their trip, and this year's superhero movies. My shoulders feel a little lighter as I inhale fresh air. I even feel cheerful enough to wave to the mailman as his truck rumbles past.

Eventually, when Rajesh starts to flag, we head back to the Patels'. Their slate gray house blends into the snowy landscape, but the cherry red door is like a beacon. I knock the snow off my boots onto the porch. There's a small towel right inside the door, which I use to loosen the clumped snow on Rajesh's paws and belly fur. Then I shed my snow gear, draping it over the old radiator. I head to the kitchen, my sock-covered feet padding against the hardwood floor. Both the Patels are in there; Mrs. Patel is grating ginger into a pan on the stove. When she sees me, she envelops me in a warm hug, and I release a shuddering breath.

"Long week?" she asks sympathetically.

"The longest," I groan. "I can't wait for senior year to be over."

Mr. Patel laughs. "But then you have college. It is much harder than high school."

I make a face, and they both chuckle. Mr. Patel and I settle at the small, round breakfast nook table as Mrs. Patel adds the masala spices—toasted cardamom, clove, anise, and nutmeg, if I remember correctly from when she once narrated as she prepared the chai.

"Tell us, what will you be studying?" she says.

And just like that, the song floods back in with its ominous notes. I swallow the lump in my throat.

"Um, I'm not quite sure yet," I say, forcing a smile. "Something related to food, I think. I was leaning towards culinary school, but now I'm not certain. Maybe journalism so I can be a food writer or a critic."

"That would be interesting. A business degree might be useful with that. You could run your own magazine," says Mr. Patel.

My smile grows more natural. The Patels' son triple-majored, and now he has a prestigious job in D.C. Their daughter, though, is an art teacher. They value more creative fields, as long as there's a practical element, and I appreciate their invested interest in what *I* want to do.

Once the chai boils the first time, Mrs. Patel sits beside me. The tea must come to a boil again, so we have a few minutes to chat before it's time to serve. I ask about their children, and they ask about Madeline's wedding. I tell the Patels it's going to be a late morning wedding and my sister has chosen shades of blue and yellow, since they're friendly and bright.

That afternoon, I warm my hands with a cup of chai,

and the grayness that crept up around my heart recedes just a little. Something about this change of scenery has helped. I will figure things out—both about college and March. It's just going to take a little time.

CHAPTER SEVENTEEN

Joel catches me in the hall between morning classes. We make eye contact, so I can't run the other way and pretend I didn't see him. Normally I wouldn't have that reaction to one of my friends, but every time I see him, I'm terrified he'll ask why I've been distant and not myself lately. Even though I only have eight minutes to make it to the other side of the building and get settled in my seat for class, I pause.

"Hey," I say, tightly gripping my backpack straps.

"I haven't seen you much lately," he says. "You doing—"

Matthew slides up beside us, and I swallow hard. A lump like a glob of peanut butter is stuck in my throat.

"Hey, man," Joel says, smiling congenially and slapping Matthew on the shoulder.

"So, I was thinking about running out and grabbing lunch as soon as this period is over. Wanna come with?" Matthew angles himself away from me, closing me out of the conversation.

"Yeah, that sounds fun!" Joel's eyes flick to me.

I start to drift away, since this doesn't involve me. Joel's eyes narrow; he doesn't want me to get away that easily. Matthew, seeing where Joel's gaze is, turns to me.

"I'd invite you, but I was thinking we'd go to Jersey

Mike's." His smile looks unkind. "And I figured you turn up your noses at most places like that."

I flinch. Guess he's no longer taking the subtle approach to his hatred for me. "It's fine," I lie. I twist my feather ring around my finger. "I brought lunch from home, and I wouldn't want to waste it."

Matthew shrugs.

I look back at Joel. "I, uh, better get to class. See you later."

"Okay, but we're gonna finish talking then," he says firmly.

"Sure," I say, knowing I don't mean it. I force a smile, then hurry off. I pause just around the corner to catch my breath and shake off my obsessive thoughts before class.

What did I do to Matthew to make him hate me? Surely he's not still hung up on the Hickory party? Or, even if he is, that was one isolated incident. It couldn't cause more than a little disgruntlement, could it?

I hope he doesn't invite me to his party, just so it's clear what kind of person he really is.

I stack our bowls on the counter by the sink, then peek at the apple cobbler in the oven. Madeline stretches before clearing the rest of the table. She puts the salad dressing in the fridge and refills our water glasses.

"Leave the dishes. I'll do them later," she says with a wave of her hand.

I nod and cross to the living room area. A sliver of the Richmond skyline is visible through the half-wall of windows. As the sun sinks further down the horizon and streetlights come alive, I smile. It's homey here.

Once the cobbler is ready, I dish out two large portions. Madeline has made tea, since she knows I don't usually drink coffee. We curl up on opposite ends of the couch, facing each other.

"Do you think you could make that soup by yourself?" I ask, referencing the dinner we just had. I used a recipe of Mom's, one that calls for stew meat, potatoes, mushrooms, and red wine, among other things.

"I think so." Madeline nods slowly. "And overall, the meal isn't too complicated to put together—soup, salad, bread."

"Yup. And it's super nice on a winter night." I gesture outside at the snow-covered trees.

"This cobbler, too." Madeline gestures with her spoon before taking an extra-large bite.

My cheeks warm with the praise. We're quiet for a moment, and the wind whistles outside. It was surprisingly nice to come to Madeline's after co-op today, to do something that didn't remind me of Matthew/March in the slightest. I chose a good recipe, too, because that soup is like an edible version of aromatherapy that smooths all troubles and makes them seem insignificant.

"Did you like college?" I ask, turning to another of my problems.

"Yeah," my sister says softly, and her gaze becomes distant as she remembers. "It was a formative time. It wasn't always happy or easy, but I appreciated it for what it was and what I learned. And for the friends I made."

I think about Madeline's bridesmaids and realize only one is a friend from before college and adulthood.

"Is it hard to…maintain your high school friendships?" I don't look at her, afraid to see her answer painted on her face.

"Yes." That's Madeline for you—brutally honest. Thankfully, she goes on, "Both people have to make an effort, yet your friendship can still change. Also, I know people always praise long friendships, but it's okay if they fizzle out or only last a couple years. And trust me, you'll make *great* friends in college, too. Amber is my best friend, and we didn't meet 'til junior year."

"I just… I believe you, but it's hard to see that. I don't want to lose the friendships I have," I reply.

"I know." Madeline's voice is gentle. "It's not fun, but it isn't always bad. Sometimes, they just fade away instead of ending in a massive fight. Sure, that hurts, but you're left with better memories of each other, and you could still get along as acquaintances."

I nod. I think of the people I consider my friends—Ro, Holly, Joel, Kylie, Dylan, Sam, and Owen. I'm not sure March is in that category anymore, which makes my heart ache. Holly and Joel have been there the longest, and Sam is the newest, but I honestly don't want to let go of any of them. They all mean something different to me.

Madeline rises from her chair, stirring me from my thoughts. "Wanna start a puzzle?" she asks, and I nod because it seems like the right thing to do. It'll draw me out of the melancholy that has settled over me yet again.

I smile at my sister as she sets a box on the table, and she returns it. It does strike me as ironic, that just as my friendship with March is wobbling, my relationship with her is growing stronger.

CHAPTER EIGHTEEN

Getting out of bed for co-op the next week is hard after my late night. But, if the brownies I made will cheer Ro up, it'll be worth it. With so many siblings, she tends to get lost in the mix now and again. When she was already having a hard day, a boy rejecting her made it worse. There was only so much I could do over text, and although I don't think she minded, I did.

The thing about being down in the dumps is, if one of my friends feels worse—or seems to at least—my problems suddenly don't matter. I have to do whatever I can to cheer them up. I can wallow later; Ro takes precedence.

So even though I was already in pajamas, I climbed out of bed at 11:30 p.m. and preheated the oven, then paged through my recipes for Ro's favorite raspberry cream cheese brownies. Mom and Dad didn't wake up, I don't think. If they did, they're used to my bouts of late-night energy, so they didn't feel the need to check on me. They know I won't burn down the house.

I used to think baking was the same at any time of the day, but there's a different energy about being in the kitchen alone late at night. The windows are dark, and it feels wrong to turn on too many bright, fluorescent lights so I use only the lights under the cabinets. All my movements are slow and quiet—even the clink of a spoon against a glass bowl is muted. I always make a cup of tea while whatever recipe I chose is in the oven. It warms my soul as much as the smells that fill the kitchen.

At breakfast, I begged Mom to be ready early because I want to meet Ro before our second period classes. I don't want to make a big deal out of Ro's feelings if she wants to keep them private, so I'd rather give her the Tupperware quietly instead of at lunch with our inquisitive friends.

I lean nonchalantly against the wall. Ro's American history class is right down the hall from my French classroom, so I shouldn't be late. I study my phone while I wait; I don't want to get caught up in a conversation with someone else and miss my best friend.

"Audra?"

She's a few steps away, wearing jeans and a cozy navy blue sweatshirt, which is odd because she usually wears sleek blouses with her jeans. She doesn't want to stand out today, I realize. When she reaches my side, I hug her. Ro's arms wrap around me—which is a big sign something's wrong, because she's not usually touchy-feely—and her breath sounds shaky.

"Shouldn't you be in class?" she asks, stepping out of the hug.

"I'll head there in a minute. I won't be late," I tell her. Then I unzip my backpack and pull out the Tupperware. "Here. These are for you."

She takes the container automatically but holds it like she doesn't know what to do with it. Then she pops the lid, and her confusion slides into surprise. Her frown glides away, and her mouth trembles a little.

"You okay?" I ask, ducking my head so I can look her in the eye.

She nods. "This was just…so nice of you." She meets my gaze, and her eyes are shining.

I shrug. "I wanted you to feel better. Chocolate's always good for that."

Ro closes the container and wraps her free arm around me. "Thanks, Audra."

"No problem." I return her hug, savoring this moment when my best friend initiated the physical contact.

"No, really, I appreciate it." She pulls back. "I know you haven't been yourself lately, so the fact that you baked for me…"

"I'd do anything for you." I blink rapidly. "Anyway, boys suck. Trust me, he wasn't worth your time."

She nods. "I know. It just…" She sighs. "It doesn't feel great right now, that's all. I thought he liked me."

"I've been there. You're allowed to be upset, but I wanted to cheer you up a little, if I could." Then, since she still looks a bit weepy, "Anything else you want to get off your chest?"

Ro shakes her head. "I don't want to dump anything more on you."

I roll my eyes. "Please. I'm pretty sure I owe you a million times over for all the rants and baggage I've dumped on you."

"Maybe." She shrugs. "But there's plenty of not great stuff I've put on you, too. Friendship isn't about paying debts and being square. It's about listening, giving advice, and supporting. So what if sometimes things are uneven?

It balances out in other ways. No one else bakes for me just because. You notice me. My parents love all of us, but since I'm a 'good kid'—" She puts air quotes around that part—"I kind of get lost in the fray sometimes, even when it would just be nice for someone to tell me my outfit looks nice or to congratulate me on that A I got on a test. Or just ask how my day is going. And you manage to do all those things."

"I wouldn't be a good friend if I didn't," I reply, brushing off her high praise. She makes it sounds like it's a burden for me to do those things.

"And you *are* a good friend." Ro stretches her arms and sighs. "Sheesh, I didn't mean to turn that into such a cry session."

Madame Gibert sticks her head out in the hall and spots me. "Audra! *Venez-vous?*"

I straighten. "*Oui*, Madame." I touch Ro's arm in what I hope is a reassuring way, then head to my classroom.

Just as I reach the door, I hear Ro say, "Hey, Matt."

I look over my shoulder. Matthew pokes at the container of brownies and says something I can't hear. Ro playfully pulls it away from him, as if he were about to steal one. I smile despite the melancholy rising up. At least Ro will be okay soon.

Matthew glances my way. We make eye contact before I dart into my classroom.

I used to spend my weeks looking forward to Stony Point, and now I dread co-op days. Today, I manage a bit better than these last few weeks. At lunch, I sit between Joel and Ro, and although they don't realize it, I feel like I'm flanked by bodyguards.

"Hey, so everyone got the event invite, right?" Matthew says.

I've been avoiding Facebook, so I wouldn't know if I did or not. But, if he's openly asking the group, I must have gotten one. It's good to know he wouldn't be that rude.

But I'm not sure I want to go to his Oscars party if he doesn't really want me there. I play with my bag of chocolate-covered pretzels instead of answering.

"Do you want us to bring anything, like drinks?" Joel asks.

"Audra *has* to bake something," says Kylie before Matthew can respond to the question.

My head shoots up. I glance at Matthew, but then I return to staring at the floor.

"I mean, I think we'll have everything covered food-wise—" he starts.

"Dude," Dylan cuts him off. "You haven't had Audra's baking, have you? She's amazing."

"You should make those mini cheesecakes you did for the Labor Day barbecue," Ro says. She nudges me and shimmies a little. "The key lime ones were my favorite."

"I, uh…"

In my peripheral vision, Matthew shrugs. "I guess if you want to."

I slide my clammy hands into my lap. "I, um, might have a family…obligation that weekend, so I might not be able to come. I could bake, though, if I do come. If you want me to."

He lifts one shoulder. "They all want you to, so that would be fine."

I can read between the lines: he doesn't want me at the party, doesn't want me to bake, but he doesn't want everyone else to see him for the jerk he is. He'll do what they want.

So I force a smile. "Okay. Does everyone want mini cheesecakes like Ro suggested?"

My friends nod. That settles that. I should go anyway. I'm sure Matthew will avoid me, and I don't want to miss out on what could be one of the last parties pre-college. It would be better to be slightly miserable for one night just so I don't feel left out, right?

I sit down at my computer and let my fingers hover over the keys. There's another email in my inbox, but I ignore it.

I don't know how to do this. How does one start a food blog? I've read tons of blogs on a variety of topics, from movies to books to food, but no one really tells you how to go about starting your own.

It needs a name obviously. And it needs to look professional, which probably means I'll need someone's help designing it. And then I need to think about my first post. Do I only want to share recipes, or do I want to talk about my favorite restaurants, too? Since I'm considering food writing at a magazine or something, non-recipe posts would be good practice and showcase my versatility. But it would be good to start with a recipe. I'll thumb through my cookbook later and pick one that'll start things with a bang.

But a name… My blog can't exist without one. If only I had some ideas.

I sigh and rest my chin on my hands. I wish I could ask March for help. He's usually good at coming up with something that would be a play on words and catch people's attention.

Everything I think of is too simple. Cooking With Audra is the only thing coming to mind, and there's no way I can go with that. It's too basic. Wouldn't draw any attention.

I lean back in my swivel desk chair and close my eyes. What would March say? I get into a March-like frame of mind and consider that for a long moment.

He'd tell me to make it literary sounding or incorporate one of my other loves like Taylor Swift or movies.

The Bowl and Spoon...From the Silver Screen to the Kitchen...Taylor's Treats...

My eyes fly open, and I sit up straight. I think I have the perfect name.

I pull up a blogging website and start looking through the free themes. I find a woodsy, medieval-like theme that solidifies my choice.

Buttercup Bakes.

It's imperfect since I do more than bake, but it alludes to my favorite movie. This means I could play with *The Princess Bride* references in my posts, too—maybe even make MLT sandwiches some time.

I'll get everything officially set up later. For now, I pull out a notebook and start brainstorming post ideas. I have to share pie and waffle recipes of course. Risotto, too. Maybe I could even talk about wedding cakes; I'll know a lot about them after all of Madeline's wedding planning.

I feel my shoulders relax although the tension hasn't completely left them. Things are looking up. Now all that's left is figuring out how to tell Mom and Dad I don't want to go to culinary school anymore. My hand pauses in writing down post ideas. I haven't been looking forward to that part, but it's gotta happen soon. There's a lot I need to stop putting off.

CHAPTER NINETEEN

The laundry machine rumbles loudly, and I slump over on the couch and groan, then rub my forehead. I've been trying to get my calculus homework done, but it's not happening. I'll have to text Madeline and ask her to help when I go to her apartment on Wednesday night. She explains the concepts just like Mrs. Powers does. When Mrs. P explains them in class, everything makes sense, but then I get home, and I somehow forget everything.

I gather up my notebooks and head upstairs. I'll work on French assignments instead.

"Your phone's been going off," Mom tells me from the kitchen table where she's grading my English homework.

"Oh, thanks." I grab my phone off the counter. I left it up here so it wouldn't distract me from calculus. Didn't do much good, though.

There are a couple texts from March, which I don't even read. There's an email from the Culinary Institute, which makes my stomach churn. Then there are two texts from Sam. Definitely the safest option.

SAM
Hey this is kinda last minute
but some of us from Hickory

are gonna go bowling tonight.
Wanna come?

SAM

I can pick you up if you need a ride.

My thumbs twitch. My mom would want me to get out of the house. She'd probably even let me take the car, if I asked to go somewhere other than church, co-op, or Madeline's. I press my lips together. It *would* be nice to hang out with people who can't tell I'm not 100 percent me.

"Hey, Mom?" I say, still looking at my phone. "Can I go bowling tonight with some friends?"

"Who all is going?" she asks, setting down her pen and rubbing her wrist.

I shrug. "Sam didn't say."

"Sam?" She raises an eyebrow.

"Yeah, he goes to Hickory. He and I saw a movie together a few weeks ago?" When she continues to give me that look, I roll my eyes and say, "We're friends."

"Okay." Her voice is sing-song in that disbelieving way. "It's fine if you two are more than that."

"I know. But I don't like him like that."

Maybe there was a tiny crush on my part back in December, but that's gone, thanks to March. No matter how much I don't want to, I have feelings for March. But if I keep avoiding him, maybe they'll go away.

"Anyway," I say, shaking my head a little, "we're off-topic. Can I go?"

Her smile grows. "Of course! Do you need me to drive you?"

"Could I maybe drive myself?" I ask, shifting from my heels to my toes.

Mom holds my gaze. I'm a good driver, but she's reluctant to trust me with the car sometimes. Mom and Dad have never said so, but I have a feeling Madeline wasn't a great driver when she was my age. I can practically see this battling with her desire for me to do something outside the house.

"Okay," she finally relents. "But you have to text me when you get there and when you're heading home."

Seems fair. I nod and hurry off to reply to Sam.

ME
Hey, that sounds like fun! I
don't need a ride, but thanks.
Which bowling alley?

SAM
The one on Broad,
south of 64.

ME
Ok!

SAM
See you there at 7?

ME
See ya!

I head out around 6:45, which is maybe a little late, but I don't want to seem too punctual. I shake my head to clear my thoughts. I'm treating this like a first date when that couldn't be further from what I want. His friends will be there, so it's really not a date.

What if Sam thinks this is a group date?

"Crap," I say to the empty car.

Plenty of homeschoolers are only allowed to do group or double dates; maybe Sam is one of those. Still, he hasn't expressed an extra interest in me, so I shouldn't be vain enough to assume. We message occasionally, though, and we slow-danced twice, and he held my hand. Maybe we're in that weird pre-dating stage? Which isn't where I want to be either. I want to be friends—nothing else. Sam is funny and interesting, but he's not who I want to date. There's nothing wrong with him, not really, but my heart isn't drawn to him.

When I park, I take a moment to collect myself. There's a group chat message on my phone from Sam, saying that he's waiting by the shoe rental counter. Someone I don't know replied with a thumbs-up emoji. I count five other names and recognize Holly's friend, Emily, and her classmate from algebra, Caleb. Sam won't be the only person I know, which is a good thing. I think.

He's inside where he said he would be, chatting with two guys. I take in his ginger hair and easy stance. A fleeting wish darts through my mind—that he was March. Everything would be simpler then.

"Hey," I say when I get over to them.

Sam's smile reaches his eyes, and they crinkle at the corners. He gives me a quick hug.

"I hope you're an excellent bowler," he says by way of greeting, "because you're gonna be on my team, and I've told Brandon and Aiden we're gonna blow them out of the water."

"Um..." I laugh.

One of the guys snickers. "Tough luck, O'Hara."

"I'm not *terrible*," I say. "I wouldn't be offended, though, if you want someone else for your team."

Sam shakes his head, scrunching his nose a little. "Nah, we can get Stephanie to join our team too. She'll be our ringer. Do you know her? Stephanie Espinosa?"

I shake my head.

"She's great," Sam says like he's confiding Richmond's Best Kept Secret. "I couldn't survive pre-calc without her."

"Glad to hear I'm invaluable," a girl behind us says.

We turn, and Sam immediately hugs a tall Latina girl.

"You," he tells her, "are on Audra's and my team. Don't let them—" he points at the boys with his thumb—"tell you otherwise."

Stephanie appraises them. "Considering Brandon needs bumpers to score over one hundred, I think they need me more."

The three boys erupt in hoots and hollers. I roll my eyes good-naturedly. I feel a little like I'm crashing a tight-knit group, but thanks to Sam, I don't feel too much like an outsider. While he tries to convince Stephanie she belongs on our team, I sneak a glance at my phone. March usually texts me in the evening. There's been nothing since those messages earlier. Maybe he finally got the hint that I don't want to talk to him anymore. Not that I would say that directly to him. No, that would only prove him right about how rude I am.

Caleb and Emily show up, hand-in-hand, which is news to me. Emily greets me and gets a brief hug from Sam, who also exchanges a bro-hug type thing with

Caleb. Emily, ever the peacekeeper, announces that she, Stephanie, and I will be a team against all four boys.

"They don't stand a chance," she says with a mischievous smile.

"I'm glad you have confidence in my bowling skills because I don't," I tell her.

"You can't be worse than Brandon," Stephanie says, tossing her dark curls.

I shrug. "I haven't bowled in a couple years, but maybe I've improved since then."

Sam hands me my shoes, and I realize he paid for me. Crap, he probably does think this is a date. He leads the way to our lanes where the other two girls and I huddle up.

"Okay, just don't suck," Stephanie tells me, "and this should be easy. Yeah, we're at a disadvantage since there's four of them, but we'll average the team scores at the end. So if we focus and don't goof off, we'll beat them, no problem."

"Don't pressure her!" Emily laughs.

"Yeah, don't psych me out." My smile is teasing, so Stephanie knows I don't mind her bluntness.

"Sam and Caleb are really good," Emily adds, "so if we can somehow keep Brandon and Aiden from doing well, we could win."

Apparently she has a competitive streak, too.

"Are we only playing for glory? 'Cause, not gonna lie, that's not very motivating," I say as we turn to analyze our ball options.

Sam, who's come up beside me, shakes his head. "We're playing for our normal stakes—losers pay for food after this."

"Oh, then that's definitely enough motivation to win," I say, grinning. I heft a shimmery black ball. "Y'all would bankrupt us with how much you eat."

"You're not wrong. I've seen Sam eat enough food for four people on numerous occasions," Caleb interjects as Sam blushes.

"I've seen Emily eat almost as much!" he blurts.

I turn towards Emily, who's skinny.

She shrugs. "I swim," she says.

That, I understand. I've been friends with Dylan long enough to know how much food swimmers can put away.

We settle into the game, and I manage to not humiliate my team. I even manage to get a spare, something I've only managed once or twice before.

After one of my turns, I sit at the table by our lanes. Sam's friends are pretty cool. Brandon and Aiden are a bit much, but they are funny, and Stephanie is chill while also coming across as effortlessly put-together. Right now, though, she's arguing with Aiden about whether he stepped across the line on a throw that knocked down eight pins.

Sam plops down beside me. "Hey."

I smile. "I'm having a good time."

"Yeah? I hope we're not too much for you." His hands fidget.

"Nah, y'all are fun. It's kinda nice to see that my friend group isn't the only weird one."

He makes a tiny face, then shifts so his hand is almost brushing mine. I inhale a bit sharply and open my mouth, but he speaks first.

"Looking forward to graduation?" he asks.

I shrug. "Hmm, I guess. I, uh, still need to decide where I'm going after, though." That's a little easier to say now that I'm getting closer to telling my parents about the change in plans.

"Me, too. I really like this school in Wisconsin, so maybe I'll go there."

"Do you know what you want to study?" I ask, resting my clasped hands on the table.

"Audra, you're up!"

I jump up. "Hold that thought," I tell Sam, then go take my turn. He takes his, too—and bowls much better than I do—and then we settle at the table again.

"Haven't quite decided on my major yet either," Sam says. He's across from me this time—my doing—and he leans back against the booth. "I like history, though. And communications would be okay. Or education. I think it would be cool to help kids find something they're passionate about."

I can't help but smile, which seems to happen a lot when I'm around Sam.

"What about you?" he asks.

I bury my face in my hands. "Ugh."

"What is it?"

I look up, and he's so earnest and sweet, that I can't help but want to confide in him. I say, "I thought I wanted to study culinary arts, but I'm leaning towards journalism now."

He raises his eyebrows. "That's a big switch."

"It's been a hectic few months." I laugh nervously as I

say it, then explain, "I'd like to write about food, even if I don't want to cook it for a living."

"That...makes sense." The creases on his forehead smooth.

"I'm starting a food blog," I tell him.

"That's cool!" His face lights up.

It's both of our turns again, so we hop up and then end up staying by the lanes with our teams until the game is over. The scores are averaged, and somehow Stephanie, Emily, and I come out on top. Aiden and Brandon sucked, as the other girls predicted, and despite a few good throws, Sam seemed off his game tonight.

Emily declares we're going to Cheesecake Factory since the boys are paying. I like their cheesecake, although nothing about that restaurant is normal in the slightest. That decor is the weirdest mix of ostentatious and *The Lord of the Rings*. It's at the mall down Broad Street, so I text my mom to tell her where we're going. By some twist of fate, Sam and I are the last to leave. He walks me to my car, then hesitates even after I've unlocked it. I glance at him as he twists up his mouth.

I take a deep breath. Might as well ask now; otherwise, I'll never work up the courage. "Sam? Do you—are we—is this a date?"

I keep my gaze fixed over his shoulder, as if that'll make this any less awkward. His breath catches, and my eyes flit to his face. His eyes have widened a little, and I worry I've completely misread the situation.

"Only," his voice wobbles, "only if you want it to be one."

I close my eyes. I should've known this was coming.

I don't know how to let him down easily, but he doesn't deserve a broken heart. So I shake my head ever so slightly.

"I don't. I'm so sorry," I whisper.

"Hey." He touches my arm, and I open my eyes. "Don't be. You're my friend first and foremost. I hope so anyways. I started wondering what it would be like to be something other than that, that's all."

"I might've wondered that myself back in December," I admit, "but I have feelings for someone else."

Sam nods and leans against the car next to mine. "I understand." He scuffs his shoe against the ground. "Sorry if I've made it weird."

"You haven't, I promise. You're great, and I want to be your friend. Being friends with you is easy, even though I haven't known you all that long."

He smiles, but it doesn't quite reach his eyes. Rejection isn't painless, even if the other person is wonderfully kind about it. I'm sure Sam isn't mad, just a little disappointed, which is perfectly valid.

I wish Sam were the guy I liked romantically. It would be so much easier.

But March isn't easy to quit. Even now, not replying to his texts leaves a gaping hole like one in my favorite sweater that I wish wasn't there. But I either have to repair the sweater or throw it out.

I haven't decided which is the best option yet.

"I, um…I think I should head home," I say.

He straightens. "You okay?"

"I just… I don't want to make you uncomfortable. If being around me is hard or whatever."

"Audra," Sam says with a small laugh. "I'm fine, I promise. I told you—you're my friend. It's not like I'm head-over-heels in love with you. I just started wondering what if. It's not going to work out, and that's okay. I'd rather learn that now than have you be unhappy. But come to Cheesecake Factory. Please?"

I look at him for a long time. I've heard so often about boys that don't handle rejection well that I've only prepared for that scenario. I squint in suspicion. For as long as I've known Sam, he's been nothing but sincere. Now shouldn't be any different, so I nod.

He ducks his head a little. "I don't want to pressure you, sorry. If you really want to go home, that's okay."

"No, I'll come with y'all. If you promise things won't be awkward, I'll be okay."

"Life is awkward," he says with a shrug. A tentative smile creeps across his face. "But I'll try not to make it more so."

"Good." I open the car door. "See you there!"

"Yeah." He pauses mid-step. "My friends'll ask what took so long. I'll say we had to jump my battery, if that's okay with you? They don't need to know what we talked about. They'll just tease us."

I nod slowly, wondering if Sam's actual motivation is that he doesn't want them to know he got rejected.

"None of them know how I feel," he adds, "so it'll be easier for both of us if we don't give them the real explanation."

As I settle in my car, I think about how different tonight was. It was almost like a taste of what college might be like—new friend group, not being driven around by parents, carefreeness. I've never been out without my parents, sister, or friends. I kind of like the strangeness of it. This type of unfamiliarity is exhilarating.

The radio plays low in the background Sam's face pops into my mind. I really do wish my feelings were for him. But maybe Sam and I wouldn't work out, if we tried. I need someone who will push back, who won't be such a cinnamon roll. Sam is perfectly nice, but he's too passive for me. He'd let me boss him around too much, which wouldn't be good for either of us. March calls me on my crap, and I appreciate that.

My stomach flips. I was so mean to Matthew. He could never like me in the same way I like him. Maybe he has feelings for Feather, but he'd certainly change his mind if I told him who I am.

I shake my head to myself. We made such a mess of everything.

Sure, neither of us was catfishing the other—which could've been a whole other giant mess—but we haven't been completely honest about who we are either. I made up stories, and he didn't act like himself in person. I reacted badly, and so did he.

But everything before that was better; we disagreed but never detrimentally. We never damaged our friendship. I don't know why Matthew acted like he did when he got to Stony Point, but I could've been less belligerent. I could've followed Ro or Joel's example. Maybe it's too late, but I have to try to make up for being so rude. It may not have results I want, but that shouldn't be the only reason I'm nice to Matthew Harwell.

Soon, I tell myself. Once I've talked to my parents, I can focus on being a better friend to Matthew. He may not reciprocate at this point, and I'd deserve it, but I can at least start to make up for what a jerk I was last fall.

Buttercup Bakes

MINI CHEESECAKES FOR A PARTY

Posted February 25, 2017 by Audra

I'm often the person asked to bring treats to parties. If you bake a lot, you've probably experienced the same thing. I occasionally try something new, but more often than not, my friends request one of my go-tos. For this particular soirée, my best friend wanted mini cheesecakes.

They're basically what they sound like—I make a graham cracker crust, which I press into muffin papers in a muffin tin. Then I fill the cups with cheesecake mixture. You can go the basic route—plain cheesecake, with perhaps a berry compote on top, or you can get a little adventurous. My favorites are key lime, Oreo, and strawberry swirl. Let me break down the recipe for you…

COMMENTS:
Holly February 25, 2017 at 1:09 PM:
Omgsh, you're finally sharing your secret recipe??
Sam February 25, 2017 at 5:47 PM:
Dude these sound so good.
Ro February 26, 2017 at 12:38 PM:
I'M SO EXCITED TO EAT THEM TONIGHT.

CHAPTER TWENTY

"I'm not going," I tell Ro as I shift my phone to rest between my ear and shoulder so I can pick up the laundry basket. "Tell them I've suddenly come down with the stomach flu or something, but I'm not going."

She sighs. "You said this two days ago and then changed your mind back."

"Well, I changed it again."

"Haven't you already baked the mini cheesecakes?"

"Yes… But I'm sure my mom and dad will help me eat them."

"Well, what about your FOMO? That was the whole reason you were going, wasn't it?" she says as I walk up the stairs from the basement.

"My…what?"

"Fear Of Missing Out. What if something exciting happens, and you miss it?"

I sigh. It feels like I'm dragging my soul up the stairs after me; I'm so weary after this whole mess with Matthew/March. "I just…can't be around him, Ro."

"Who?"

"Matthew!"

"I thought you guys were getting along now."

My laugh is bitter as I plop down on my bed. "I did, too."

"Oh geez, what happened?" I can picture her face-palming.

"It's a long story. Tell you later?"

"Okay. But you should still come. When else do we get to dress up and pretend to be adults? Plus aren't you curious to see the Harwells' house? I know I am."

"Yeah, but...I don't know."

"I'll miss you if you don't come."

"You will. I'm not sure everyone will."

Ro sighs tiredly. "Don't be like that."

I pause. "Sorry."

"Please come? You can stay by my side all night. Matthew can't possibly bother you then. And didn't you have the perfect dress all picked out? When else will you get to wear it?"

I look at the lacy black dress hanging on my closet door. She has a point.

"Okay, I'll come."

"Great. I promise, if you don't have a good time, you can nag me for all eternity." We both laugh. "I'll see you at seven-thirty, okay?"

"Okay."

I hang up, then stare at my dress a little longer. I really hope Matthew can keep it together tonight; any eye roll in my direction will probably send me over the edge.

Ro will be here soon to pick me up. I grab my phone to stick in my purse; there aren't any new texts, but March—*Matthew*—emailed again yesterday. My fingers move almost of their own accord, opening my mail app. As I pull up his email, my heart pulses with guilt. I should tell him the truth soon. But, at the same time, I don't want to have to deal with the fallout of him not liking Audra but liking Feather.

From: idesofmarch117@gmail.com
To: feathergirl1389@gmail.com
Sent: February 25, 2017, 7:38 pm
Subject: You ok?

Feather,
Just checking in. Did I do something to upset you? If so, please tell me so I can make it up to you. Is everything ok with your friends and family? I hope everyone is safe and healthy.
This semester has been kind of rough. My dad expects me to get my college applications in soon, but I'm considering not going... at least for a year. I don't know what I want to do with my life yet. You're lucky to know exactly what you want. I mean, I want to work or travel for a year, but that's not a long-term career goal. My dad wants me to have one. I wish I knew you'd reply to this. I need your advice; you're good at that.
Please write back, even if it's just a quick message to let me know you're ok. Or why you haven't been answering any of my texts or emails.
-March

I feel like even more of a jerk, and yet also annoyed he's expecting so much from me. Am I the only friend he can talk to about the pressure from his dad and college struggles? Can other guys not talk about that or something?

The doorbell rings. I run downstairs and gather up my things—jacket, purse, shoes, and the dessert I'm bringing—while my mom greets Ro. I hurry into the hallway. Ro is wearing a dark green dress and ballet flats. I feel appropriately dressed now.

"Be home by midnight, all right? And text when you get home," my mom says. "Your dad and I will probably be at Professor Norfleet's party until twelve, twelve-thirty."

"Okay, Mom." She gives me a side-hug, and then Ro and I head out.

"Drive carefully!" Mom calls, and my best friend responds affirmatively.

We're quiet on the drive over. Ro focuses on the road— she's an anxious driver after dark—and I'm trying to maintain a semblance of calmness. I don't want to ruin this party for anyone, so I have to pretend everything is fine when it's decidedly not.

We're about halfway there when Ro says, "So…it's later. Why aren't you and Matt getting along anymore? Does it have something to do with why you haven't been yourself lately?"

I should've known Ro would be perceptive enough to figure things out.

"Apparently we never got along," I mutter.

She side-eyes me. "Don't be vague. What's wrong?"

"Well, first of all, I know who March is."

"What?! How did you find out?"

"That's an even longer story. March is…Matthew."

Ro is silent for a minute. "Holy crap. I did *not* see that coming, not after we ruled him out last fall. I would've bet good money on him being that guy, Sam, at Holly's co-op."

"Yeah, well, it's not Sam." I tug at my hem to smooth out my skirt. "But anyway, Matthew and I aren't on good terms. Back in December, March told me there was this girl at his co-op that he disliked. He thought she was stuck-up and annoying, and he needed someone he could complain to about her."

"Let me guess—he was talking about you."

I blink and shake my head a little. "How did you know? It took me a week after I knew he was March to figure that out."

We hit a red light. Ro smiles sheepishly as she turns to look at me. "He never looks that happy to see you. See if you notice it tonight. But wow, I'm surprised he invited you if he dislikes you that much."

"Gee, thanks."

"You know what I mean."

"I guess he doesn't want me to know. I would've realized something was up if I was the only person not invited."

"True. Well I hope he's not a jerk tonight. And maybe he hasn't had the chance to see the real you. 'Cause you're not stuck-up. I don't know why he thinks that."

I shift in my seat. "You're my best friend, Ro. I know you're supposed to make me feel better, but I want you to tell me the truth, too."

I stare out the window as we pull up in front of a massive red house. Ro puts the car in park and turns to look at me again. Another car pulls in behind us, and we let the people get out and walk by before we say anything else.

Ro takes a deep breath before saying, "Sometimes you speak without thinking, and you're pretty picky. I guess I can see how that would come across as snooty or something."

I chew on my lip. She's not wrong; especially after how I treated Matthew at the Hickory dance. Still, he disliked me before that.

"Why haven't y'all ever said anything before?" I ask, crossing my arms over my chest. "If you're my friends, shouldn't you help me see my flaws and become a better person? I feel like I try to do that with y'all. Not in a mean way, of course. But I think friends are supposed to call each other out when they're being jerks."

She shrugs. "I don't think the way you are has ever bothered me. Like, I always know you're teasing and that your pickiness about food is coming from a good place. But someone new, who doesn't know that and maybe doesn't want to see the best in everyone, would interpret it differently."

I nod, although I'm not sure how to respond to that. Maybe I should try to be more careful when I tease the others. I don't want it to ever be misconstrued as meanness because I would never purposefully be unkind to any of my friends.

Ro grabs her purse from the backseat. "Come on. Let's have a good time with our friends. I mean, look at this house! I'll bet it's even cooler inside, and can you imagine the food Mrs. Harwell made?"

I look out my window again. I guess it would be interesting to see how March—Matthew—lives. Besides, Owen, Kylie, and the others will be inside. I can just talk with them and avoid Matthew.

I reach over and squeeze Ro's hand. "Thanks for being honest with me."

The group that passed us, a couple of guys and a girl, close the house's dark wooden front door as we get out of the car. I don't recognize them. I didn't realize Matthew was inviting people from outside our co-op. Maybe that'll keep both of us on our best behavior, though.

A boy who looks like he's in middle school answers the door when we get there. I almost freeze in my tracks when I see him; he looks so much like Matthew that I can picture March when we first started talking—short for his age, hair sticking up and badly in need of a trim, and a smile always just a blink away.

"Hi. You go to the same co-op as us, don't you?" We nod, and he holds the door open a little wider so we can step inside. Then he calls, "Matt! Some more of your friends are here!"

I take in the Harwells' house. It's painted in earthy tones, and the lights are more yellow than white. The foyer is narrower and not as tall as I expected; it's homier. Matthew's brother scampers off down the hall, and my gaze follows him. I catch a glimpse of the kitchen and practically hyperventilate. It's a wide-open space with a long wooden island and beautiful faux-brick tile floors. It's basically everything I didn't know I wanted in a kitchen.

A woman emerges from around the corner. She's tall,

curvy, and perfectly polished, from her sleek chin-length hair to her steel gray kitten heels.

"Hi, I'm Meg Harwell," she says, extending a hand to first Ro and then me. "I've seen you two at Stony Point Homeschool Academy, but we haven't had the chance to meet."

"I'm Rowena Stenger, but I go by Ro."

"Rowena! That's a charming name."

Ro has pasted on her polite smile. Adults love her name, but she doesn't. "My parents are really into the Romantic period of literature."

"They have good taste. *Ivanhoe* is one of my favorites. And you are?"

"Audra Dunne. Ma'am," I add.

"Oh, yes, I met your mother when we joined the co-op! Well, welcome to both of you. I don't know where my son has run off to, but everyone else is gathering in the kitchen." She notices my food carrier. "Right, Matthew told me you were bringing a dessert. He says you're an excellent baker?"

I hand over the mini cheesecakes and consider this bit of praise. Matthew hasn't tried anything I've made, so I don't know why he would tell his mom that. "I try," I finally say. "I'd like to think I'm pretty good."

I'm not sure what to think of Mrs. Harwell. From what March has implied, she's become more involved with the family business than with her kids. But she seems warm, like the mustard color on the walls, and she seems involved enough in Matthew's life to care that his party runs smoothly.

We follow her into the kitchen. I try not to drool over the state-of-the-art appliances and elegant dishes. What I wouldn't give to cook in a room like this. It's fancy without being untouchable; it's meant to be used. It's much different from my grandma's kitchen, though— the place where I most love to cook. Grandma's window hangings are blue-and-gold-checked, and her ice blue refrigerator looks vintage, not at all modern like this stainless steel one.

There are introductions all around that pull me out of my admiration. Matthew's theater friends are kind enough, and both his brothers—Thomas and George, Mrs. Harwell calls them—hop around and sneak food off the platters as we make surface-level conversations with Theo, Chris, and Leah. I notice George, the younger boy, is wearing a Spider-Man shirt; I ask him about superheroes, and we talk about that for a while. Matthew finally makes an appearance, remote in hand.

"Sorry, I was getting the TV ready," he tells his mom. He greets the other guests and, when he gets to me, I watch his reaction like Ro suggested. I'm terrible at reading emotions, and I could be imagining it, but his smile looks less than genuine.

Something cold and wet presses into my knee. I startle back and look down to find a dog that looks like Winn-Dixie, shaggy with pointed ears and a wagging tail.

"Oh, sorry," says Matthew, grabbing the dog's collar. "Come on, Kelly."

"No, she's fine," I say as I bend down to pet her silky ears.

I hesitate for the briefest moment before running my hand over the dog's head. This is the dog March has mentioned for years; I'm finally meeting her. Kelly pants happily and thumps her tail.

"She likes you." He sounds surprised.

"Dogs generally do," I say. I think I manage to not sound smug.

"Let's head to the rec room," he announces to the whole group. "Mom, when everyone else arrives, send them that way, okay?"

Once the rest of our group arrives, I perch on the edge of a leather sofa and stay close to my friends. Matthew introduces us to his friends from theater and church, and they seem nice, but I'm too on edge to make more than small talk. We return to the kitchen, fill plates with little appetizers—although I give the mini quiches a wide berth—and grab wine glasses filled with sparkling apple cider. Then we all settle in the rec room, which I think used to be the garage. It's spacious, filled with leather furniture, and painted in cooler tones than the rest of the first floor.

The Oscars start at 8:30, and then everyone's focus is on the ceremony. I'm curled up on a giant couch between Ro and Owen. Matthew settles on Owen's other side, and I can't resist glancing at him every now and then. During one of the commercial breaks, his gaze catches mine, and I quickly look away before my eyes dart back to his of their own accord. He watches me with an unreadable expression, and I stare back. I wonder if he can tell that I know the truth.

"You know," he says, leaning over Owen, "I have a friend who loves food, too. You two should talk sometime."

I blink, confused. Then it sinks in—does he mean Feather? I laugh uncomfortably as my thoughts race. Has he figured it out? Does he know I'm Feather?

"I'd always love more friends that cook," I say. I worry that my words sound as forced as they feel, but nothing looks amiss on Matthew's face. Then again, he's an actor. He's better at hiding things than me.

I excuse myself to go get more food. No one else is in the kitchen, so I take a moment to collect myself. Bracing my hands against the island, I take deep breaths.

He doesn't know, I tell myself. *He's just trying to be nice. You should do the same.*

Once I've composed myself, I refill my glass and put some fruit and fancy cheese on my plate. Back in the rec room, I retake my seat as one of the presenters tries to make a quip onscreen. I smile as if nothing is wrong. Because nothing is.

Right?

At the next commercial break, Owen turns to me. "What historical sites have you been to? Here in Richmond, I mean."

"Not many," I admit. "I've gone to the Byrd Theatre a lot, and I've been to, um, the Capitol and St. John's Church on field trips. Why?"

"It's cool to live in a place with so much history. Tuscumbia didn't have that, ya know? Anyways, I was wondering what the good places to visit are, and I thought you might know because of your dad."

"He's tried. Tours bore me, though."

"Oh." Owen looks disappointed.

I hesitate before nudging him. "What?"

"Would you want to go to some of them with me? I only have a few months before I go off to college and I want to appreciate Richmond while I can." He glances at Matthew, who's fiddling with his phone. "Matt and Ro should come, too. It's nice to have a friend group like this."

After a pause, I say, "Sure, that sounds fun."

"Cool." Owen smiles.

"Which did you—"

Matthew shushes me and points at the screen. His beloved Oscars are back on. I bite back a sharp retort; Ro would be proud of me.

Later in the evening, I go to refill my glass again, and Ro asks me to grab some dessert for her. While I'm in the dimly lit kitchen, Matthew strolls in, bearing a couple empty plates. He dumps them in the sink, and I try to ignore him. Except he doesn't have the same idea. As I fill Ro's and my plates, he leans back against the counter and folds his arms over his dark blue button-down.

When the silence has stretched too long, I side-eye him and say, "What's up?"

He shrugs. He's wearing contacts instead of glasses tonight, and I realize I never pictured March as a glasses-wearer. With that thought, I adjust my frames; they often shift so that they sit crooked on my nose.

"We don't talk much, so I feel like I don't know a lot about you," he says.

I don't know how to respond to that. I reach for the

bottle of sparkling cider, but it's empty. Matthew grabs a fresh one out of the double-door fridge and pops it open before handing to me.

"Thanks." Once I've poured a glass, I half-lift myself onto one of the stools around the island just so I don't have to remain steady on my feet anymore. I'm still not used to the idea that I'm talking with March in person.

"Do you have any pets?" he asks, out of the blue.

I turn to look at him. "Um"

"I'm trying to get to know you," he says. "You met my dog, so... Do you have a dog?"

I shake my head. "No pets."

"That sucks," he comments before eating a tortilla chip.

I shrug. "My parents say they don't have time for one, and I'll be away at college in the fall so..."

"Do you want a dog? Or a cat?"

"A dog. Eventually. I like dogs more, but my parents prefer cats."

"My mom doesn't like either. My dad and I talked her into getting Kelly."

It's like she heard her name, because she wanders in, her tag jingling softly and her nails clicking against the brick-tile floor. I slide off my seat, and my fingers reach for her. She lingers by me for a quick pat and then lumbers to Matthew's side, and he strokes her head. Animals are a safe topic. March and I rarely talk about them, except when Kelly does something funny. If we start talking about food or movies, I'm scared something will click in his mind like it did for me, and he'll realize I'm Feather.

"Ro's probably wondering what's taking me so long,"

I say. I pick up the two plates, then realize I can't carry my glass, too.

Matthew reaches over and takes Ro's plate. "Is she your best friend?"

"Ro? Yeah. One of them, I mean. We've known each other since I joined Stony Point in sixth grade." We walk back towards the rec room.

"That's a long time."

"Yeah, I guess. It feels like she's always been a part of my life, though. What about you? Do you have a best friend here, or is he back where you used to live?"

"What makes you think it's a 'he'?" Matthew raises an eyebrow, and my cheeks flush.

"Well Joel's and Dylan's best friends aren't girls, so I assumed," I shoot back, trying to sound not rude but playful.

"I'm just teasing. The guys here are cool, but, yeah, my best friend is back in Ohio. I got to see him over break."

"Do you miss your old home?"

As I wait for his answer, I notice we're standing outside the rec room—we have been for a couple minutes—and our conversation is staying civil. Matthew is acting like he never disliked me at all.

"Sometimes," he says. "It's hard to move before your senior year. But it's not bad here."

"I've lived in the same city my whole life so I can't imagine what that's like."

"You like Richmond a lot, don't you?"

A smile creeps onto my face of its own accord, and I nod.

"Why are you going to college out of state then?"

It surprises me that he knows that. "My college plans are... They may've changed," I admit. "I'm not really sure right now what I want to study or where I want to go."

I can't believe I told him that. Maybe it's because I already told March something similar, but I haven't even told Holly or Ro how I'm feeling. So why am I telling the guy who said he could never be my friend?

His smile is rueful. "I'm kind of in the same boat. I mean, I want to be an actor, but my dad won't pay for me to study that. So I'm trying to figure things out." He laughs bitterly. "Joel, Dylan, Owen, Kylie... They all seem to have things figured out, so they don't understand."

I sigh. "I thought I had things figured out."

We're silent for a couple minutes. I can't stop thinking about March, and I can feel Matthew studying me. I don't want this conversation to end—I want him to get to know me and like me—but at the same time I'm afraid I'll say something without thinking, and it'll reverse everything that has changed for the better tonight.

"Ro will probably come looking for me soon," I say before pushing away from the wall and heading back into the rec room. Neither Owen nor Ro say anything when we rejoin them, although I feel their eyes on me when Matthew hands Ro her plate.

I stay quiet the rest of the evening, numbly tracing the stem of my glass but not drinking a drop. I couldn't even say who won Best Actor, Best Actress, and Best Picture, though everyone is clearly buzzing about some drama that happened during the ceremony. My thoughts are consumed with Matthew and how he treated me tonight, how he seemed to gradually warm up to me, and how he both is and isn't March.

Mrs. Harwell brings us our coats, which she whisked away to places unknown earlier. Last conversations take place in the foyer, although Matthew's mom reminds us to be quiet since the younger Harwell boys are in bed.

As I watch my friends chatter away, I realize Matthew is right. Dylan's already been scouted by several collegiate swim teams. Joel will study agriculture and business at Virginia Tech; he's dreamed of running the family farm since we were still eating Goldfish around a little blue table in the church nursery. Kylie will probably end up as a photographer or an event coordinator. That's more of a plan than either Matthew or I have right now.

We say our good-byes, and then Ro and I head out. She's too focused on driving to chat, which I'm glad for. The sky outside the car is the darkest shade of blue, lit intermittently by the headlights of other cars. Pop music plays softly on the radio, and we hit mostly green lights. The streets are more peaceful than my chaos of thoughts. I can't get Matthew off my mind.

Maybe I can tell March who I am. At the very least, I've got to stop ignoring his messages. But maybe everything would be okay if I stopped keeping secrets, too.

CHAPTER TWENTY-ONE

From: idesofmarch117@gmail.com
To: feathergirl1389@gmail.com
Sent: February 27, 2017, 1:58 am
Subject: Miss you

Dear Feather,
Still haven't heard from you, and I wanted to make sure you're ok.
It's been weeks and this isn't like you. Maybe your phone broke
or you have a lot of homework or someone in your family is ill, but
I'm not used to not talking to you. I'm kind of worried.
Remember that girl I kind of hated? She came to the Oscars party
after all, and I thought things would be weird, but they weren't.
She was…Well she was different. She was nice to my mom and
brothers, and she almost seemed more nervous and shy than
rude. We talked for a bit, just the two of us, and I can see why the
others like her. I thought about why I thought she was stuck up
and rude, and I guess she's just honest and not fake. So I guess
all of this is to say first, or second, or even third impressions can
be wrong.
Have you ever misjudged someone? Please tell me I'm not alone.
Please write back soon. I miss talking to you.
-March

From: feathergirl1389@gmail.com
To: idesofmarch117@gmail.com
Sent: February 27, 2017, 7:07 pm
Subject: Re: Miss you

Dear March,

I'm sorry that I wasn't replying to your messages and emails. Things have been hard these last few weeks and, while I know talking with you usually helps me work through things, I needed to deal with all of this on my own. Everyone in my family is okay, so it's nothing like that. But I can't really go into detail. Sorry.

To answer your question, yes, I have misjudged someone. I like to think I have pretty good judgment, so usually if I dislike someone, it's because they're not a good person. But all my friends seemed to like this person, and I trust my friends so I tried to keep an open mind and I realized I had been wrong. It happens to the best of us.

I saw your email from a couple days ago. If it helps any, I'm working up the courage to tell my parents about my changing career goals. I'm sure they'll be supportive, but I like certainty and stability. I wish I knew where I should go and what I should major in.

I'm sorry about your dad, though. Really sorry. We're at that age where we're supposed to still be figuring things out. I was lucky to think I knew what I wanted to do; my friends are lucky to have some semblance of a plan. Your dad needs to understand you're not an adult yet. You haven't even finished high school, for goodness' sake!

I want to be all organized and adult-y and tell you what to do, but you need to figure it out on your own. If you ever need to talk

things out, though, I'm here for you. I promise I won't disappear again.
You know what we haven't done in a while? Watch the same movie and message each other while we're watching. Wanna do that tonight or tomorrow?
-Feather

P.S. I missed you, too.

He texts me barely fifteen minutes after I send that email. I get up and close my bedroom door, so my parents can't interrupt.

MARCH
So everything's ok?

ME
It will be.
ME
Are you going to talk to your dad?
Maybe if you to sit down and have
a conversation, you can work
things out. If he can see how
you feel, maybe he'll compromise.
ME
*two sit

MARCH
I don't think he'll understand.

ME
You don't know until you try.

MARCH
I know, I know. So are we gonna
watch a movie or not?

                             ME
               Yeah. What are you in the mood for?

MARCH
Nothing too highbrow. I got
too much of that before the Oscars.

                             ME
                  We haven't watched Princess
                       Bride in a while.

MARCH
As you wish.

We've done this more than two dozen times over the years. We'll get all set up with snacks—I have popcorn and white-chocolate-covered pretzels, and then we'll try to start at the exact same time and text each other our reactions. Tonight we quote our favorite lines and chat about little things in *The Princess Bride* and outside of it. He tells me about his Oscars party (most of which I knew, of course), and I complain about the paper I'm writing for English class.

As the credits start to roll, and I wipe away my tears—I'm a nostalgic sap when it comes to *The Princess Bride*—I try to work up some courage. I want to bring up us meeting, but maybe it's a bit too soon after his email. After all, he's just decided he doesn't dislike me anymore. I don't want to jinx things. I don't want to lose March for good. But maybe there's a way to approach it, see how he feels…

> ME
> Remember how we talked about
> meeting and decided it wasn't
> the right time?

My heart races and my palms sweat as I wait for his reply. I start to reach for my ring, then remember I haven't worn it in a few weeks. If I understood him, March appreciates that I'm honest. Maybe that'll make this easier.

MARCH
Yeah. I think that was the right choice
I like our friendship how it is, and
I don't want things to change yet.

> ME
> Oh, okay.

MARCH
Why?

> ME
> I've just been thinking it might
> be easier if we didn't have to be
> so careful of what we said, if we
> knew each other…

MARCH
Do you want to meet?

> ME
> Kind of. I know I was hesitant
> before, so this is probably weird.

MARCH
Nah you're fine

ME
If you're not ready, then I
understand and we don't
have to meet. You didn't want
me to be uncomfortable, and
I want the same for you.

MARCH
I want to wait. But we can talk
about it again soon. Like
maybe this summer.

ME
Sounds good. I'm scared, too.
That meeting you will change
things, I mean. But our friendship
can't stay the same forever.

MARCH
yeah

ME
Change is inevitable.

MARCH
So is oblivion.

ME
I see you finally read
The Fault in Our Stars.

MARCH
Your nagging got to me. I couldn't
hold out any longer.

MARCH
Plus I got bored over Christmas
break. Especially during my flights

I can't stop from grinning. Guess we both did something for each other over Christmas break. Not that I'm gonna tell him about watching *Star Wars*, especially since I haven't watched the prequel trilogy or the latest movie yet.

ME
It's a good book! I usually prefer
historical fiction and fantasy, but
TFIOS is amazing.

MARCH
It was okay

ME

ME
Also I hate you for making
that reference.

MARCH
Did you want me to lie and say
I gave it 5 stars, it was earth-
shattering, the best book I
ever read?

ME
Yes.

MARCH
I gave it 5 stars. It's the best
book I ever read, and I'm

going to give everyone I know
a copy and make them read it,
too.

ME

That is exactly what I
wanted to hear.

MARCH

It's your turn to read one of my
recommendations

ME

What do you want me to read?

MARCH

Something off that list I sent you
this summer. Do you still have it?

ME

Hang on, let me check

I find his email after a few minutes of scrolling through
Gmail on my computer. We talk about books for a while
longer.

MARCH

Do you ever go back to a place
you used to visit all the time
and it doesn't feel the same
anymore?

MARCH

Because I visited all my friends
in December and it was good to
see them but nothing felt the same

ME

Everyone changes

MARCH

It wasn't them. We've texted and
all so they didn't seem any different.
It was more the places we went
and things we did. We went to my
favorite restaurant and I didn't
recognize any of the staff. And I
didn't actually "go home." I
stayed at a friend's house.
Nothing felt right.

ME

I'm sorry. That doesn't sound fun.
We've lived in the same place my
whole life, so I don't know what to
tell you. Except that it really sucks and
I wish it didn't have to be that way.

MARCH

I hope college is better. I need
a place that feels like home again.

I try not to be bothered that he doesn't feel at home in
my city, the place that means we can actually meet in the
not-so-distant future. I'm sure moving isn't fun; I wouldn't
want to be uprooted my senior year and leave the places
I know best and all my closest friends. Sure the Internet
would still connect us, but it's not the same. So I guess I can
imagine how March feels.

It's getting late, but it's like neither of us wants to

say good-bye now that we're talking again. I reply to his messages after I get into my pajamas and curl up in bed, with my chenille blanket tucked around me, and there's a delay in his responses where I imagine he's brushing his teeth or saying good night to his brothers. We're falling back into comfortableness, and that's what I want most.

CHAPTER TWENTY-TWO

It's been a month since I started planning what to say to my parents. I think I had it all finalized last Tuesday, but I spent another week working up the courage to talk to them after I could get March's advice.

Tonight's the night, though. Dad brought up the deposit for the Culinary Institute at dinner, and I had to fake my way through that conversation. (10/10 would not recommend.) I have March's support, so that makes this a little easier.

I help clear the table, which doesn't go unnoticed. I usually set the table and contribute to the meal itself, so I only clear the dishes when I want my parents in a good mood. Mom gives me a look, the one that says she's onto me and she knows I want something. Dad stands and reaches for his briefcase while I'm loading the dishwasher. I panic and hit my knuckles on the salmon-pink-and-black granite countertop as I scramble for words. Once he starts grading tests or papers, Dad can't be interrupted. I spin around, wincing at the pain in my hand.

"Wait!" I blurt. "Um, can I, uh, talk to you guys?"

"What's up, sweetheart?" Mom says, pausing the dish rinsing.

I dry my hands on the towel hanging by the sink. "Can

we, well, sit...?" I gesture to the table. I don't want us standing for this discussion, but I've forgotten the words to ask.

My parents exchange a look.

"Sounds serious," Dad says as he lowers himself back into his chair.

My hands grow clammy. As I move over to the table, I play with the hem of my shirt. I open my mouth, but nothing comes out. Mom and Dad stare at me. The clock by the door clacks loudly, and my heartbeat increases with every tick and tock.

"Audra?" Mom prompts.

"Right, um, so here's the thing. I don't want to go to culinary school anymore," I say all in one breath.

They stay silent, although Mom raises an eyebrow.

I send up a silent prayer a little too late that I can explain this in a calm, clear, rational manner. Then I take a deep breath.

"I've been thinking about it a lot, and I'm not made to... withstand the pressure of a professional kitchen," I say. "The cooking class is going better, but it still stresses me out. I know they're kids and working around adults will be different, but I honestly think it'll stress me out more. This has been on my mind for over a month, so this isn't a hasty decision. And I've been figuring out what I'll do instead."

I pause for a breath. My parents are unreadable, although Dad's brow is furrowed. So I press on.

"Food is still my passion, and I want to do something related. Maybe food writing, like as a critic or for a magazine," I explain. I move my fidgeting hands to my lap where they'll be out of sight. "And thankfully most of my back-up schools have good journalism or writing programs. I haven't decided which one I should go to yet, but at least I have options. Thank you for making me apply to other schools besides ones with culinary programs. But anyway, um, I guess that's everything. So…yeah."

Well, that wasn't so bad. Maybe my prayer wasn't too late.

The silence is unbearable, but I need them to talk first. I've read about negotiation and interrogation tactics, and often, the first person to speak will end up conceding more. I have nothing left to give, so it can't be me.

"Are you *sure*, Audra?" Mom says.

"Yes," I say firmly, although her question sends doubt through me. "As sure as anyone can be. Besides, I'm not even eighteen. Why do I have to have everything figured out already? Maybe someday I'll go to culinary school, but this is a better path for me. For now."

Her hazel eyes are filled with doubt. "Culinary school has been your dream for so long. How can it change so quickly? How can you be certain journalism is a better choice?"

"I…can't," my voice falters. "But it gives me more options. I can always take some pastry courses, get my certification on the side, that kind of thing."

Mom shakes her head. "This is so late to be changing your mind. You've got to think about financial aid and housing. You haven't even decided where you want to go instead! And we have to try to get our deposit back from the CIA."

My heart sinks, but I hold firm. I look Mom right in the eye as I say, "Would you rather I stay on the planned path and hate it, or can I chart a new course where I can explore something better for me?"

Dad has been awfully quiet this whole time, which terrifies me. I can't even meet his gaze, out of fear that I'll see only disappointment in his brown eyes.

"I just think we need to talk more about this, that's all," Mom says. She folds her hands on the table.

"Okay, but what's there to talk about?" I frown hard to keep myself from crying with frustration. "I've realized I'm not cut out to be a chef, and I've made my peace with that."

"I don't want you to regret giving up your dream," she says so fervently that I can't help but wonder if she's speaking from some secret experience.

"I'm not giving it up!" I shove back from the table slightly, and the chair legs scrape against the floor. "My dream is changing, that's all."

"This seems so sudden." She shakes her head again. I want to scream because how can my mother still not get it?

"I wish you'd told us sooner," Dad finally says, and I know I've lost if he's siding with Mom. But then he adds, "It sounds like this has stressed you out, kiddo, and I hate that you had to deal with it alone for so long. Your mom and I are always here to support you."

He takes one of Mom's hands and wraps it in his own. His smile, which he directs at both of us, is gentle.

"Let's see how we can work this out, okay? There're a

few things to decide. First, I'm sure we can get our deposit back, Kathleen. It's barely March."

Mom nods, and Dad turns to me.

"Do you feel settled when you think about this new direction?"

"Yeah. It's like…" I gesture vaguely, as if that'll explain what I'm trying to say. "It's like I don't have to hold my breath. I'm not scared of the future anymore."

"Then I don't see why you shouldn't pursue this new path. What schools are you considering?" he asks.

"Well, U of R—" Dad reflexively grins, and I can't help but roll my eyes. I list the rest, using my fingers to count. "Emerson, a tiny school in Kentucky called Asbury, Washington and Lee, and that last college… I'm blanking on the name… Uh, it's in Wisconsin?"

"Foxwood?" Mom supplies.

"Yes, that one!"

"Okay, that's a solid list." Dad nods. "You should decide soon, so we can get moving on everything. I don't want you to miss out on the best school because you waited too long. But your mom and I are here for you every step of the way."

Mom nods. "Despite my misgivings, I'll support you, sweetheart. I really do want you to be happy."

"Thanks." I get up and hug them both.

"Why don't we set a deadline for your decision?" she suggests. "That way you don't put it off."

"Okay…"

"Let's say no more than three weeks? That way it'll be settled before spring break." She gives me a very mom-esque look, exerting her authority.

I nod, realizing I should compromise at least a little. She reaches up and hugs me again.

When I go upstairs, I know I should message March, but I text Ro and Kylie first in our group chat, and then I shoot Holly a message.

My head is still swimming, but there is a weight gone from my shoulders. Now I have to pick what college I'll attend. No pressure.

Of course, just the thought of that makes my hands sweaty again. It doesn't help that I feel like I just ran a mile. Still, now that my college plans are moving in the right direction, I can turn my focus to other worries and projects that need tweaking.

I text March/Matthew an update about the conversation with my parents, then lean back against my pillows. His feelings about me are definitely something that needs tweaking.

CHAPTER TWENTY-THREE

Matthew is down in the dumps. The others don't notice—they're planning stuff for their spring break road trip—but I do. I'm not sure what's wrong, though; he hasn't let onto anything in his messages, so it's probably not that serious. Maybe he thinks he bombed a test this morning or something.

I shift, my knee bumping into Kylie's. She barely notices since she's so caught up in talking with the guys and Ro. We're sitting in a circle on the multipurpose room floor; March—the month—came in like a lion this year, so we can't have lunch outside yet. I start to reach for my phone—maybe I could discreetly text Matthew or something—but then I stop. I can't always help him as Feather. Besides, he already likes her; he needs to like me as Audra, too.

An idea hits me. I brush crumbs off my lap and stand.

"Bathroom," I say when Ro pauses and looks up at me.

I stash my lunch containers in the big tote bag my mom keeps with her at co-op before wandering down the hall. I haven't been to Stony Point's vending machine in a long time, but I think they have what I'm looking for.

I pass a couple middle schoolers sitting under the coat racks in the hall. They're playing a game on an iPad, and I smile. Ro and I used to do that when we were their age.

Well, we'd read books, but we'd sit out here where it was quieter, and her siblings couldn't bother us. We'd complain about classes, gossip about classmates, and rave about our favorite books. I kind of miss those days.

Don't get me wrong: I'm glad we're in high school, and our friendship has grown with us, but things felt so much simpler then.

I wait for a couple kids to make up their minds at the vending machine, and then it's my turn. First, I get peanut M&Ms—I prefer Sour Patch Kids, but vending machines often don't have those—and then I scan the candy selection for the kind Matthew told me in December he liked best. I remember this machine having it last fall, but maybe the operators have cut them by now...

There. On the second-to-last row.

I feed another dollar into the machine, then press the code for Airhead Xtremes.

As I walk back to the lunchroom, I clutch the candy. The wrappers crinkle. Maybe I should've gotten everyone candy so it wouldn't stand out that I got Matthew something.

It's too late for that, though. I don't have enough money anyway.

My friends are packing up their things when I return; they won't notice what I'm doing and make a big deal out of it then. I grab my backpack from where I left it between Kylie and Owen and smile at them and Ro as they head off. I watch Matthew, who has one earbud in as he watches something on his phone, pack up his bag. As Joel and Dylan drift off to their classes, I seize my opportunity.

"Hey," I say, pushing hair behind my ears and stepping to Matthew's side.

"What," he says. Despite our burgeoning friendship, his tone is flat.

"I noticed you were—" I pause when I see the superheroes on his phone screen. "Sorry, is that Wonder Woman?"

"Yeah, it's the new *Justice League* trailer. You like Wonder Woman?" He pauses the video and removes his earbud, but he doesn't make eye contact.

"Only with every fiber of my being. She could punch me, and I wouldn't care," I say as we walk.

It occurs to me that this is like last fall, except I'm the one more interested in this conversation than him. Guilt bubbles up. I should've been nicer to him before now.

"She probably would punch you," he mutters, although it sounds half-hearted. He winces.

"I'd deserve it," I cheerfully reply, despite my heart plummeting fifty feet. I had hoped we were past the biting comments.

He stops at the foot of the stairs. "You wouldn't. I'm sorry I said that." He shoves a hand into his hair, ruffling it and making a few strands stand on end.

My smile is tentative. "It's okay." I fiddle with the hem of my tunic-like shirt, then tell him, "I, uh, got you some candy."

His eyebrows shoot up. "Well now I *really* feel bad for what I said."

I hold out the package, but Matthew doesn't take it yet.

"Why?" he asks, staring at my hands. He tightly grips the straps of his backpack.

I scoot over to the side so we're not blocking the stairs, and he follows my lead. Lucy Kurtz gives us a weird look as she passes, and I shake my head at her. If she starts gossiping about this, I'll make her regret it. Once she's gone, I turn back to Matthew. He's close enough that I catch a spicy-citrusy scent wafting from him.

"You didn't seem like yourself today." I shrug. "I didn't know if this would help, but I wanted to cheer you up."

His eyebrows are still raised.

"I, um…"

I force the candy into his hands and start up the stairs. Matthew follows. I think I'm about to escape the awkwardness when he touches my arm.

"Really, thank you." His smile doesn't quite reach his eyes. "The others didn't notice, and I thought I was okay with that, but sometimes it's hard keeping everything to yourself."

The halls are clearing out. I should get to class, but I hesitate. Maybe Matthew needs a friend more than I need to be in calculus. There's a little sitting area at the top of the stairs, and I move over there. I balance on the armrest of a couch; Matthew leans against the wall.

As I fiddle with the straps of my backpack, I ask, "Can I help?"

He shrugs. "Eh, you don't need to hear all my crap."

"Abridged version then?"

"My dad doesn't get me. I know a lot of teenagers say that, but it's true, and it sucks."

I really lucked out in the parental department, so I'm not sure how to help him. Even as Feather, who knows more details about the situation Matthew is referring to. I try an approach Feather hasn't. "Can your mom mediate?"

"I think she agrees with him but doesn't want to get involved."

He crosses one leg over the other. I study his face; the usual twinkle is gone from his russet brown eyes. He screws up his mouth momentarily before asking, "What do you do when you and your parents don't see eye-to-eye?"

"I try to come prepared to the discussions. Um, and I try to stay calm because my parents respect that more. And I guess it helps that they want to reach a compromise."

He nods, then looks down at the package in his hands. "I love Airhead Xtremes," he says.

I sigh to myself. Typical boy, changing the subject when he doesn't want to come across as vulnerable anymore.

"You told me," I say. When he tilts his head, I explain, "In December at the, uh, costume party."

Great, now he's going to remember how awful I was to him that night.

"Huh. I don't remember that, but I'll trust you," he says, playing with the end of the wrapper.

I shift on my seat as my cheeks warm. "Yeah, I'm sure you remember other stuff from that night more." I pause. "I'm sorry I was so rude. You didn't deserve it."

He waves his hand. "All's forgiven." He slides the Airheads into his backpack and looks like he's about to push off the wall and go to class, but he changes his mind. "Um, just wondering, but what did I do to upset you? Like what about what I said that night wasn't okay?"

I sigh again. I suppose we had to unpack this sooner or later. "All last fall, you made comments about my opinions of food, and they didn't feel nice, so I just…snapped. Plus, I, um, kind of had a crush on Sam, and I felt like you'd embarrassed me on purpose, so he was going to think I was weird."

Matthew's jaw twitches. "Oh. I'm sorry I crossed a line in teasing you. If I do it again, tell me, okay? I want to be friends, and that means I shouldn't hurt your feelings on purpose."

I nod.

He glances at his watch. "Well," he says, with a little laugh, "I guess it's too late to go to class now."

"Oh, darn," I laugh. "Guess we'll have to skip."

I drop my backpack on the floor and slide onto the couch. As I fix the hem of my tunic shirt, Matthew plops his backpack beside mine. He hesitates for only a second and then sits beside me. My fingers curl involuntarily at his proximity. His arm brushes against me as he settles in his seat, and I turn so I'm sitting cross-legged and facing him.

It takes everything I've got to hold my secret inside and not yell out, *I'm Feather! I'm right in front of you, and you're my best friend, and I have a crush on you, and please notice that I'm your friend from online.*

It still baffles me that he hasn't noticed yet. He came so close at his party, when he brought up the food thing. I know I didn't notice he was March, but I didn't want to see it. Does he not want me to be Feather? Or does he not know me well enough as Audra to see all the similarities?

"You ready for the Idlewoods concert?" he asks, fiddling with his smart watch.

"Definitely. I've been playing their stuff all the time so I can sing along." As I answer, I think about the defining things he knows about Feather: her love for Taylor Swift and for food, and that she has an older sister. I don't think I've ever talked to Matthew about Taylor, so maybe that's the missing puzzle piece.

"We should go to the beach first, make a whole day of it. Do you think Joel would want to?"

I shrug. "You can ask. He might have to work that morning, though. It would be fun. Cold, though."

"I've swum in the Great Lakes. I think I can handle it." He gives me a patronizing look that I can tell is fake only because I've been on the receiving end of the real thing.

I hold up my hands in mock defeat. "If you say so."

We're quiet for a couple minutes. I check my phone before sliding it back in my bag.

"What, uh, what other music do you listen to?" I ask, messing with a strand of my hair. I remember that I haven't listened to a Fleetwood Mac song yet today, so this could be my opportunity.

"Hmm, I kind of like indie rock and some old stuff. Fleetwood Mac is my favorite, though."

"I've been meaning to listen to more Fleetwood Mac." That's not really a lie.

He sits up a little straighter, and his eyes light up. He grabs his phone. "Which ones have you heard?"

"Hm, the stuff that's on those oldies stations mostly," I tell him as I push my sleeves up.

"Then you probably haven't heard this one." He pauses and meets my eyes. "Do you mind listening to one of their songs?"

I shake my head. "I have my earbuds," I offer, looking towards the classrooms through the double doorway.

"Awesome."

I plug them in and take the right earbud. He queues up the song and puts the other earbud in his left ear. Stevie Nicks's voice comes through clearly, accompanied by piano and guitars.

When the song ends, Matthew looks at me expectantly.

"I like it." There's still a smile on my face, and my toes wriggle in my shoes.

"What type of stuff do you listen to?" he asks. We're still attached by my earbuds, and that spicy-citrusy scent from before drifts around us. I must be close enough to smell his aftershave.

"Um, some pop. I like Ed Sheeran. Broadway musicals. Um…I like instrumental stuff, too, but not like classical. I like to listen to film soundtracks while I bake," I reply, choosing the route that seems a little safer. I'm not sure I could keep myself from fangirling over Taylor, and that would be a dead giveaway that I'm Feather.

"What's your favorite soundtrack?" He opens up a streaming service on his phone.

I can't tell him my actual favorite—*Pride and Prejudice*—because that, too, would be a blaring signal. Maybe I could say *Star Wars*. I may not have liked the movies, but the music is iconic. And I liked the scores for Narnia and *Inside Out*.

"Ooh, that's really hard." I rub at the bridge of my nose in thought. "I like stuff Rachel Portman's done, like *Belle*. And I like the feel of the *Guardians of the Galaxy* soundtrack with all the classic songs from the '70s and '80s."

He nods. I watch as he pulls up the *Guardians of the Galaxy* soundtrack. Then he looks up at me. With a shy grin, he asks, "Wanna listen?"

"Uh, absolutely."

We listen to a few songs off the soundtrack, and then Matthew suggests an indie artist he thinks I might like called Happenstance. We listen to the band's latest album, and he's right—I do like the sound and the feeling of those songs.

"Hey, guys!" I twist around to see Kylie, Owen, and Dylan by the stairs.

Owen's smile looks different than usual, like there's a little bit of a smirk to it. "What are y'all up to?" he says.

"Just listening to music," Matthew tells him.

Kylie's eyes widen. "Did you guys skip class?"

"Yeah, we, uh, got caught up talking and then we decided it was too late to go," I reply, reaching for my backpack. If they're out of class, I'd better head downstairs to the kitchen to prep for the cooking class. It's a good thing Matthew still thinks I'm only the assistant for the cooking class; otherwise, I'm sure he'd know instantly that I'm Feather.

Kylie grabs my arm when I get to her side. "Audra, you *never* skip class."

I shrug. "It's not a big deal."

I turn to Matthew, hoping he'll back me up. He nods, which isn't the strongest support, but I'll take it.

"Okay, well, I've gotta go. See y'all next week," I say.

Matthew's smile looks genuine, and my heart beats a little faster. The others linger upstairs, but I really do need to get to the kitchen. Mom and Mrs. Cho will have started setting up, but this is my class after all; they shouldn't have to do all the work. Kylie hurries down the stairs beside me.

"You and Matthew hung out? Just the two of you? Voluntarily?" She shakes her head, sending her long dark hair flying.

"Um, yeah...?" I don't see what the big deal is. Yeah, he and I didn't get along for a while, but Kylie never knew how bad it was, unless Ro told her. I doubt she did, though; Ro isn't a gossip.

"How did that happen?"

"It just...did. We got to talking, forgot about class, and then decided to hang out. We listened to music like he said. He *really* likes Fleetwood Mac."

"Sounds like someone else you know." When I glance at her, I catch a smirk on her face.

"Yeah..." I'm reluctant to follow that conversation trail, since we don't have time for me to tell her what I found out two months ago. "Um, and we listened to some indie stuff, too. And then y'all showed up, so..."

Kylie looks impressed. "I didn't think Matt shared music with anyone."

We're almost to the kitchen, but apparently this conversation isn't over.

"What do you mean by that?" I frown.

"Oh, nothing," she says airily. "You must be special, though."

I roll my eyes. "Okay, Kylie." I peer into the kitchen. Some of my students are already gathering. "I need to get in there."

She crosses her arms over her chest. "All right. But we're gonna talk more later."

"I don't think there's anything else to discuss, but okay."

I dart into the kitchen and apologize to Mrs. Cho and Mom for running late. I quickly wash my hands and finish the prep work. But of course, since I'm me, my mind keeps catching on what Kylie was saying—and not saying. Was she implying that Matthew and I like each other romantically? Just because we skipped class and hung out together? It wasn't like we planned it, so that's a big leap to make. Besides, how does she know he doesn't share music with anyone? He shared music with both versions of me; there are so many songs I listen to because March told me about them, and I've returned the favor.

Yes, I like him, but he doesn't feel the same way about me. *Maybe* he likes Feather, but I doubt he sees me as anything other than a friend, which is fine. There's nothing wrong with or lesser about friendship.

I frown and rub at a crease in my forehead.

"Miss Audra." I glance down. One of my students, Isabella, is at my side. She's one of the youngest and smallest in the class, but she always has a smile for me. "Are we going to start class?" she asks.

I nod and return her smile, although I'm sure mine is a little more tired. Today was a big step in the right direction for Matthew and me, but why do I still feel weird about everything?

CHAPTER TWENTY-FOUR

Ro's birthday was two days ago, and she's invited all her friends over, plus her massive family, for a casual backyard party. March weather is just as unpredictable in Virginia as it is in most states, but on this Saturday, the weather has decided to play nice. It's a good day for a party.

The adults sit on the patio while Mr. Stenger mans the grill. The younger kids—Ro's youngest siblings and cousins—are screeching and chasing a random dog. I don't even know where it came from; the Stengers don't have any pets. The rest of us are scattered around the yard. I've claimed the tree swing; Joel was up in the tree, talking with me, a few minutes ago, but now he's trying to rescue the poor dog. I'm watching Dylan and Matthew throw a Frisbee around, but I'm trying to be subtle about it. Both Matthew and I have made an effort these last couple of weeks. He's been getting to know me, and I've found he's not so irritating and spoiled after all. Maybe he was just nervous when he started at Stony Point—

"Hey," Owen's voice startles me, and I blush, knowing he caught where my gaze was. He leans against the tree before saying, "Ro has a *lot* of siblings."

I laugh, relieved. "You didn't notice that at Stony Point?"

"I guess not."

"There're seven of them."

"Seven?! Wow." He shakes his head. "I'm an only child; I can't imagine that."

"Yeah, I feel like an only sometimes."

"So…" he says after a moment. "You and Matthew?"

"What?" Then I remember Owen caught me staring at Matthew. I shake my head and laugh uncomfortably. "Oh, uh, not really. I was just, uh, thinking and not really focusing on where I was looking."

"Right." Owen side-eyes me.

"Trust me, there's nothing there. If you haven't noticed, he and I have only been friendly for, like, three weeks."

"Okay, so you and Dylan then?"

"Owen Bell, are you trying to set me up with everyone?" I exclaim. "Anyways, Dylan and Kylie have been dancing around each other for years. There's no way I'd interfere with that, and I don't think of Dylan as anything but a friend."

Owen's gaze flits from Dylan to Kylie, who's sprawled in the grass with Ro. "Huh. I've been hanging out with y'all for six months, and I had no idea."

I start to swing back and forth. "That's 'cause you're a boy; you wouldn't notice something unless it hit you in the face."

Maybe that's what March—Matthew—meant when he said I was too harsh.

"Sorry, that was mean," I say, slowing the swing.

"It's all right." He pauses. "Guys are kinda oblivious, aren't we?"

"Girls can be, too," I offer, but the look Owen gives me says he knows as well as I do that I'm just trying to be nice, even though what I said was true. There's a lot I haven't noticed—about Owen, about Matthew, about my own sister.

"Are you guys gonna play nice while we're gone?" Owen asks. The college road trip group leaves early tomorrow morning for Kentucky.

"Of course we will!" I feign offense that he'd even ask. "Joel will be here to keep us in line."

It's admittedly kinda weird to be left behind, when normally I'd spend most of spring break with all my friends. But Joel, Matthew, and I already have plans to stay busy, including the concert down in Portsmouth. I'm sure, too, that the Hickory friend group will invite me to hang out at some point.

Joel calls Owen's name, and he glances at me, but I wave him on. I don't mind sitting alone and watching everyone. Today is Ro's day; I don't need to be in the middle of things, monopolizing all her attention when her family is here.

I let the swing rock back and forth with the breeze. I've been trying not to think about it these last few weeks, but I need to decide what school I want to go to.

I mentally run over my options. The university in Kentucky has a good communications program, but I like Emerson's writing program more. Plus, New England has always appealed to me. And Foxwood—I'm pretty sure Sam is going there, so at least I'd have a friend if I chose that school. I know my dad is hoping I'll choose the University of Richmond, but I'm ready to leave, at least for a little while. I love Richmond, but it can't be my whole world; I want to explore and see what else there is.

And then suddenly, just like that, I know.

I want to go to Emerson. I want to see New England autumns and be able to wear boots earlier in fall and live in a different area of the country. I want to wear royal purple with pride and join the Emerson alumni ranks around the world.

"Hey, Audra," Matthew says, startling me out of my thoughts. He's picking his way across the grass to me, with his hands shoved in his jeans pockets.

"Hey," I reply, smoothing a strand of hair behind my ear. Then my hands tighten around the swing's ropes.

"What's up?" he asks, shifting from one foot to the other.

"Not much. Just thinking about some things." I know I'm unintentionally killing any conversation he may be trying to start, but I can't help it. Now that I know he's March, the guy I like as more than a friend, I have trouble talking to him despite our blossoming friendship the last couple weeks. Between this and how harsh I've been, he probably thinks I'm some abnormal person who can't function in polite society.

"Oh."

He starts to ease away, like he thinks I want to be alone. I fumble for something, *anything*, to say that'll keep him here with me.

"How's your dog?" I blurt out.

"Oh, uh, she's…good. Nothing unusual."

"That's…good." Could I be any more awkward?

"Did you bake anything for today?" he asks, glancing over at the tables of food.

"No, Mrs. Stenger and Helen had it covered." I want to ask if he's talked to his dad yet since that's a conversation that won't end in two sentences, but it's a question that would be best coming from Feather. "You excited for spring formal?" I finally ask.

Stony Point and Hickory always team up for a spring dance, which juniors and seniors are both invited to, but since we're homeschoolers, we apparently can't call it prom. It's like how Hickory can't host a costume party in October; the uber-conservative parents would riot. Stony Point barely gets away with the Fall Fancy.

"Eh, maybe. You planning to go?" he replies, and I nod.

I try to remember if he's ever mentioned a movie or TV show, one that he hasn't just talked to Feather about. Then my gaze alights on his shirt. I gesture to the words, *O, Captain, my Captain!*

"Is that a Walt Whitman reference?" I never pictured March reading nineteenth-century poetry.

He looks down and huffs a laugh. "Oh, kinda. It's more of a *Dead Poets Society* reference."

"What's that?" I ask. *Is it a book?* I wonder to myself.

Matthew's eyes widen. "You've never seen *Dead Poets Society*?"

A movie then. One I somehow never heard of. I shake my head in response.

"Oh man, you're missing out." He gestures wildly with his hands. "We've gotta fix that. You and I should watch it later this week."

I laugh a little. "Do I get no say in this?"

"Nope. Until you've seen *Dead Poets Society*, your education is lacking."

"If you say so," I say, continuing to giggle.

He steps closer and grabs the swing's ropes, so my movement ceases. "I say so."

Our eyes meet, and my breath catches. He stares at me with such intensity. This is the closest I think I've ever been to March. He starts to lean in, like I have a magnetic pull he can't resist.

What is happening? Matthew couldn't stand me a month ago, and now he's inches away from, what, kissing me? I startle, and my feet kick off the ground, sending the swing back into motion. My knees hit his legs, and he stumbles back. He blushes and runs a hand through his hair.

"I'm gonna, uh, see what Ro is up to," I say before leaping off the swing and running across the yard to the safety of my best friend's side. She gives me a curious look, but I smile as if nothing is wrong. She, Kylie, and her cousins are talking about spring break plans, so I fall into their conversation.

For the rest of the afternoon, I try and keep my gaze off Matthew, but it's harder than I think, especially when he stands across from me when we're all singing "Happy Birthday" to Ro. Our eyes meet a couple times, and my cheeks flame. Maybe Kylie's observation that Friday afternoon was right.

CHAPTER TWENTY-FIVE

I'm packing my purse for tonight when my phone buzzes. I double-check that I have a bottle of water, then look at the message.

JOEL
I've got stomach flu or food poisoning or something.

ME
Oh no! I'm sorry you're sick.
ME
Have you told Matthew?

JOEL
Yeah. Y'all should still go!
Don't miss out on my account

My fingers hover as I contemplate another text. Matthew is driving us and I have the tickets, so there's no reason our plans have to completely change. Being alone with him for more than an hour terrifies me, though. What if we can't get along without Joel as a buffer? And he doesn't even have my phone number; it was easy enough to push all our communication through Joel so Matthew wouldn't find out he'd already been texting me as Feather. Ugh, everything is so complicated.

JOEL
I could give him your number
so y'all can text directly.

> ME
> Omg, please don't.
> ME
> I can't explain why, but he
> can't have my phone number.

JOEL
Ok......

> ME
> It's a long story.

JOEL
Once I'm better, I
wanna hear it.

> ME
> Maybe...

My hands are sweating from that close call. Matthew
can't know I'm Feather—not yet and not like that. I have to
find the right moment to tell him.

But that's not going to be tonight, which is only
reaffirmed when I hop in the passenger seat of his SUV
a few hours later. He drops his sunglasses in the console
between our seats. I sneak a glance at his face; today is
another contacts day, it seems, which fits more with how
I pictured March. Slowly, though, I've gotten used to the
idea of a glasses-wearing March. A Fleetwood Mac song is
blasting. Until now, I was too wrapped up with worrying
about Joel, but my thoughts screech to a halt and focus on
one thing.

I'm in Matthew Harwell's car. I am in *March's* car. I am in a car alone with March.

"Hey," he says, and I don't think I'm imagining that his smile is genuine.

"Hi."

We don't say anything more while I buckle in and he backs the car down the driveway. Then we're on our way, and I stay quiet so Matthew can pay attention to the GPS guiding us to I-64 East. Once we're past the downtown area, he offers the aux cord.

"You want a turn?"

"Oh, uh… I'm fine with Fleetwood Mac," I say. It sounds like he has *Rumours* on since it's still Stevie Nicks singing.

He shrugs. "Ok, but don't say I didn't give you the option to get away from my Fleetwood Mac obsession."

I laugh, then turn up the radio. We're flying down the highway, the sun is shining, and we're on our way to see the Idlewoods. Despite Joel's absence, I'm having a good time.

I turn to look at Matthew. A gray bandana headband is holding his hair off his forehead. He's wearing his sunglasses and a smile and singing at the top of his lungs to "Go Your Own Way"; I can't help but smile, too.

Yeah, he's March. I can see it now.

My phone rings, and when I see Madeline's picture pop up, I gesture for him to turn down the music.

"Hey, Mads, what's up?" I ask, turning towards the window slightly.

"Trevor and I can't pick a cake flavor. We both like the chocolate with chocolate mousse and the lemon with vanilla buttercream and raspberry filling. When you're back in town, would you be our tiebreaker?" she says all in one breath. "You know cake, so I figure you can tell which one our guests will enjoy more."

"And there's no way I can talk you into pie?" I ask, hoping Madeline can hear the smile in my voice.

Madeline chuckles. "I don't care either way, but Trevor wants cake. But he doesn't care what kind. We're so indecisive."

It's nice that she wants to include me on such a big detail. I tell her, "That's what I'm here for then. I'll help y'all when I get back."

"Thanks, I really appreciate it. I'll let you get back to your trip. Sorry to bother you!"

"No, it's fine," I reply. "We're just hanging out right now. But I'll talk to you when I get back."

"Sounds good."

Once I've hung up, Matthew asks, "What was that about?"

"Oh, just wedding stuff for my sister," I say.

"Ah, mawwiage," he says, and I can't help it, but I burst out laughing.

"It's a *Princess Bride* reference," he says, looking mildly hurt.

"No, I know, I just didn't expect it," I say, still giggling, "and, you have to admit, you sounded really funny."

"Oh yeah, didn't you dress up as Buttercup for that costume party last semester?" he asks.

"Yup! It's one of my favorites."

Then we're bantering back and forth in movie quotes.

Warmth fills me, and my toes curl. I always wanted to quote *The Princess Bride* to March and have him return the line after. I mean, we did it a few times in our messages, but this feels different—in a good way. Suddenly, I want to tell him who I am, but I catch myself. Things are good between us right now—both in person and online. I can't predict how he'd react if I told him I'm Feather; it might ruin everything. No, it's better to wait until this summer when we'll have no reason to see each other, in case everything crashes and burns.

The rest of the drive is quiet with occasional moments of talking about our classes or the pictures our friends sent yesterday. We go through the Cook Out drive-thru for dinner, which results in a debate about fries vs. tater tots vs. hush puppies. Thankfully, we agree that onion rings aren't even an option.

He offers the aux cord to me again when we're about half an hour out from the amphitheater. I consider one of my Taylor Swift playlists but instead go with my generic spring playlist, filled with what I've been enjoying most for the last few weeks. There are, of course, a few Taylor songs, but it's also got some oldies from my parents and stuff Matthew introduced me to that Friday afternoon.

Then we're pulling into one of the downtown Portsmouth parking lots. My heartbeat quickens as we get out of the car. The Idlewoods may be a fairly new band for me, but I haven't gone to many concerts before so each one is a new thrill.

"What gate do we need to go to?" Matthew asks, hefting our lawn chairs a little higher.

I pull out one of our tickets to see if it says. "Ugh, it's painful how far away our seats are," I say. We had to go with general admission on the lawn.

"'Life is pain. Anyone who says differently is selling something,'" he replies.

I feel my cheeks flush. That quote was the first thing March ever said to me. I'm so preoccupied with the thought that I don't watch where I'm going, and my toe catches on an uneven patch of pavement. I pitch forward, but Matthew's hand grabs my wrist, wrenching me back.

"Are you okay?" he asks.

His long fingers are still wrapped around my wrist, and I'm terrified he can feel my out-of-control pulse.

"Yeah," I say. As I catch my breath, I can hear the pre-show playlist drifting out of the venue. I pause and tilt my head a little as I listen. "Is that 'Guiding Light'?"

He looks up. "Oh. Yeah, I think it is. I'm surprised you know the song. I haven't met anyone who knows of Foy Vance."

"You mentioned it last fall." The words are out of my mouth before I can stop them, but I've remembered *March* told *Feather* about that song. Shit.

His brow furrows. "I did?"

I have no clue how to recover from that slip. "Um…" I say.

Quick! I tell my brain. *Think of another* Princess Bride *quote! Distract him!*

"Humperdinck!" I splutter instead.

I want to die from embarrassment.

"What?" he replies. He looks down, then releases my

wrist and our chairs and folds his arms over his chest. "Audra, what's going on?"

"Right, well, here's the thing…" I begin. There's no way to avoid this now, despite my best efforts. I just have to hope for the best now.

"The only person I remember mentioning that song to is…" he says at the same time. His eyes widen, and he backs away.

I could laugh and play it off, tell Matthew we've both got it wrong and that, really, he mentioned it a few weeks ago when he was introducing me to Happenstance and other indie artists. But I'm tired of lying and keeping secrets. It's so frustrating that, every time we talk, I can't reference something only Feather and March have talked about. It kills me that he's my best friend but doesn't know it. I take a deep breath.

"Hi, March," I say. I cross my arms to hide how my hands are trembling.

"Is this some kind of joke?" he exclaims. "Did you, like, go through my phone or something?"

I blink. Does he think that poorly of me? "No, why would I do that?"

He stares at me for a long moment before saying, his tone flat, "You're Feather." When I nod, he asks, "How long have you known? That I'm March?"

"Since January," I admit. Maybe I'll get points for being honest.

"*January*? You've known for months and didn't say anything?"

"I was upset!" My whole body is shaking now.

"So you found out I was March and realized I wasn't who you wanted him to be. Great, awesome. Glad to know you think so little of me." He laughs bitterly. "Oh and I bet that's why you pretended you didn't think it was a good time to meet."

"No, I wanted to meet you at first, really. But then I found out you hated me."

He freezes, and I forge on, "Yeah, I know I was the girl you kept ranting about." His cheeks redden. "So excuse me for not wanting to tell my best friend that I was actually the girl he hated!"

"How did you find out?" he mumbles.

"That day you called me at Starbucks, you mentioned her—me—and it wasn't too hard to figure out who you meant. You weren't very subtle about it anyway. Ro—and the others, too, I'm sure—could tell you acted differently around me." I keep going, unable to stop anything from spilling out. "You're a jerk, you know that? I can't believe you thought I was stuck-up." I don't mention the fact that he changed his mind about me; everything he said in his messages before that still stings, and anyways, he'd judged me too harshly.

"Yeah, well you weren't that nice to me when I joined Stony Point, so can you blame me?" he shoots back.

"Because you acted like a…like a spoiled douchebag." I throw my hands up. "It's no wonder you felt like my friends didn't want to include you. *I* definitely didn't."

He recoils. That was a below-the-belt shot, but I'm too worked up to care. If I could think straight, I'd calm down and maybe apologize, but this whole thing has spiraled into disaster.

"You assumed I was an asshole," he retorts.

I plant my hands on my hips. "And you assumed I was stuck-up. Why do you get a free pass? I couldn't look at you, couldn't text you for weeks because it hurt me so badly to find out my best friend thought I was awful," I say.

"*That's* why you ignored all my texts and emails?"

"Can you blame me?" I parrot his words from earlier.

"You could've said something. You could've told me as Feather that I was..." He gestures, at a loss for words. "Being too harsh and should give the girl another chance. Or, I don't know, you could've straight up told me you were...you, and maybe I would've realized I'd been wrong, especially because I liked Feather. She was—you were— my best friend, for Pete's sake."

"Yeah, that's exactly how it would've gone," I say sarcastically. His words echo in my ears; he said I *was* his best friend. But I'm too upset to dwell on that just yet. "Trust me, you would've stopped talking to me and then I would've lost my best friend, and I couldn't bear that."

"So you lied to me instead. And now you *have* lost your best friend, so congratulations, you didn't keep that from happening." Matthew turns on his heel and stomps down the row of cars.

I can't hold the tears back any longer. I stand there and cry, albeit quietly so maybe no one else will overhear. Although they probably heard that whole argument, so it's a little late for privacy, I guess.

"Are you coming?" he calls without turning around. "I may be angry, but I'm *not* a douchebag, no matter what you think. I'm not going to leave you stranded."

I stumble after him, and he stays a few paces ahead of me. I swipe at my eyes, trying to keep the tears from getting all over my glasses and blurring my vision. The car ride back to Richmond is painfully silent. My hiccupping breaths as I try to calm down are so loud, but they don't produce any reaction from him.

"I think we need some space," I murmur finally, as we near my neighborhood. "With Joel sick, it's not like we'd be expected to hang out anyways."

"Fine by me," he mutters. "I don't want to be around a liar anyhow."

I wince at the steel in his eyes. As soon as the car is in park, I flee into my house. It's dark inside since my parents are at Madeline's and weren't expecting me back until late. I want to be alone anyway.

CHAPTER TWENTY-SIX

A headache pulses at my temples, and I bury my head further under the pillows. My phone vibrates, and I want to ignore it, but I'm pretty sure it's Ro and Kylie, checking in at Joel's suggestion. Probably to make sure Matthew and I didn't kill each other on the way to or from the concert. So I emerge from my blanket cocoon, pop earbuds in, and answer the FaceTime call.

"Hi!" Kylie says, leaning closer to the screen. "Are you home already? How was the concert?"

I rub at the bridge of my nose before propping my phone against a book on my nightstand. "I'm home, but we ended up not going."

"What happened? I thought you guys were gonna go without Joel," Ro says. She nudges Kylie over a bit, and I notice her freckled cheeks are slightly pink like she got too much sun. "Did Matt say something mean again? I thought y'all were on good terms now."

I groan and pull my knees up to my chest before resting my head in my hands. "He found out."

"Found out what?" Kylie says.

"That I'm Feather," I whisper. "And that I knew he's March."

Kylie swears, and Ro swats her arm. Then Kylie blinks

and shakes her head a little. "Wait, Matthew is March?"

I nod. "I found out a few months ago. It's a whole giant mess."

"He didn't react well," Ro guesses, and I nod again. She rolls her eyes. "Ugh, boys aren't worth the effort sometimes." She pauses. "Most of the time."

"I said hurtful things, too," I say, shifting to sit cross-legged.

"Reach out then? I'll bet Matt regrets what he said. You can both apologize," Kylie encourages.

I shake my head. "I don't want to be rejected again. 'Cause that's what he did—rejected me. He didn't want me to be Feather."

Kylie screws up her mouth in thought, but I don't want to talk about anything to do with Matthew anymore tonight.

"So how was your college visit today?" I ask. "You guys were in Lexington, right?"

Ro frowns but doesn't try to change the subject back, for which I'm grateful. "Yeah, and we can't chat for too long, unfortunately, since we're staying overnight in the dorm."

They show me around the common room, which is almost completely deserted at this hour. They explain this dorm is the suite-style one, so four to five girls share each bathroom and then there's a kitchenette for the whole hall to use. The walls are cinder blocks painted yellow, which looks a little too sterile for my taste, but the couches look comfy, and the residents have hung up twinkle lights and posters with inside jokes and a bunch of pictures.

"They have a really good communications program here," Kylie tells me. "The art program seems a little weaker, though, so I probably won't apply."

"That sucks."

She shrugs. "Eh, it'll make my application process easier."

Ro tells me more about the communications department, as well as the psychology program. She hasn't settled on her exact major yet, but she seems enthusiastic about the options at this university. The group drives to Chattanooga tomorrow, where they'll have a brief tour of another college in the afternoon. Their week is almost halfway over, but they still have a lot on their agenda. I nod and smile supportively as Kylie chatters about the beach day they're hoping to get on Friday. It's easier to focus on my friends' plans than my downward spiral.

But sooner than I'd like, they have to hang up and go to bed since they're leaving early tomorrow morning. We exchange goodbyes, and I put on a brave face.

I stay curled up a while longer, and then I text Madeline, who says to call her since Mom and Dad have left for the evening.

"Hey, what's up?" My sister sounds vaguely distracted, and I start to second-guess this phone call.

"Um, if you're busy, it can wait," I tell her. I rub part of the bedspread between my fingers.

Her tone clears, as she says, "No, it's fine. What's wrong? You don't sound the same."

Wow, I really am a bad actor if my sister can tell over the phone that something's up.

The whole story spills out in an awful jumble, and I'm sure Madeline is horribly confused. To her credit, she asks only a few questions.

"I need to get away for a few days," I whisper while she's still processing everything.

"Okay," she says instantly. "But I think Mom and Dad would be—"

"I don't want to tell them why. They still don't know about March. Can you help me come up with an excuse?"

"Hmm..."

It hits me that I wouldn't have asked Madeline for a favor like this even four months ago. How wonderfully our relationship has grown.

She sighs and says, "Trevor and I just had a fight. I was figuring out how I could get some space when you called. I'm sure he and I will be fine, but he's just being so nonchalant about stuff like budgeting and whose place we're moving into after the wedding, and ugh, I'm just so frustrated. So I'm trying to get my boss to send me up to the New York office for the rest of the week. That way I won't have time to even think about the wedding."

"Can I come with?" I ask immediately. "I can do my own thing and not get in your way. I just gotta get out of here. I don't want to be all alone at home, moping."

Madeline is quiet for a couple minutes. I hold my breath and fidget. Finally, she says, "Let me talk to my boss in the morning. Then I'll talk to Mom and Dad, if she says yes. I'll tell them the truth about why I'm going, and I'll say I want you with for sisterly support."

"Thank you, thank you, thank you!" I exclaim despite

my lingering headache. "I can pay for my own plane ticket."

"Don't jump the gun. We haven't gotten a yes yet. But go ahead and start pricing flights and trains while you wait. I'll call you back when I have an answer," Madeline tells me.

"Okay." I nod emphatically even though she can't see me.

We hang up, and I take a deep breath. My spring break can still be salvaged. Even if Madeline can't go to New York, I'm sure she'll find a way for us to spend time together. Then we can support each other, just like I always hoped we would.

I check prices like she told me to, writing down the best deals. And then, while I wait, I start an email. What I told Ro is true—I can't face Matthew. But she was right, too: I have to apologize and try to explain.

Dear March, I start. Then I backspace and change it to *Dear Matthew*. That's whom this email is to, the boy I owe an apology. After everything he deals with at home, he didn't deserve my lies, too.

Dear Matthew,

I'm sorry for the things I said tonight. Most of them were said out of anger and intended to be cruel, and that wasn't right. I'm sorry I didn't tell you sooner when I found out who you were, but I wasn't lying when I said I didn't want to lose my best friend. I was all set to tell you until I learned what you thought of me, and I got scared. I wanted space and to keep the secret rather than lose you completely. Although I didn't do a good job

*of maintaining that friendship for a few weeks there either. I'm
sorry for that too. I didn't handle my emotions well.*

*I'm hoping maybe you just weren't expecting this, and that's
why you reacted how you did. Then again, I'm probably not who
you wanted to be Feather, which is fine.*

*I don't want this to divide our friend group so can we try to get
along when the others are back? I hope you can forgive me, if
not understand why I did what I did.*

-Audra

I press send, but I have little hope of him replying,
despite what Ro said. Based on what he said earlier, I
doubt Matthew will ever want to be my friend again.

My sleep is rough. I can't stop mulling over everything
Matthew said and the look of betrayal on his face. Not
even a soothing playlist can tune out my thoughts. When
my phone chimes at five a.m., I roll over and squint at the
bright screen. My glasses are within reach, and I fumble to
put them on. I'm not sure what I expect but certainly not
an email, let alone one from Matthew.

I open it, unsure what to expect. Yeah, I sent that
apology, but I didn't think he'd actually respond, at least
not this soon. My curiosity gets the better of me, and I
start reading.

Dear Feather, it starts.

*Or, well, Audra. I'm still having trouble thinking of you as the
same person. Maybe you had the same problem when you*

first found out I was March. But first, I want to apologize. You ranted, as Feather, about several people, so I guess I felt comfortable doing the same. I already admitted I misjudged you—Audra—but I shouldn't have assumed you were an awful person. Really, I didn't know you all that well, but I thought I had the whole picture and I had you pegged as this snobby girl who didn't know how to be kind unless it benefitted her. But I of all people should realize there are parts of ourselves we don't show to everyone. With how you felt about me, it's no wonder you tensed up and didn't act like yourself. Ro texted me earlier, and she set me straight about a lot of my incorrect assumptions. She went kinda mama bear on me, if I'm being honest. You should be glad to have a friend like her. You've done a lot for Ro that I didn't know about, stuff that wasn't my business so why would I know about it? And I know the others think the world of you.

But anyway since I didn't know all the facts before, I should've kept my opinions to myself. Or talked to you directly about how you had offended me. That would've been way more mature. I'm sorry I jumped to conclusions and hurt you.

You mean the world to me. You're one of my best friends, and I would never intentionally ruin that. You get me in ways that no one else does, and I don't want to throw away four years of history just because I'm a stubborn idiot.

You don't need to apologize for keeping that secret and not telling me who you were sooner. To be honest, I probably would've done the same thing, if I'd figured out you were Feather just because it would've terrified me to realize I already knew you. This whole situation is weird, and it's hard to know what to do, and I think we're both the type of person who doesn't want

*things to change if the change isn't guaranteed to be positive.
So I can't blame you for not saying anything sooner. I'm sorry I
got so upset with you about that. I was shocked and didn't react
well, but that's no excuse for the things I said.*

*I didn't know who I wanted to be Feather. But now I can't
imagine her as anyone else. And I want to get to know you
better as Audra because... here's the thing. I've fallen in love
with my best friend. I think it happened a year or so ago, but
I didn't figure it out until I realized just how much I missed
talking to you back in January and February. But I assumed
you didn't feel the same way and we didn't know when we'd
meet so it didn't matter. Until now. And I guess I just hope you
feel the same. But if you don't, I'll respect that. I don't want to
lose Feather as a friend, and I want to get to know you better
as Audra. I said that already, but anyway, I've been trying to do
that since my Oscars party, if you hadn't noticed. Please don't
hate me. Please give me a second chance to be less of a jerk.
If it's any consolation, I've been awake most of the night, mad
at myself for how I treated you.*

*Can we talk later today? In person? As much as I like emailing
you, we should do this face to face.*

Yours,

Matthew (You can keep calling me March, though, if you want)

My ears fill with a ringing silence as I focus on nothing
else but one sentence. In the background, though, I hear
ukulele music and a warm, deep voice singing through
my earbuds. But I don't hear the singer's words, just that
sentence of Matthew's over and over in my mind.

I've fallen in love with my best friend.

I've fallen in love with my best friend.
I've fallen in love with my best friend.
Me, too, I think.

I have to write back—or text him at the very least and tell him I *would* like to talk. But first, I need sleep, and now I feel like it could happen. Isn't that ironic?

"'And I think to myself, what a wonderful world,'" the singer warbles as I stare at my phone.

I lock the screen and flop back on my pillow.

CHAPTER TWENTY-SEVEN

The first thing I do when I wake at 9 a.m. is call Matthew. I hold my breath as the phone rings once…twice…three times. Then he picks up.

"Hello?"

Crap, he actually answered. Which I wanted to happen, but still.

"Hey, March," I say.

It may be my imagination, but I think Matthew inhales sharply. "Audra?"

"Yeah. I, um, got your email, but replying that way didn't feel right. I wanted to ask when you wanted to meet to talk," I reply. When he doesn't respond right away, I add, "Do you still want to talk?"

"No, yeah, definitely," he says. "Um… Do you have plans today? I know it's last minute, but the rest of this week is kinda busy for me, and I don't think we should put this off." His voice trails off.

"I'm not busy. I just…don't have a car. My parents need them both for work today."

He pauses, then says, "I could come to you. You're close to the church where Stony Point meets, right?"

I don't even know how he knows that. "Yeah. That would be okay." I tell him my address, and he says he'll be here in half an hour.

That gives me enough time to change into something other than lounge pants and a T-shirt that inexplicably still fits me, even though it's from seventh grade. I brush my teeth and also my hair, and swipe on some mascara, but not enough to make me look like I'm trying too hard. Just as I start pacing—nowhere near the front door, though, since I don't want Matthew to see—I realize I should text my mom. I've just finished the message, telling her Matthew and I are having a last-minute study session and I'll be home by early afternoon, and started pacing again when Matthew knocks on the front door.

"Hey," I say after I open the door. I gaze up at him—he's shorter than I expected March to be but still taller than me by a few inches.

"Hey," he replies, shoving his hands in his pockets. "Um, so do you wanna go some place or stay here?"

"Let's go somewhere. I'm not allowed to have guys over when my parents aren't here."

He looks surprised only for a moment before saying, "Right, I knew that." I tilt my head, and he adds, "You mentioned it online at some point."

"Oh." An awkward silence follows. I clear my throat, then say, "Um, well, there's a café nearby. Unless you want to go somewhere else."

"Nah, that's fine."

I've had the screen door shut between us this whole time, and he opens it for me, holding it until I've locked the main door and crossed to the edge of the porch. We walk down the brick steps side by side, and I glance at him out of the corner of my eye. He's wearing his glasses today, and, heaven help me, he's really cute.

When he starts the car, music blares from the radio. Matthew scrambles to turn it off, but my hand shoots out to stop him.

"Oh. My. Gosh. You were listening to *1989*?"

"No, it was just on the radio," he says, but I see right through his lie.

"Nuh-uh, they never play 'I Wish You Would' on the radio. I *knew* you liked Taylor more than you let on." I poke his arm. "C'mon, admit it."

"*1989* is pretty good," he says begrudgingly. "But I like *Red* better."

If I didn't already love him, that would do it for me. I could kiss him.

I turn the radio louder, and we listen to Taylor sing until we get to the café. Neither one of us speaks again until we have our drinks and breakfast and are sitting on the patio.

"I don't hate you," I begin.

Matthew's gaze softens as his eyes flit across my face, like he's memorizing every freckle, every crinkle, every blemish.

"And it's abundantly clear that I misjudged you, too. Apparently, my gut instinct isn't always right. Anyway, I'm sorry I was so mean to you when you first joined Stony Point. You didn't deserve it. Oh, and for the record, none of my—*our*—friends hated you," I say.

He looks sheepish. "Yeah, I'm a bit insecure, if that wasn't obvious. It's hard making friends your senior year, and I thought you guys were putting up with me."

"Trust me, we weren't." Well, I was for a while there, but he knows that already.

We're quiet for a moment. Then Matthew says, "I should've known you were Feather. The food thing is a dead giveaway. I wondered if you were her, but then you said you didn't have any pets, and Feather told me she had a cat, so I ruled you out."

"Oh, Sherman died two years ago. I never mentioned that?"

He shakes his head. "That explains a lot. And here I was, looking around for a girl with a cat…"

"Y'know…I ruled you out as March. Last fall."

"Why?" His voice lilts up, and his brow furrows.

"You hated that Fleetwood Mac song. I thought March loved them all," I tell him.

He laughs. "I *hate* 'Don't Stop.' But, c'mon, there has to be a Taylor Swift song you don't like."

I consider his statement, then admit, "Yeah, there're a couple. Okay, I guess I shouldn't have ruled you out immediately. But at that point, I still thought you were obnoxious, so I didn't want to believe you were March."

"I was trying too hard. Geez, I can't believe you and the others wanted to hang out with me. *I* wouldn't have wanted to be my friend."

"I'm glad Ro, and Joel, and the others looked past all of that." When he doesn't respond, I study him. "I never pictured March with glasses. I like them."

His cheeks flush, and he reaches up to adjust his glasses. Then he plays with his drink before picking up his vibrating phone. He laughs lightly at something on his screen and then holds it up for me to see a chain of messages from Dylan, including a video of Owen snoring against the car window.

"I'm almost sad we're not there," I say, laughing too.

Matthew types a reply, then puts his phone away. "It would've been fun. Today especially. Chattanooga looks cool, and I would've liked to hike outside the city."

"Maybe Owen or Dylan will decide to go to school there, and you can visit them next year," I suggest.

"Yeah, maybe."

He's quiet for a moment, and I'm working up the courage to bring up the rest of his email. You know, the part where he said he loves me. But then he clears his throat.

"So, uh, have you decided where you're going yet?" he asks, looking up at me through his lashes.

"Yeah, I'll be in Boston at Emerson College."

Something, I can't tell what, shifts in his face. "Oh," he says, his tone shifting to something cold and indecipherable. "Boston."

I'm puzzled. What does he have against Boston? Is he vehemently anti-Red Sox or something? I pick up my lemonade and gulp it down, just to give me time to think. We were doing so well... At least, I thought we were. But I'm looking at him, and he has that façade up again, the one that says Matthew only. There's not a hint of March in him right now, and my heart sinks a little. It's like he still doesn't fully trust me. I feel my tentative happiness recede.

He pulls his phone back out and looks at it. "Sorry to cut this short, but I should probably get home. My mom says I need to watch my brothers since she and my dad have a board meeting," he says.

"Oh. Okay," I say, feeling confused.

I trail Matthew back to his car after clearing my dishes. The air between us is still. The silence rings in my ears, since he doesn't turn the radio back on. He's got to be as uncomfortable as I am; March mentioned once that he hates silence and likes background noise. I don't mind quiet as long as it's comfortable, which this isn't. There's still so much unsaid between us, and I don't know how to put any of it into words.

Why can't I vocalize anything? He said he loves me, for heaven's sake. The least I could do is tell him I feel the same way, or *he* could bring it up himself. His email put the ball in my court, but I shouldn't be the only one to bring things up. I feel myself growing more and more cross, and I don't like it.

When we pull into the driveway, I turn to Matthew, but he avoids looking at me.

"Are we okay?" I ask.

His brown eyes finally look my way. "Yeah."

"Okay then," I say, even though things don't feel okay at all. "I'll, uh, see you next Friday."

I hop out. He doesn't pull away until I'm inside the house, but I wish he hadn't left at all. I was so hopeful when I called him and now my heart aches with the letdown.

Days pass, and Matthew doesn't contact me. I decide things can't be left like this, so I sit down to email him.

From: feathergirl1389@gmail.com
To: idesofmarch117@gmail.com
Sent: April 11, 2017, 3:10 pm
Subject:

Dear Matthew,

I'm not sure what happened last week at the café, but I felt the mood shift. Because of that, I didn't say everything I wanted to, but I still think some of those words deserve a face-to-face conversation. So this email won't address everything.

With that said, March and Matthew might be two different sides, but I'm starting to see you as the same person. That day when we skipped class, and in the car during spring break, you were March. And now that I know the truth, I see a teeny bit of Matthew in every message where you pretended you didn't care. And I'm so glad you're you because I wouldn't want March to be anyone else. You know how to at least be polite to people you don't like—unlike me—and you're fiercely protective of those you do. You're a wonderful big brother, and you're funny, and you're charming. I'm starting to realize you're the first person I turn to when I'm upset, and you make me so happy.

Please don't shut me out.

-Feather

CHAPTER TWENTY-EIGHT

The timer on my phone beeps, and I clap my hands. The kids, who have been chattering away in groups, turn to me, and I inwardly sigh with relief. Ever since that first week, each class has been better than the last. My dad was right; it just took time for them to respect me as the new teacher, and I've found my footing now. I still don't want to run a kitchen, but I don't hate this. The semester is almost over, too, and then someone else will have to teach the class.

"Okay, the pizzas should be done, so with Mrs. Dunne's and Mrs. Cho's help, you'll each take yours out of the oven and put it on the plate with your name," I announce. "I'll help you cut them into slices, and if you want to add pepper flakes or Parmesan, I can help you with that, too."

The fifteen preteens chatter with excitement and shuffle into a crooked line. I'm so glad to have my mom and Mrs. Cho around; kids and hot ovens do not mix well, so I always get nervous during this part of class.

The students come by my station next, where I slice their mini pizzas. I find something nice to say about each one, like, "You arranged your peppers so artistically," or "Ooh, Canadian bacon and pineapple is my favorite, too." (Not a lie; it's amazing. Haters gonna hate.)

Everything smells so good, and I'm expecting at least a few people to poke their heads in, hoping for extras. It's become a regular occurrence, and it's not just my students' parents; anyone who happens to wander by the kitchen will peek in. I glance up as the kids gather around the table at the far end of the kitchen, and my suspicion was correct: there's someone in the doorway—but I wasn't expecting to see *him.*

Matthew leans against the doorframe; his arms are crossed, but he's smiling a little. I meet his gaze and smile back.

"Audra," says Jenny Sung, Kylie's little sister, pulling me out of my thoughts. "Could I have some Parmesan on my pizza?"

"Absolutely," I say as I expertly slice her mushroom-and-sausage pizza into four pieces. Then I hand her the shaker filled with cheese. "Here you go. Just remember: a little goes a long way."

I want to look back and see if Matthew is still there, but my focus is on my students. As it should be. But some of my thoughts wander. I thought he left for the day after the last period. Did he read my email? Does he want to talk again? Does he still love me, or did he change his mind, or did I do something wrong, or—

I pull myself off that rabbit trail. That's a dangerous path to wander down. What matters most is my friendship with Matthew. Hopefully he's ready to work things out.

Class finishes in a blur. My students stream past Matthew into the hallway, and I turn to survey the messy kitchen. Even though the kids helped pack up the leftover ingredients, the countertops are a mess, and a bunch of dishes are piled in the sink.

"Need some help?" says Matthew. He's already pushing up his sleeves and eyeing the dirty dishes.

"Um, sure," I reply, blinking more times than is necessary.

Then it dawns on me that he might be creating an opportunity to talk, so I turn to my mom and say, "Hey, Mom, didn't you need to talk to Mrs. Mitchell about something? You'd better go catch her before she leaves."

When she frowns and starts to respond, I widen my eyes at her and flick a glance at Matthew. She seems to catch on, thankfully, and makes a hasty exit, although she can't help but study him. As far as she knows, he and I are barely more than acquaintances. She likes Mrs. Harwell, though, so that must count for something.

To Mrs. Cho, I say, "Matthew and I can handle clean-up. Thanks so much for your help today."

Her expression is a little more suspicious, but she leaves, too. Then I'm all alone with March. I take a shaky breath before gathering up the rest of the dishes. I bring them to the sink, which Matthew is filling with soapy water.

"You wash, I'll dry?" I say.

He looks at me and nods. "I like your hair like that," he comments before picking up a bowl and rinsing it.

I reach up and touch the messy topknot. My hair was down earlier, but I needed it out of the way for this class, and a bun was easiest. Still, this isn't the nicest it can look, so the fact that he likes it… Warmth fills me from my head to my toes and reenergizes the butterflies in my stomach. Maybe I should look up some video tutorials for buns later.

"I'm, uh, sorry about last Wednesday. How I shut down and cut the conversation short," he says.

"It's okay."

We're quiet for a couple minutes until he says, "I got upset that you're going off to Boston this fall and hadn't told me. Told March. You're going to be so far away, having adventures, and you'll make new friends and forget about me. I don't want to lose you," he admits.

I want to laugh out of relief and surprise, but I hold back since that would hurt his feelings. "Matthew, you don't need to worry! I hadn't told you yet because I decided literally the day before they all left for Kentucky. In fact, I barely messaged March at all that week." Then I relax. "I could never forget about you. You're one of my best friends. Besides, won't you have adventures at... Have you decided where you're going to school?"

"I don't know. Maybe. My dad wants me to go somewhere, anywhere, but I want time to figure things out. I want to take a gap year, which means while you and Joel go off and experience new things, I'll be stuck here, living the same, boring life."

"So go to college! Most schools are fine with you being an undecided major your freshman year. Then you can have adventures, too."

"But I don't want to go somewhere I don't really want to be."

I shake my head and let out an exasperated huff. "You can't resent me for going to Emerson then," I say, my voice low. "I'm not stopping you from living your life."

He pauses, his hands stilling on a baking sheet. "I'm not mad at you. I'm jealous."

"Why? You could afford pretty much any school you

wanted. Do you want to go to Emerson, too? Did you apply and not get in?"

"No! No, that's not it. I'm jealous because you have everything figured out. Even those months when you didn't, you had ideas and you knew your parents would support you no matter what. My dad is so fed up at this point that he'd let me major in anything, but I know he'd constantly be on my case until I switched to…business or something like that." He sighs. "I'm not sure I could put up with that."

I don't have a good response for that. All I can say is, "I'm sorry."

He shrugs, his cheeks a little pink. So he won't feel embarrassed, I scramble to change the subject to something that most definitely needs to be addressed.

"Well Boston's only, like, a two-hour flight from Richmond."

"Yeah…?" he says slowly, like he's unsure where I'm going with this.

I roll my eyes. I'm not going to spell it out for him, even if he's an oblivious boy. I shouldn't have to do all the work. So we fall into silence as we finish washing the dishes.

"I just… Why didn't you say anything about the second half of my email?" he blurts out.

I blink and set down the dishtowel. "What?"

"I told you this big thing, and you haven't even brought it up. Are you embarrassed? Because, really, it's fine if you don't like me back. I'll get over it. But I at least need to know how you feel." He finishes with the last measuring cup, and he turns to me, his hands dripping. He looks so lost, and without thinking, I reach out and grab his hand.

"I was getting to that! If you hadn't shut down at breakfast, I would've brought it up," I tell him.

He has the decency to look properly abashed. "Sorry. I didn't get any sleep, so I was exhausted. I just... I thought about you leaving, and I didn't like the feeling. I didn't react well in the moment, which seems to be a recurring problem. But it's because I'll miss you."

I can't be mad at him, not when he says things that make my heart race. I study him as his eyes flit across my face, trying to read my expression. I smile despite myself before pulling my hand from his and reaching up to touch his rumpled hair. It's as soft as I always imagined March's hair feeling. He sucks in a sharp breath before leaning into my touch. My hand slides down to rest on the side of his neck, my thumb brushing his jaw. He rests a wet hand on my raised arm, but I don't mind the dampness.

I've been thinking a lot about what to say to him, the boy who snuck into my heart without either of us realizing it. "You're my best friend. I know I've said that a million times, but it's true. And I know you want to get to know me, but I'm not so different from Feather. When I'm her, I'm better at thinking before I speak, but I'm sure a lot of people are like that on the Internet. *Anyway.* I know you better than I ever thought I did, and I'm so glad you're March. You infuriate me and make me happy and understand me, and I'm so glad you're in my life." I take a deep breath. "I listen to Fleetwood Mac songs every morning, and I ask myself, 'What would March do' when I'm trying to be braver, and I watched all of the Star Wars movies, and I didn't even realize til January that I was doing all of that because I love you."

He freezes. "You do?"

I nod. He inches closer to me, moving like he's afraid I'm going to vanish. But I don't move at all, and soon, he's close enough that our noses brush. I tense up a tiny bit as I realize what's about to happen and how this will change everything.

For once, I don't care if everything changes, I realize.

His eyes are shut, and his eyelashes flutter against my cheek. My eyes close, too, just as his other hand lands on my waist. I wait for his kiss, but he lingers, letting his breath tickle my face.

My hand slides to the nape of his neck, and my fingers curl into his hair as I huff, "Kiss me already."

"As you wish," he whispers.

A laugh escapes me. "You're so cheesy," I say right before his lips meet mine.

After a moment, he pulls away a little bit, but I follow him, not wanting this to be over. This time, he doesn't break the kiss as he moves back until he's leaning against the counter. I grip the side of his shirt and memorize the way his lips feel against mine, knowing I will never forget this moment. Kissing Matthew is like waffles on a Sunday morning, Christmas mornings by the fire, or June days on the sunny hillside of my backyard.

Then someone wolf-whistles. Matthew and I jump apart. I look over to find Dylan standing in the doorway and flush instantly.

"Took y'all long enough," he says before disappearing around the corner.

I look up at Matthew, befuddled. We both laugh, embarrassed, and I bury my face in his shoulder to hide my red cheeks until they return to a normal shade.

"Do I even want to know what he meant?" Matthew says.

"Probably not," I reply, shaking my head. For a moment, I consider how our friends have looked at us over the last few weeks and how they encouraged us to hang out during spring break. I'm pretty sure I'm going to have to give Ro and Kylie an earful later, but that doesn't matter right now, not really.

He reaches for my hand, and I let him hold it. His thumb brushes patterns over my palm, sending tingles up through my veins. I'm pretty sure my cheeks are never going to be anything but bright pink again.

"Wait," he says suddenly, and our eyes meet. "You watched Star Wars? What did you think? Did you like it? Who's your favorite character?"

I laugh, tossing my head back a little. "Oh my word. You kissed me like that, and all you can think about is *Star Wars*?"

"You said you watched them because of me! That's why I thought of it."

"Can we go back to kissing?" I say with an innocent smile as I play with his fingers laced in mine.

He pulls his hand from mine and frowns. "You didn't like them."

"No...not really," I respond sweetly, scuffing my shoe against the ground with a sheepish grin. "But I like you."

He sighs, but a smile plays on his face. "You're lucky I like you too." I lean up and kiss the corner of his mouth.

Matthew wraps his arms around my waist to keep me close. I lean in, amazed that I get to enjoy such warmth and comfort with him, especially after everything we've been through.

"I, um. I want to take you on a date," he says, chewing on his lip. "I was thinking we could go to the Byrd one evening next week. Do you want to?"

I smile and kiss his cheek because how could I not? "I would love to," I tell him. He picked the perfect place for our first date: a gorgeous historic movie theater in Carytown.

My phone buzzes in my pocket, and I want to ignore it. It's probably my mom, though, so I slip one hand off Matthew's back and reach into my pocket. She has a habit of interrupting my moments with him.

But it's from Kylie instead.

KYLIE
A little birdie told me you and
Matt were making out in the SP
kitchen. Get it, girl!

"Oh, for Pete's sake," I mutter. I show Matthew my phone, and he just laughs.

"Owen has been trying to get us together for *months*," he tells me. "I always told him I liked another girl. And by that, I meant Feather."

I admit, "Kylie thought there was something between us like a month ago, but we were just becoming friends then." I glance towards the door, as if Dylan were still there. "To be honest, I think all our friends were trying to set us up for a while."

He wrinkles his nose. "Did they really have a hand in this, though?"

I consider that. He watches me and pushes a loose strand of hair behind my ear. I take in every detail of his face: long eyelashes hidden slightly by his glasses, the tiny freckle on his cheek, his slightly crooked smile, his rumpled hair, which, I realize with pleasure, is my handiwork—

"Audra?" he prompts.

I shake my head. "Right, well, I don't think they did. Them just shoving us together wasn't going to solve anything. We didn't like each other, and you had valid issues with how I treated you. We had to want things to change between us for anything to ever happen. And of course, it helped that I liked March. Like, a lot."

One of his eyebrows quirks up. "Yeah?"

I shove at his chest and laugh. "Don't go getting a big head now."

"I don't think I can," he murmurs. "Not when I'm constantly amazed that you chose me."

We both lean in at the same time, but we're immediately cut off by my phone buzzing again. I groan.

"Go ahead," he whispers.

I pull it out to find a text from my mom, asking if we're done cleaning and saying she's ready to go whenever. I show it to Matthew.

"I don't want to keep your mom waiting," he says and brushes my cheek with a kiss. "We can talk later."

"Okay," I sigh. But then, because I'm not ready to part ways yet, I ask, "Do you think things would be different if I hadn't realized you were March when I did, and we had met up before your Oscar party like you originally suggested?" I hold my breath until he answers.

"Oh, yeah, of course. But I don't know how they would've been different. I'm not sure I would've reacted well. I didn't know *you* then, so..." He hesitates. "I don't think I would've been as nice to you as I should've been. So I'm glad things worked out the way they did, even if it didn't go perfectly this way either."

I study his expression—wide eyes, the way he's biting his bottom lip slightly.

"I guess we'll never know for sure," I agree. "But I'm happy with where we are now. I wouldn't change that at least."

He takes my hand and squeezes it three times. "I'll text you when I get off work tonight, okay?" he says, and his brown eyes flit across my face.

"Call me instead?" I ask. Now that I can, I want to hear his voice all the time.

"Yeah, of course."

I go up on tiptoe and kiss his cheek before he leaves with a wave. I put all the dishes away and wipe down the counters one last time before going to find my mom. I wander for a bit through the halls, my thoughts on nothing in particular. This week ended so much better than I thought it would. It hits me, just how lucky we were. How all the little coincidences added up and brought us to this point where we got to become more than just friends on the Internet. March is a part of my life beyond my computer screen, and I can't imagine it any other way.

Buttercup Bakes

A FOODIE'S ADVENTURE IN CHICAGO
Posted July 13, 2017 by Audra

Last weekend, I went with my dad to Chicago. While he spent his days at a conference, I explored the city with a friend. I enjoyed the museums and attractions, but the best part of the trip was, of course, the food. We sampled deep-dish pizza, hot dogs, popcorn, and more (although there were no mutton-lettuce-and-tomato sandwiches to be found...), and we spent the better part of a day at Taste of Chicago, which was like living my best dream. Let me give y'all a run-down of what Chicago has to offer on the culinary front...

COMMENTS:

Julia July 13, 2017 at 10:14 AM:
I've always wanted to go to Chicago! Glad you had such a good time.

MC July 13, 2017 at 12:05 PM:
Oh, yum. Everything you ate sounds so good.

Sam July 13, 2017 at 12:17 PM:
You only went to Gino's East? Oh man your missing out on way better deep-dish. Lou Malnati's has the best.

> **Audra** July 13, 2017 at 3:07 PM:
> I'll go there next time! Promise!

Matthew July 13, 2017 at 3:15 PM:
A friend, huh? ;) What did he/she think of Taste of Chicago?

> **Audra** July 13, 2017 at 4:42 PM:
> You would know better than I do. ;)

Matthew July 13, 2017 at 7:13 PM:
We should go on another adventure next weekend.

>**Audra** July 13, 2017 at 9:02 PM:
>As you wish. :)

ACKNOWLEDGEMENTS

I am so excited that this book is finally making its way into the world, and I'm so thankful for each and every reader. And now there are a few people I need to thank by name.

Thank you to Dr. Erin Penner, Dr. Devin Brown, and Dr. Daniel Strait. You inspired me to be passionate about what I do and proved that you can make a living by being an English nerd. And a special thank you to Dr. Brown for never considering YA to be lesser.

Thank you to Emery Lord, Morgan Matson, Ally Carter, Emma Mills, Laura Weymouth, Jennifer Iacopelli, Stacey Lee, Heather Vogel Frederick, and so many other authors, who formed me as a reader and a writer.

Thank you to my parents, for not discouraging me from wanting to major in creative writing. Thank you for being with me every step of the way and helping me find realistic ways to pursue this dream.

Thank you to Alexa Mamoulides for being an excellent beta reader (and also putting up with all of my shenanigans in the summer of 2018). And thank you to Sarah Yung, the bestest writer friend and editor.

Thank you as always to Mary-Courtney, Kelly, Melissa, Beka, and everyone else I consider part of my squad. I still can't believe you all chose to be friends with someone who creates characters based off of you and then kills them off for kicks and giggles. Thanks for sticking around.

I can't neglect to thank Tom Hanks, Meg Ryan, and the late Nora Ephron for the excellent movie that inspired this book. I visited Café Lalo, and several songs from my book playlist played while I was there, so it was definitely fate. Also I think more of us should live our lives by the mantra "What would Kathleen Kelly do?" And thank you to Taylor Swift, for all the sleepless nights and amazing songs. Feather wouldn't love your music if I didn't.

Thank you to Catherine Tinker, playlist creator extraordinaire and namer of Buttercup Bakes. You have become the biggest supporter of my writing, and I love that I can reciprocate. You are a rockstar, and I can't wait to see your multitude of funny, relatable YA books on shelves someday.

Tegan, dearest little sister, I'm so glad I found you. Thank you for always pushing me to be kinder and better, even when we both want to give into our goblin tendencies.

Thank you to Elise Jackson, the pasta mom to my moss dad—I am so very glad God put you in my life. Thank you for reading all my crappy first drafts, pushing me to write amazing stories, and answering any music-related questions. And now I'm going to say a bunch of words/phrases that make zero sense to anyone but the two of us: popcorn, Candace laughs, Jim-Bob Shakespeare, reindeer, Royals.

And finally, to God be the glory. Thank You for blessing me each and every day and writing the ultimate story.

www.ingramcontent.com/pod-product-compliance
Lightning Source LLC
Chambersburg PA
CBHW021752190726
48290CB00008B/2593